Evening Bags and Executions

Books by Dorothy Howell

HANDBAGS AND HOMICIDE

PURSES AND POISON

SHOULDER BAGS AND SHOOTINGS

CLUTCHES AND CURSES

TOTE BAGS AND TOE TAGS

EVENING BAGS AND EXECUTIONS

Published by Kensington Publishing Corporation

Evening Bags and Executions

DOROTHY HOWELL

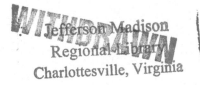

KENSINGTON BOOKS
http://www.kensingtonbooks.com

KENSINGTON BOOKS are published by

Kensington Publishing Corp.
119 West 40th Street
New York, NY 10018

Library of Congress Card Catalogue Number: 2013936487

ISBN-13: 978-0-7582-5334-7
ISBN-10: 0-7582-5334-6
First Kensington Hardcover Printing: July 2013

eISBN-13: 978-0-7582-8929-2
eISBN-10: 0-7582-8929-4
First Kensington Electronic Edition: July 2013

10 9 8 7 6 5 4 3 2 1

Printed in the United States of America

To David, Stacy, Seth, Judy, and Brian with love

ACKNOWLEDGMENTS

The author counts herself extremely lucky to have the love, support and encouragement of many people. Some of them are David Howell, Stacy Howell, Judith Branstetter, Brian Branstetter, Seth Branstetter, Martha Cooper, and William F. Wu, Ph.D.

Many thanks to Evan Marshall of the Evan Marshall Agency, and John Scognamiglio and the talented team at Kensington Books for all their hard work.

And special thanks to John Lennon, Paul McCartney, George Harrison, and Ringo Starr.

CHAPTER 1

The girl who had this job before me was murdered.
That should have been my first clue.

But, honestly, that little chunk of info hadn't seemed like a big deal when I'd applied for the position. And the fact that I'd been hired pretty much over the phone didn't seem significant, either.

So I, Haley Randolph, with my worthy-of-a-romance-novel-cover dark hair, my I'm-enviably-tall five-foot-nine-inch height, and my too-bad-they're-mostly-recessive beauty-queen genes, had accepted a position as an assistant planner at L.A. Affairs, the biggest, coolest event-planning company in Los Angeles.

I mean, jeez, what else could I do? I needed a job—or, really, a paycheck—plus I owned eight fully accessorized business suits left from a job I'd had a few weeks ago—long story—that I absolutely had to wear *somewhere*.

Everybody has their priorities.

My life had taken a lot of hits in the last month or so, but I'm proud to say I'd rolled with all of them. Some other person might have been knocked for a loop at losing the best job in the entire world, as I had, or been devastated beyond belief at breaking up with their totally hot boyfriend, as I had. But not me. Oh no. In fact, I was doing way better now than before those things happened. Really.

My whole future had suddenly crystallized—like when you see a to-die-for Louis Vuitton satchel in the display window and *know* that, no matter what, you're going to buy it—and I knew exactly where my life was headed and how I was going to get there.

So here I was facing down birthday number twenty-five pretty soon—the dreaded hump year on the downhill slide to the my-life-is-over-I'll-never-have-fun-again big three-oh—and I was perfectly okay with it. I swear.

That's probably because, at long last, I'd settled on the career I wanted. It didn't even bother me that it required that I finally get my bachelor's degree.

The decision had come to me in a flash at three o'clock one morning when I was sitting alone on my couch, eating Oreos stuffed with M&M's, dipped in fudge, and topped with chocolate chips—my own personal recipe—and watching television. I'd discovered the History Channel—do they have interesting shows, or what?—and believe me, a lot of fantastic ideas can spring up during those all-night documentary marathons.

I'd decided I wanted a career as a corporate buyer. I mean, jeez, it seemed like a natural fit for me—I loved to shop, I had great taste in absolutely everything, and I wasn't intimidated by crowds, even on Black Friday.

I'd actually been hired to work as a buyer, sort of, a few weeks ago at a fabulous company downtown. I ended up working as their corporate event planner instead—long story—but everything had turned out okay. Kind of.

That life-altering, future-defining decision made, I'd registered for four classes at College of the Canyons—most of them were online, but they still counted—and was loving every one of them. Really.

My life was rolling along great now. I had my totally cool apartment in Santa Clarita that was about thirty minutes north of downtown Los Angeles. It needed a little fixing up but was still fabulous. My best friend Marcie Hanover and I were giving killer purse parties, though, really, I hadn't had much time lately to plan a party. I had tons of really great friends, even though I hadn't seen any of them in a while. I still had my part-time sales clerk job at Holt's Department Store and, yeah, I only made about eight bucks an hour, but it was okay. And the best part of my life was that my mom and I were getting along great.

I left my Honda in a parking garage off Sepulveda Boulevard in Sherman Oaks and headed for the building that would be my new home away from home. It was a gorgeous Southern California morning in September. Nearby were lots of office buildings, banks, apartment complexes, and the Sherman Oaks Galleria with terrific shops and restaurants.

Showing up for the first day on the job could be intimidating for some people, but not me. Let's just say that I'd done this quite often in the last few years. I'd worked as a lifeguard, receptionist, file clerk, and two weeks at a pet store before moving on to a fantastic job in the accounting department of the Pike Warner law firm last fall. Things hadn't turned out as well as I'd hoped—there was that whole administrative-leave-investigating-pending thing—but I'd moved on.

The one constant in my life, employment-wise, was my job at Holt's. I'd taken a part-time sales clerk job there about a year ago and, well, there had been a few—okay, more than a few—problems, but every job had its moments, didn't it?

That's where I'd met my boyfriend, Ty Cameron. He was the latest in five generations of his family to own and be completely obsessed with running the chain, plus he'd opened several boutiques he'd named Wallace, after some ancient ancestor, and had just finished negotiations for Holt's International.

Ty is—was—a way hot boyfriend. He looked fabulous in his expensive suits and drove a totally cool Porsche. Our breakup was something we decided on together, and it was for the best. Really. So I'm perfectly okay with it. Perfectly okay. Perfectly.

The lobby of the building that housed L.A. Affairs was all glass and red marble. A lot of well-dressed men and women streamed into the elevators carrying briefcases and messenger bags, everybody seemingly anxious to get into their offices and start the day.

I'd selected a black business suit—one of the eight Marcie had helped me shop for a few weeks ago—for my first day on the job, and carried my Louis Vuitton satchel and day planner. Marcie had offered to come to my apartment last night and help me pick out my outfit, as a best friend would, but I'd told her not to.

I'd been offered a job here at L.A. Affairs a few months ago but had blown it off to go to London with Ty. After my fabulous job had ended a few weeks ago, Marcie had suggested I contact them and see if they were still interested in hiring me, and since Marcie was almost always right about things, I gave them a call. They got back to me right away with an offer. The woman in H.R. hadn't even asked to see my updated résumé, which was a real break for me—long story.

I got out of the elevator on the third floor and walked down the carpeted hallway to the double doors that had L.A. Affairs printed on them in gold lettering. I pushed my way inside and spotted the receptionist standing behind her desk. She jumped when she saw me.

"Oh! My!" She waved her hands as if she were doing a jazz routine, and said, "Are you ready to party?"

I remembered her from when I'd been in the office a few months ago. She was probably somewhere on the high side of forty with blond hair sculpted into the shape of a football helmet, a little on the heavy side, and dressed in one of those tweed suits that make you look like you're wearing a carpet.

She giggled and clasped her hands together. "They make me say that."

"I'm Haley Randolph," I said. "I'm starting work here today."

"Oh! My! Well, you really are ready to party, aren't you?" she said, and laughed. "Welcome. I'm Mindy."

I saw no reason to remind her that I'd been in here a few months ago asking about the girl who'd been murdered.

"Nice to meet you," I said.

Mindy's smile faded. "I haven't worked here long. My husband left me."

I was pretty sure she'd told me about her marital situation the last time I was here.

"He just left me," Mindy said. "Out of the blue. No warning. He just left."

"Sorry to hear that," I said.

"But I'm working here, so everything is fine," Mindy said. "Well, not really. Everything is sort of, well, it's not fine."

Jeez, what was with her? Why hadn't she gotten over her husband as quickly as I'd gotten over my breakup with Ty?

Maybe I could give her some pointers later.

"Which way to H.R.?" I asked.

"Oh! My! That would be Edie's department. I'll call her," Mindy said.

She eyed the telephone console on her desk that had enough buttons on it to coordinate U.S. naval operations in the Pacific; a half-dozen red and yellow lights flashed frantically.

"Oh, jiminy, now let me see if I can find her," Mindy said. She picked up the handset and hit a button. "Hello, Edie? This is—oh, it's not? Are you sure? Yes, okay, I'll try—which extension? Oh, yes, that's right. Okay."

Mindy pushed another button. "Hello, Edie? This is— oh, it's not? Oh, jiminy, are you sure?"

I walked away, figuring that, sooner or later, I would stumble across the Human Resources department.

A cube farm sat in the center of the room, and along the wall was a line of glassed-in offices where, presumably, L.A. Affairs' upscale clientele and the rich and famous of Los Angeles—or their personal assistants—came to discuss upcoming parties and events. The whole place was decorated in chic, sophisticated shades of beige, cream, ecru, and white.

I turned right and walked along another corridor and found a cluster of offices. All of them had little nameplates on the door. I stopped when I saw the one that read EDIE FRANKLIN, HUMAN RESOURCES.

Through the open door I spotted a tiny woman with supershort, pale blond hair rocking a Michael Kors dress and accessories sitting behind the desk. I rapped on the door, and she looked up. From the crinkles around her eyes, I figured forty was in her rearview mirror.

"I'm Haley Randolph," I said.

Edie's eyes widened and she threw herself back in her chair.

"You're here. You actually came," she said, and scrambled to her feet. She rushed around the desk. "Come in, Haley. Please sit down. I can't tell you how glad I am that you're here."

Wow, I hadn't expected such a warm welcome. This job was starting out great.

Edie ushered me into the chair in front of her desk. "Can I get you anything? How about some coffee? Would you prefer tea?"

"Coffee would be nice," I said.

Edie leaned out the door and screamed, "Kayla!"

She gave me a wide smile and said, "This won't take a minute. Just make yourself comfortable."

"What the hell?" A young, dark-haired woman in a YSL suit, whom I presumed was Kayla, walked through the door.

"This is Haley, our new assistant planner," Edie said, presenting me as if I were a Marchesa gown only just arrived from a Milan runway show.

Kayla looked at me with an I-can't-believe-it expression, and said, "You're kidding."

"Would you get Haley a coffee, please?" Edie asked, forcing a smile.

"Does she know about—"

"Just get it. *Now!*"

Kayla hurried away, and Edie turned back to me with her plastered-on smile firmly in place once more.

"Let's get you settled in, shall we?" she said, and took a seat behind her desk. She pulled a large packet from her drawer and handed it to me. I knew from my extensive experience that this was my new-hire info.

"We're starting you out as an assistant planner. I realize that when we spoke on the phone I mentioned the senior planner position," Edie said.

The senior planner position had belonged to the girl who'd been murdered a few months back—long story. I guess I should have been irked that Edie was offering me a lower position now, but I was really okay with not taking a dead girl's job.

Call me crazy.

"I see you moving up to senior planner in no time," Edie said. Her smile widened. "No time at all, really. And that, of course, means a significant increase in your salary, plus a company car—your choice of color—profit sharing, an assistant planner of your own, a quarterly bonus, a membership in a health club, a weekly spa visit, and a clothing allowance."

Wow, this was a fantastic job, all right. I'd have to give Marcie a big thank-you for insisting I apply here.

Kayla dashed into the office, sans coffee.

"Haley needs to come to the breakroom with me," she told Edie.

"I haven't finished going over her benefits," she replied.

Kayla's eyes widened and she leaned forward.

"Immediately, Edie. Haley needs to come with me *immediately*."

"Oh!" Edie popped out of her chair. "Run along with Kayla, if you will, Haley. I'll get back with you on benefits later today."

She shooed me out of her office, and I walked down the corridor with Kayla. We turned a corner and I heard a door slam behind us, followed by a woman screaming at the top of her voice.

"Who's that?" I asked.

Kayla rolled her eyes. "Vanessa Lord. She's our top event planner. Brings in all the high-dollar clients. L.A. Affairs would be circling the drain if it weren't for her—and she knows it. The rest of us just have to put up with her."

"She doesn't sound very happy," I said.

"Vanessa is never happy," Kayla said. "Nothing suits her. Ever."

"I feel sorry for the assistant planner who has to work under her," I said.

"Um, well, actually," Kayla said, "you're her new assistant."

Oh, crap.

CHAPTER 2

"Okay, look, I realize this isn't your fault, *technically*," Vanessa said. "But you need to resign. *Today*."

I sat across the desk from Vanessa in her immaculate office that overlooked Sepulveda Boulevard. I figured she was only a few years older than me. She had on an exquisitely styled, black Armani suit. Her dark hair was in a sophisticated updo. Her makeup and nails were perfect.

I couldn't find a single thing wrong with her appearance, which was really irritating.

We'd met two minutes ago when Edie—fresh from her screaming match with Vanessa—had introduced us, then left to have her Zoloft prescription refilled, no doubt.

I could easily see how Vanessa had made the decision that she didn't like me so quickly because, already, I knew I didn't like her, either.

I saw no need to share that revelation with her since I really wanted to keep this job—at least long enough to wear each of my eight fully accessorized business suits a minimum of one time. Collecting a paycheck would be nice too, since I'd received a troubling e-mail from my bank a couple of days ago.

"Why do you think I should resign?" I asked.

"Because I don't like you," Vanessa told me.

Jeez, no wonder H.R. was so quick to hire me.

"Don't take it personally," Vanessa told me. "I liked my last assistant. She quit. I want her back, but H.R. refuses to meet her demands."

I figured those demands included providing her with a cross and an unlimited supply of garlic to sleep with.

"As long as you're here, H.R. has no incentive to rehire her," Vanessa said. She pulled a sheet of paper from her drawer and slapped it down in front of me. "You can write your resignation on this."

I was tempted to write something, all right—two choice words came to mind—but I didn't.

"I'm not going to resign," I told her.

"Yes, you are."

"No, I'm not."

"Yes, you are."

Jeez, what grade were we in?

"Look," I told her. "I'm going to keep this job until *I* decide to quit. And there's nothing you can do about it."

Vanessa gave me serious stink-eye and pressed her lips together so tight, I thought cartoon steam might actually come out of her ears.

"We'll see about that," she said.

Vanessa stomped out of her office and screamed, "Kayla! Where is Edie? *Kayla!*"

I went to my office.

Kayla, who was probably hiding under a desk somewhere right now—not that I blamed her, of course—had showed me around the office complex while Vanessa had been screaming at Edie earlier. I'd gotten spoiled by having my own private office at my last job, so I was really glad to see that I had one here, even if it was right next door to Vanessa's office.

It came with a neutral-colored desk, chair, credenza, and bookcase, and was accented with splashes of vibrant blues and yellows in the wall prints. I gazed out the window down Sepulveda Boulevard, hoping to spot a Starbucks—home of my all-time favorite drink on the entire planet—nearby. I knew one was located in the Sherman Oaks Galleria, but that was about a five-minute walk from here—I preferred something under three, in case of an emergency.

I sat down at my desk and realized the morning was flying by and essential matters absolutely had to be taken care of. I pulled out my cell phone and made lunch plans.

Luckily, Marcie had anticipated my first day on the new job and had taken off a half day from her job at a bank downtown—is she a terrific BFF or what? We met at the Cheesecake Factory at the Galleria.

"So, how's it going?" Marcie asked after we sat down.

Marcie and I were a mismatched pair of friends—I'm tall and dark haired, she's short, petite, and blond—but that's okay because between the two of us, we can wear absolutely anything.

"Great," I said, looking over the menu. "Everything's going great."

"Really?" she asked. "The first day on a new job can be kind of intense."

"No problems," I said. "Wow, this Godiva chocolate cheesecake looks great. So does the chocolate mousse cheesecake."

"Remember that girl we went to City Walk with last year? The one who wore that dress with the stripes and the gold sandals?" Marcie asked. "She's having a party on Saturday. We should definitely go."

"I'll think about it," I said.

The waiter approached our table.

"I'll have the chef salad," Marcie said.

"I can't decide between the Godiva chocolate cheesecake and the chocolate mousse cheesecake," I said. "Bring me both."

"Sure thing," he said, and left.

"One of the girls in the insurance department came by

my desk this morning asking when we can schedule a purse party," Marcie said. "How about Friday night?"

"Maybe," I said, and gazed across the restaurant. "Where's that guy with my cheesecake?"

"What do you think of the new Enchantress evening bag on the cover of *Marie Claire* this month?" Marcie asked. "Isn't it awesome?"

"I didn't see it," I said.

Marcie gave me her I'm-your-best-friend-and-I'm-worried look, and asked, "Haley, are you sure you're feeling all right?"

"I'm fine. Perfectly fine," I said.

Marcie shook her head. "You've hardly been anywhere in weeks, and every time I mention scheduling a purse party, you don't want to talk about it. That isn't like you."

I shrugged. "I just haven't felt like doing much lately."

"And you haven't even noticed that gorgeous Enchantress bag," Marcie said.

"It's no big deal," I said.

"It is a big deal. Haley, you need to get out and have some fun." She narrowed her eyes at me and said, "Are you sure you've really dealt with your breakup with Ty?"

Dealing with a breakup could be handled in one of two ways. The first required numerous crying jags, beer, chocolate, and late-night conversations with friends whereby everyone agreed the guy was a scumbag, he wasn't good enough for you, and they're glad you broke up. The second way called for stalking your ex and your ex's new girlfriend, spying on their every move, and telling everyone—including strangers standing next to you in checkout lines—that he was bad in bed, whether it was true or not.

Just because I hadn't worked my way through either of those get-over-him processes didn't mean I wasn't, in fact, over Ty. Because I was. Really.

"Haley," Marcie said, "you never even cried."

I had cried over the breakup. Marcie just didn't know it.

The day that Ty and I had broken up—our mutual decision—he'd left my apartment where he'd been living—
long story. I'd just started thinking about tidying up the
place when Jack Bishop pounded on my door, demanding
to be let inside, shouting that I owed him, he'd decided
what he wanted, and he wanted it right then.

Jack Bishop was a totally hot, gorgeous private detective I'd met at the Pike Warner law firm last year. We'd
helped each other out with cases from time to time—but
that was it. Nothing more ever went on between us—Ty
was my official boyfriend, and I was a real stickler about
that sort of thing—though that day when Jack came
pounding on my door, all of that could have changed.

Except that when Jack walked into my apartment, I
burst out crying. He held me and listened while I told him
about the breakup, got me tissues, brought me beer, cud-
dled me against his chest while I sobbed some more, and
carried me to my bed after I passed out on the couch.

So, even though Marcie didn't know all the details, I'd
actually dealt with the breakup right after it happened—
which was why I was perfectly all right now.

"How about if I come over to your apartment tonight?"
Marcie said. "We can hang out and catch up on things."

"I'll think about it and text you later," I said.

The waiter brought Marcie's salad and my two slices of
cheesecake. I never could decide which I liked best, not
even after I ate both of them.

"Text me later," Marcie said, as we walked out of the
restaurant. "Let me know about tonight."

"I will," I said, and headed back to work.

The rest of the afternoon stretched out before me with
nothing to do—which was the beauty of the first day at a
new job—so I settled behind my desk enjoying the pros-
pect of spending several leisurely hours until quitting time

rolled around, doing nothing, accomplishing nothing, contributing nothing, and getting paid for it. My serenity was shattered when Vanessa barged into my office.

"This is yours now," she told me, and tossed a portfolio onto my desk. "Since you think you're such a hot assistant planner, I'm turning this event over to you *completely*."

I looked at the portfolio, then back at her.

"And don't even *think* about asking me questions," Vanessa said.

The only question that came to mind was to ask why she was always such a bitch.

I decided to hold off on that one for a while.

Vanessa glared at me for a few more seconds as if actually wishing I would ask her a question—which I didn't, of course—then stormed out of my office.

So much for my quiet afternoon.

I opened the portfolio and saw that the event Vanessa had turned over to me was a party hosted by someone named Sheridan Adams. I flipped through the contracts and the notes in the folder.

It didn't look like a huge deal to me; most parties weren't. The only thing that caught my eye was the bakery, Lacy Cakes, that Vanessa had contracted for a specialty cake Sheridan Adams had requested.

Lacy Cakes was known as the bakery to the stars, catering to celebrities, the elite of Los Angeles, and wealthy Hollywood insiders. They didn't do any advertising because they weren't interested in turning out twenty-dollar birthday cakes that could be purchased just as easily at a grocery store. Word of mouth brought them plenty of customers willing to pay thousands for a unique, custom-made cake.

I knew this because my mom had ordered a cake from Lacy Cakes not long ago. Mom was a former beauty queen. Really. She lived with my dad in the house I grew up in, a small mansion located in La Cañada Flintridge that had been left to her by my great-grandmother, along with a trust fund.

Mom's experience with Lacy Cakes hadn't been great, so I decided I should visit the shop personally and make sure everything was on track for Sheridan Adams's party— whomever she was. Besides, I had to do something until it was time to go home, plus I had on a fabulous suit and, really, more people should have the opportunity to see me in it.

I got my purse, grabbed the portfolio, and left the office.

Lacy Cakes was located on Burbank Boulevard near Kester Avenue, a few blocks from Sepulveda Boulevard, in a strip mall along with a liquor store, a mail center, a nail shop, and a used bookstore. Not exactly the classiest location in Sherman Oaks, but most of their orders came in over the Internet, by telephone, or from event-planning companies like L.A. Affairs.

I parked in front of the big glass display window that had LACY CAKES painted on it, grabbed the portfolio, and left the car. A bell chimed when I walked through the door.

The interior of Lacy Cakes looked better than the neighborhood suggested. There were several seating groups with huge, overstuffed sofas and chairs, lots of dark wood, and varying shades of brown and green. Positioned around the room a dozen exquisite, extravagant cakes for every imaginable occasion were displayed. They looked fabulous.

I wanted to lay my face on each of them and eat my way down to the platter—but who wouldn't?

I spent a few minutes salivating over the cakes, then headed to the curtained doorway in the back corner of the shop.

"Hello?" I called.

I got no response, but I figured everybody was probably elbow-deep in buttercream icing and couldn't exactly come running.

I waited awhile longer.

"Hello?" I called. "Anyone here?"

Still nothing.

I didn't have all day to stand around and wait, so I pushed the curtain aside and stepped into the back room.

I spotted buckets and vats of colorful icing and fondant—I've watched a lot of the Food Network lately—along with stainless steel ovens, several work tables, all sorts of gadgets and gizmos stored on shelves, and an office area in the corner with a desk, computer, fax machine and telephone. But no people.

Jeez, where was everybody?

I walked farther into the room.

I didn't see anyone.

I expected the place to smell sweet.

It didn't.

I got a weird feeling.

Then I spotted two legs sticking out from under one of the worktables. I circled around and saw a woman lying on the floor, a huge red stain covering the bib of her white apron.

Dead.

CHAPTER 3

"**I** should have known," Detective Madison muttered when he walked into Lacy Cakes and spotted me.

I'm pretty sure he wasn't glad to see me. I sure as heck wasn't thrilled at seeing him.

Detective Madison and I had a long history—but not the good kind. He'd investigated several murders at which I was a casual bystander—I swear—but Madison never saw it that way. He'd tried numerous times to find me guilty of *something* but never had.

I don't think that helped our relationship.

I hadn't seen Madison in a while, but he hadn't changed much. He had the belly of a sumo wrestler covered by a shirt with straining buttons, a tie with a gravy stain, and a sport coat his mom had probably bought for him when he'd graduated from the police academy thirty-some years ago.

I'd called 9-1-1 as soon as I'd found the body under the worktable and waited by the front door until cops showed up in their patrol cars. Detective Madison had arrived a few minutes later—I guess it was a slow day in L.A. murder-wise—but I didn't see his partner, Detective Shuman.

Shuman, I liked. He liked me, too—in a strictly professional way, of course—since I had an official boyfriend—whom I am completely over now—and Shuman had a girlfriend he adored. I'd helped him out with several cases and he'd cut me some slack all those times Detective Madison had been convinced I'd murdered someone.

I gazed outside at the plain vanilla Crown Victoria that Detective Madison had rolled up in.

"Where's Shuman?" I asked.

Madison drew back a little, as if I'd just asked whether he was a boxers or briefs man—ugh, gross!—then said, "Don't go anywhere."

He pushed past me and disappeared into the workroom.

I knew from experience that the investigation could take a while. I usually hid out—that is, waited—in a breakroom, but I hadn't seen one here so instead I found a spot on the sofa nearest the window and sat down.

I considered calling L.A. Affairs to let them know I'd be delayed returning to the office, but I didn't think reporting that I'd uncovered the murder of one of the company's top vendors was the best thing to do on a first day of a new job.

I thought about Detective Shuman and wondered why he wasn't working with Madison today. He could have been sick, or maybe he had a doctor or dentist appointment this afternoon. Maybe he was on vacation.

Another thought shot through my head—maybe he was on his honeymoon.

Oh my God, had Shuman gotten married?

Not that I wouldn't be happy for him, if he had. Really.

I'd met his girlfriend, Amanda, one evening during my shift at Holt's. They'd been dating for over a year now. The two of them had come in to buy a new stand mixer because Amanda intended to cook German food for Shuman. She was an attorney in the District Attorney's office, one of those attractive, competent, smart people who was impossible to dislike.

I hate it when that happens.

I liked Amanda. Shuman was crazy about her.

Still, I got a kind of yucky feeling in my stomach think-ing about the two of them on their honeymoon, all happy and in love—even though I was completely over my breakup with Ty. Completely over it. Completely.

There was a lot of commotion going on in the bakery—cops, investigators, and techs coming and going, radios squawking, raised and whispered voices—so I occupied myself by looking out the window. A lot was going on out there too, but pretty soon my eyes glazed over and I put the whole scene on "ignore."

"Miss Randolph?" someone called. "Miss Randolph!"

Jarred back to reality—jeez, how long had I been zoned out?—I recognized Detective Madison's voice. He was stand-ing in front of me, doing serious cop face.

"Do you want to explain what happened here?" he asked, as if daring me to answer.

I'd been through this several times before with Madison, as well as other homicide detectives and, oh yeah, a couple of FBI agents—long story—so I knew the less I said, the better—for me, anyway. Still, I had absolutely nothing to do with that woman's death, whomever she was. I'd sim-ply had the misfortune of walking in and finding her body. That was it. And no way could Madison spin it into any-thing more.

"I came by to check on a cake for one of my clients," I told him. "I'm working at L.A. Affairs now. It's an upscale event-planning company that handles high-profile events for an exclusive, elite clientele."

"And they hired *you?*" he said, with a definite sneer in his voice.

Obviously, Detective Madison had no appreciation for the totally fabulous, fully accessorized business suit I had on, which I had expertly styled with my awesome Louis Vuitton satchel.

His eyes narrowed. "Since when?"

"Today," I said. "Today is my first day."

"Your very first day on a new job and they send you out on something like this?" he asked.

I saw no reason to tell Madison that I'd left the office without actually informing anyone I was leaving.

He seemed to pick up on it, anyway.

"You *did* tell your new supervisor you were leaving, *didn't* you?" he asked.

"Well, actually—"

"So you sneaked away," he concluded.

Not exactly. Okay, maybe. Kind of.

"You came here to talk to Lacy Hobbs, the dead woman, didn't you," Madison said.

I gasped. The woman lying dead in the workroom was Lacy Hobbs?

Oh, crap.

"Don't deny it, Miss Randolph," Madison said. "I looked at her telephone message book. Your name was in it, followed by the word 'complaint.' "

Oh my God. I'd called Lacy because my mom had gone totally berserk over the cake she'd ordered and hated. But I couldn't tell Madison. No way was I throwing Mom out in front of that bus.

"You had it in for Lacy Hobbs, didn't you?" Madison said.

"No, of course not," I told him.

"So you got yourself a job that gave you an excuse to come here *and* made it look like you had a legitimate reason for being here," Madison concluded. "You did that so you could murder Lacy Hobbs."

"I didn't—"

"No one was here. You had the entire bakery to yourself," he said.

Were those cakes sitting around the bakery real?

"You knew the victim. You had a dispute with her—a well-documented dispute," Madison said.

How long had they been on display?

"You sneaked away from your job, came here when no one else was around, and settled the score with her—permanently," he went on.

Would anyone notice if I ate a chunk out of the back—of each of them?

Detective Madison glared at me, as if he actually expected me to confess to the murder.

"Don't leave town," he told me, and stomped away.

Like I was going somewhere—my honeymoon, maybe? I didn't have a fiancé, a serious boyfriend, not even a kind-of boyfriend, because I'd broken up with my official boyfriend—which I was perfectly all right with. Really.

I left the bakery.

I loved my apartment. I'd spent tons of money and maxed out an impressive number of credit cards to decorate it just the way I wanted. It was situated in an upscale complex in Santa Clarita just off the 14 freeway, allowing for a quick dash to Los Angeles—as long as traffic wasn't slowed to a crawl, which could happen without rhyme or reason at most any time of the day or night. Still, I loved it there.

I swung into my usual parking space and got out of my Honda. As first days went, this one hadn't been so great, but at least it was over and I was still employed. I headed for the staircase that led to my second-story apartment, pretty sure I could hear my emergency package of Oreos calling to me from my kitchen cabinet, when someone jumped out of a car parked nearby.

"Haley, hang on a minute," Marcie called.

I hadn't even noticed that she was parked a few spaces down from mine. Jeez, had she gotten a new car or something?

"You didn't text me," she said, "so I came over."

I'd forgotten that she'd mentioned coming by my place tonight when I'd seen her at lunch.

We headed up the stairs together and walked down the exterior hallway to my apartment. I opened the door and went inside.

"I checked online for the Enchantress bag," Marcie said, following me into my living room. "I looked everywhere but—*oh my God.*"

Marcie froze. Her eyes widened. She rotated her head slowly, taking in the entire room, then turned to me looking more horrified than when, a few weeks ago, a girl we knew told us she got her hair styled at one of those discount, so-called salons and actually suggested we should do the same.

"What *happened* to your apartment?" Marcie asked.

I'd told her about the changes Ty had made when he lived here. Apparently, she'd forgotten.

"These are the things Ty left here," I explained. "I told you. Remember?"

"Yeah, but—why is it *like this?*" she asked.

"He hasn't finished installing everything yet," I said, and placed my handbag and keys on the little table beside the door.

"What is that thing?" she asked, pointing to what could easily have been mistaken for a partially assembled, one-man tank sitting in the middle of my living room. It was surrounded by nuts, bolts, all kinds of metal parts, a thick orange extension cord, and several power tools.

"It's a grill," I told her. "The Turbo 2000 Mega Grill. It's got ten burners, twelve hundred inches of grilling space, side burners, a warming oven with two settings, it's all stainless steel, and has the most BTUs of any grill on the market today."

"Why is it sitting in the middle of your living room?" she asked.

"Ty hasn't finished putting it together yet," I said.

"And the television?" she asked, pointing. "Oh my God, is it bolted to your wall?"

"Ty bought it for me, after realizing my old one needed upgrading," I explained.

"Why are all those wires and cables dangling from your wall?" she asked.

"He put up the cables with duct tape because that's all he had at the time," I said.

Marcie eyed the artwork that used to hang on my wall and was now stacked up beside the sofa, and the chairs that used to form an inviting group and now sat at odd angles against the wall. She waded through the mound of bubble wrap, packing paper, and brown cardboard containers piled up near my patio door.

"Why is all of this trash still here?" she asked.

"He hasn't had a chance to take it out yet," I said.

Marcie pushed past me into the kitchen and pointed to the freezer Ty had purchased and filled with five hundred pounds of meat.

"You haven't gotten rid of this?" she demanded.

"Well, no," I admitted. "It's full of food and it would be wasteful to throw it out."

"Haley, what is going on with you?" Marcie asked.

Seeing my apartment through Marcie's eyes did give me a minute's pause. Yeah, okay, I'd let things go lately. A few things were out of place, needed picking up, but it wasn't a big deal. Really.

"I knew something was wrong," Marcie said, and began pacing back and forth across my kitchen. "I should have come over sooner."

"Nothing's wrong," I assured her. "I'm fine. Everything is fine."

She stopped and whirled to face me.

"Haley, don't you see what's happening here?" she demanded. "You've turned into a breakup zombie."

"No, I haven't," I said. "I'm perfectly—"

"Yes, you have." Marcie insisted. "You're living in breakup zombieland."

I just looked at her.

"Listen to me, Haley. I know what I'm talking about," she said. "You haven't dealt with the breakup. You're emotionally stuck. You're walking around, going through the motions, but you're really in a breakup trance—like a zombie."

I couldn't think of anything to say.

Marcie drew in a breath and straightened her shoulders. "You have to face the truth, Haley. You and Ty *broke up*. He's not coming back. And leaving all of this stuff in your apartment, pretending he's going to come back and fix it, is only going to keep you suspended in breakup zombieland indefinitely."

Marcie was almost always right about things. Oh my God, was she right about this?

My heart started to ache. My chest felt heavy. I could hardly draw a breath.

"He wouldn't just leave all of this stuff here for me to clean up," I managed to say. "He's coming back so we can . . . talk about . . . things."

"It's been weeks, Haley. Weeks. If he intended to come back, he would have done it by now," Marcie said.

"Ty wouldn't walk away from the mess he left me with," I told her. "I know him. He wouldn't do that."

Marcie looked at me for a couple of minutes, like she was judging me, trying to decide something, then said, "Look, Haley, I didn't want to tell you this, but now I feel I have to."

I didn't want to hear what she was about to say.

"It's the only way to make you see the truth," she said.

I kind of liked it in breakup zombieland.

"You need to sit down," Marcie told me.

She led me to the sofa in my living room and we sat down. She scooted to the edge and turned to face me.

"I saw Sarah Covington the other day," Marcie said.

I hate Sarah Covington.

She was the vice president of marketing for Holt's. She was pretty, smart, had her B.A., wore fabulous clothes and handbags, and made tons of money—all of which were reasons to hate her.

But the thing that really got to me was that she was all over Ty, all the time. She was forever tweeting, calling, texting, and e-mailing him about every tiny, miniscule, insignificant thing that happened at Holt's. She had to see him personally about absolutely any and all aspects of her job, and she was forever interrupting our dates, phone conversations, and what little time Ty and I had together. The worst part was that Ty never realized what she was doing, hung on her every word, and allowed her to shoehorn herself into almost every part of his life.

I hate her.

Now, with Marcie sitting next to me wearing that brace-yourself look on her face, I double-hated Sarah Covington.

"When I saw Sarah the other day," Marcie said gently, "she had on an engagement ring."

Breath went out of me. I thought I might faint. Then I got mad.

"He's engaged *already?*" I demanded, and sprang off the sofa. "To *her?* To that—that—"

"I don't know for sure that it's Ty. I didn't ask her," Marcie told me.

"Oh my God!" I kicked the pile of trash, sending bubble wrap and packing paper flying around the room.

"But you know how close they are," Marcie said. "So I just figured it was him."

I grabbed one of the television cables and yanked it off my wall.

"It was his idea," I said.

I might have yelled that.

"I came home and he was already packed. He said he couldn't be the kind of boyfriend I wanted—but he never asked what kind of boyfriend I wanted."

I'm pretty sure I yelled that.

"Do you think he wanted to ask Sarah to marry him then?" Marcie asked.

"I thought he liked this other girl—one *I* introduced him to."

I definitely yelled that.

I scooped up a shipping carton and heaved it across the room, then spent a few more minutes slamming power tools into the grill, jumping up and down on the extension cord, and pelting my walls with nuts and bolts.

Finally, exhausted, I collapsed onto the sofa again.

Marcie just sat there while I fumed, as a BFF would, then went into the kitchen and brought back two Coronas and a half-dozen frozen Snickers bars.

"At least you're out of breakup zombieland now," Marcie said.

Wow, Marcie was right. I felt like I'd been lost in a thick fog for weeks, like I'd been in some kind of trance, and now finally I was clearheaded again.

I tipped up my beer and settled back on the sofa, ready to do some serious catching-up with Marcie, when my cell phone rang. I had to climb over a small mountain of debris, but I caught it before it stopped ringing.

I looked at the caller ID screen and saw that my mom was calling.

Okay, that was weird. Why would Mom be calling me?

"Hi, Haley," she said when I answered. "I want to confirm that we're still having lunch together tomorrow."

I was having lunch? Tomorrow? With Mom?

"Well, huh . . ."

"*Our* day, as usual," she said.

We had a day? When had that happened?

"I'll meet you at one o'clock," Mom said, "at the English Garden tearoom, just as we planned."

The English Garden tearoom? I hate that place.

"We'll discuss everything then," Mom said, and hung up.

I stared at my phone.

Oh my God. I had a *usual* day set up with Mom? At that dreadful tearoom? And now the two of us were discussing *everything?*

When had all of this happened?

Then it hit me—I must have set up all of this while I was walking around semicomatose in breakup zombieland.

Then something else hit me—if I'd committed to *this*, what else had I agreed to?

CHAPTER 4

Leave it to a best friend to completely shatter your world, crush your dreams, and destroy your illusions—but, hey, that's what best friends are for. Right?

Hearing Marcie say all those things to me last night was tough. Really tough. But I needed to hear them. She was right—Marcie was almost always right. I'd been a break-up zombie.

Most of the last few weeks were still a bit fuzzy to me. The thing that stood out the most in my mind was shopping. I recalled prowling the malls, stores, shops, and boutiques, whipping out my credit cards like a quick-draw gunslinger in a Wild West shootout—a memory that was reinforced this morning when I once again received a concerning e-mail from my bank.

But the important thing was that my BFF had shocked me out of my breakup trance and brought me back to reality. I was clearheaded now and completely in control of my thoughts and actions. Marcie had even taken our friendship a step further by contacting a handyman who'd done some work at her mom's house and arranging for him to put my apartment in order.

I got off the elevator on the third floor and walked down the hall to L.A. Affairs. I'd selected a gray business suit today and teamed it with a classic black-and-white Chanel bag. I looked great, if I do say so myself.

"Are you ready to party?" Mindy exclaimed when I walked in.

Today she had on a navy blue dress with wide shoulder pads and chunky costume jewelry; she'd given herself big hair. She looked as if she'd just walked off the set of that old TV show *Dynasty* where she'd played Joan Collins's stand-in, if Joan Collins had been plus size with bad hair and worse makeup.

"Oh, it's you," Mindy said, then giggled and covered her mouth. "Good morning, Haley."

"Good morning," I said.

"I put you in the rotation today." Mindy gave me an apologetic smile, then leaned forward and whispered, "Vanessa made me."

I had no idea what the rotation was but figured I'd find out sooner or later, and I was pretty sure that if Vanessa was behind it, no way would it be good—for me, anyway.

In true corporate tradition, I stowed my handbag in my desk and headed for the breakroom where I, along with most all the employees, would spend an inordinate amount of time preparing a single cup of coffee, chat about our evening, our upcoming day, and our lunch plans, all in an effort to put off doing any actual work for as long as possible.

Kayla was in the breakroom when I walked in, along with several other women. Everyone had on a fabulous outfit, styled to perfection.

Kayla smiled when she saw me, then turned to the other women.

"Everyone, this is Haley Randolph. She just started working here yesterday," she announced.

The women smiled and introduced themselves, and a few of them gave my awesome suit an appreciative glance.

"Haley is Vanessa's new assistant planner," Kayla said.

The women all gasped and drew back, as if they thought I might have cooties, or something, and didn't want to get too close. A few of them murmured a couple of words, and they all scurried out of the breakroom.

"Don't take it personally," Kayla said, reaching for a coffee cup in the cabinet. "They have nothing against you. It's just that nobody likes Vanessa."

"I hate her," I said.

"I hated her first," Kayla said.

We both burst out laughing, and instantly I knew I'd found my BFF at L.A. Affairs.

"If you need anything today, just come ask me," Kayla said as she left the breakroom.

I fixed my cup of coffee, happy to see a generous supply of flavored coffee creamers—always a plus, in my book—and then went to my office.

While on the job I'd had a few months ago I'd developed a morning routine that had served me well—though, admittedly, not my employer—and I saw no reason to deviate from it here at L.A. Affairs.

I settled into my desk and sipped my coffee while I reviewed my e-mail. Then I read my horoscope, booked a pedi, caught up on Facebook, checked my credit card balances, and took a picture of myself with my cell phone sitting at my desk and sent it to Marcie.

A vague memory surfaced of Marcie mentioning the Enchantress, a new evening bag that had made the cover of *Marie Claire,* so I looked it up online, then nearly fell out of my chair when I saw it.

Oh my God. It was an evening clutch made from antique textiles recently discovered in a Milan warehouse, lined with Persian silk, and accented with beads and Swarovski crystals.

My heart raced. It was gorgeous—beyond gorgeous, really—and I absolutely had to have one.

I checked the Macy's, Neiman Marcus, and Nordstrom Web sites. All of them carried the bag but were out of stock. I added my name to their waiting lists. This, I knew from experience, would not be enough to actually get one of the bags. Something more innovative, cunning, and conniving was called for. I just had to think it up.

For some reason, this caused the image of Ty to pop into my head. He was innovative but not cunning or conniving, so I'm not sure why I thought of him at that moment, except that he still had a way of taking up space in my brain.

Then, along with the image of Ty, I flashed on Sarah Covington.

I hate her.

I pushed her out of my head and turned my thoughts to murder—which just shows how much I don't like Sarah Covington if I'd rather think about a dead body than her.

Honestly, when I'd found Lacy Hobbs on the floor in her workroom yesterday, I hadn't known it was her. I knew she was dead, of course—long story. I'd never actually met Lacy, though I'd gotten an earful from my mom about her and the cake she'd made for Mom's charity event that turned out to be absolutely abysmal—Mom's description.

I got out of my office chair, went to the window, and stared down at all the people and cars on Sepulveda Boulevard. Everybody had someplace to go, someone to meet, something to do.

Except for Lacy.

I thought back to yesterday and recalled finding her dead in the workroom—an astonishing accomplishment given the breakup trance I'd been in at the time. I figured her for late fifties—older, maybe, if she'd had some work done—with blond hair in a well-cut style, waxed brows, full on makeup, and a fresh manicure. She'd looked great—except for the fact that she was dead, of course.

I wondered if it would be any comfort to Lacy's loved ones that she'd died—or been murdered, actually—doing what she loved, that she'd left this world wearing her white apron with her company logo on it—a cake with a star on top—and clutching a piping bag filled with pink icing.

I'd scoped out the workroom while I called 9-1-1 on my cell phone but hadn't seen anything out of place. No sign of a scuffle. The back door was closed. Everything was neat and orderly, even the cake sitting on the worktable that Lacy had apparently been decorating at the time of her murder.

I thought a little harder and recalled that, during the commotion going on around me yesterday as I sat on the sofa and stared out the window, I'd overheard the cops mention that Lacy had been shot at close range. I conjured up the image of someone walking into the bakery, as I had done, going through the curtained doorway to the workroom, same as me, and shooting Lacy point-blank in the heart, then simply leaving.

It hit me then that perhaps I'd actually seen the killer when I'd pulled into the parking lot. I rewound my thoughts and reviewed the mental videotape of my arrival at the strip mall yesterday. Several cars had been parked in the lot and a couple of other vehicles had driven past me, but none of them seemed familiar and I didn't recognize anyone.

Of course, I'd been in my breakup trance, so maybe I wasn't remembering everything.

And where the heck was Detective Shuman, I suddenly wondered. Was he back on the job today, working the case alongside Detective Madison? I hoped so, since Madison seemed convinced once again that I had something to do with a murder and I knew I could count on Shuman to keep an open mind.

Maybe I should call him.

We were friends—though not friends with benefits—and I hadn't talked to him in a while, so it would be okay to call. He'd know it was just cover so I could ask him about the case, but hey, friends understood that sort of thing. Right?

I got my cell phone from my purse and scrolled through my address book. Shuman had two phones, like a lot of people did, and always carried both of them with him. One was his personal phone; the other was for anything that involved LAPD business.

I tried his personal phone first. His voicemail picked up, so I left a message asking him to call me. Then I tried his cop phone.

"Hello?" A man answered, but I knew it wasn't Shuman.

Okay, that was weird.

"I'm calling for Detective Shuman," I said.

"What do you want?" he asked.

The guy sounded grumpy and out of sorts. I wondered for a moment if it was Detective Madison, then realized it wasn't his voice.

"Is Shuman there?" I asked.

"No, he's not," the man said. "I can help you. What do you need?"

No way was I telling some strange guy the reason I was trying to contact Shuman. Since Madison had already decided I was a suspect in Lacy Hobbs's murder, I figured it wouldn't do me any good to say anything, even though my name had no doubt appeared on the caller ID screen.

"I'll call back later," I said, and hung up.

That whole exchange seemed odd and it made me worry that something had happened to Shuman—he was a cop, after all.

I went back to my desk and Googled his name, LAPD,

murder, and cop shooting but didn't find anything indicating he might have been hurt in the line of duty.

Whew!

Okay, so maybe he was sick and staying off work for a while.

I didn't like the sound of that either, but it was better than thinking he was dead. Still, if that were the situation, Shuman or maybe his girlfriend, Amanda, would check his messages and get back to me.

Of course, maybe Shuman was simply on vacation. Homicide detectives were allowed to take vacation, weren't they?

Or maybe he was on his honeymoon.

I wish I'd stop thinking about that.

The whole thing was bugging me so much that there was nothing I could do but find out for sure just what was up with Shuman.

I didn't have Amanda's cell phone number or her number at the District Attorney's office, but I checked the Internet and placed calls to several of the numbers listed there and finally reached someone who knew her and gave me yet another number.

"Hi, I'm calling for Amanda Payton," I said.

"Who's calling, please?" the woman asked. She sounded professional and competent, like maybe she was a receptionist or admin assistant.

"Haley Randolph," I replied.

"And what is your business with Ms. Payton?" she asked.

"It's a personal call," I told her, and envisioned her typing all my info into a message to send to Amanda.

"You're a friend of Ms. Payton?" she asked.

Jeez, trying to find out if I was seriously a murder suspect was turning into a lot of work.

"Yes, we're friends," I said.

"At what number can you be reached?"

I gave her my cell phone number.

"Will Amanda get that message today?" I asked.

"Someone will get back with you," she said, and hung up.

Someone will get back with me? What was that supposed to mean?

Was Amanda off work keeping vigil because Shuman was sick or injured, or lying in a hospital bed somewhere, hanging on to life by a thin, unraveling thread?

The scene played out in my mind. Amanda at his bedside. Shuman in a medically induced, drugged haze, plastic tubes and blood-stained bandages everywhere, machines beeping and blinking, nurses and doctors rushing around, and all Shuman can do is gaze up at Amanda, trying to communicate the deep abiding love he feels for her. And Amanda, choking back tears, trying to stay strong while his life slipped away.

Or maybe I saw that on the Lifetime Movie Network last week.

I've got to get a grip on myself.

Anyway, chances were that Shuman was fine. He had the flu, or he was on vacation, and more than likely the receptionist at the D.A.'s office told everyone who called that *someone* would get back to them, and I would hear from either Shuman or Amanda—or maybe both—before lunch.

Unless they were on their honeymoon.

Crap.

Not that I wasn't happy for them, because I was. But still.

Since I was driving myself crazy with my own thoughts, I decided there was nothing to do but get down to work.

I hate it when that happens.

I opened the portfolio Vanessa had quite literally thrown at me yesterday. When I'd glanced over it I'd seen that it involved some sort of get-together, but that was about it. Nothing much to worry about, party-wise. But now, thanks to Lacy Hobbs getting murdered, I'd have to find out from someone just what was up with the cake that had been ordered.

I read over the signed legal contract.

My heart started to beat faster.

I flipped through the notes.

My hands began to tremble.

Oh my God. This party was *huge*. Two hundred people were expected. There would be massive amounts of specialty foods, numerous musical performers, elaborate decorations, all with a Beatles theme.

The Beatles? Jeez, how old were the people giving this party?

I flipped through the file and saw that the entire event was being presented by Sheridan Adams. I'd read her name yesterday, but because I'd been mired in breakup zombieland I hadn't made the connection.

Sheridan Adams was the wife of Hollywood's highest profile, most prolific, Academy Award–winning director and producer, Talbot Adams. The man was a gazillionaire. Sheridan, a former actress, staged extravagant events at their estate in Holmby Hills to raise money for her charitable foundation. Anyone in their right mind would die— or kill—for an invitation to one of her parties.

I knew all of this because I was a vigilant reader of *People* magazine.

This was an event on a massive scale. An entire staff of planners could hardly handle all the work required to pull it off. Why would Vanessa have dumped it in my lap?

Then it hit me—Vanessa had given me this party because she knew how much work was involved. She thought I couldn't handle it. She wanted me to fail—big-time.

Oh my God. Vanessa was trying to get me fired.

When L.A. Affairs saw how bad I screwed up on this party, they would have no choice but to fire me. Then Vanessa could force them to rehire her old assistant planner.

No way was I letting that happen.

No way.

CHAPTER 5

"**M**y life is falling apart," Mom announced when I walked into the house.

Note—she hadn't said hello, asked how I was feeling, or checked on what my day had been like, which was just about all the info anyone needed to get to know my mom.

I'd texted her this morning and cancelled our lunch plans—which I still had no memory of making—but Mom had insisted I come to her place after work. So here I was, anxious to get in and out quickly because I had to work tonight at Holt's—which I did, unfortunately, still remember.

Of course, Mom didn't look like her life was falling apart. As a former beauty queen, she always dressed as if a red carpet might suddenly roll out in front of her and she would have to walk down it, smiling her pageant smile and waving her pageant wave, dressed for a black-tie awards presentation.

Today, for absolutely no reason, Mom had on a cocktail-length, strapless Pucci dress, four-inch Louboutin slingbacks, a diamond choker, and full-on makeup, with her hair styled in an intricate half updo.

Yep, that's my mom.

Actually, Mom and I look somewhat alike. We're the

same height, with the same dark hair and blue eyes. While Mom was stunning, I was merely pretty, as she'd told me many times. She'd tried for years to mold me into a duplicate of herself, and I'd spent most of my childhood taking all sorts of lessons—ballet, tap, modeling, voice, piano—with Mom coaching me, trying desperately to unearth some miniscule nugget of natural talent in me. I dropped off her radar after my younger sister stepped up and the big proton cannon that was Mom's desperate desire for a Mini-Me turned to her.

It didn't hurt that I'd set fire to the den curtains while twirling fire batons.

"You won't believe what I've been through," Mom told me, as I followed her through the house to her office—a room she'd decorated mostly with pictures of herself.

Until I'd escaped to my own apartment, I'd lived here all my life along with my dad—he's an aerospace engineer—and my older brother who's an air force pilot, and my sister who attended UCLA and did some modeling.

The house—a Spanish-style mansion in the San Gabriel Mountains near Pasadena with an awesome view of the Los Angeles basin—had been left to Mom by her grandmother, along with a trust fund. No one in the family had ever divulged—or confessed—exactly what my great-grandmother did to end up with so much wealth.

The bigger mystery, to my way of thinking, was how my mom could have possibly ingratiated herself to anyone—let alone a family member—to warrant such an inheritance. And in yet another bizarre, unexpected, and totally unprecedented twist of fate, my mother had been so grateful that she'd honored her grandmother by giving me—her firstborn daughter—the middle name of Thelma, after her.

Mom had started several businesses, none of which had ended well—long story. That was probably because her idea of running something meant coming up with an idea, then turning the whole thing over to someone with minimal qualifications and questionable credentials and ignoring everything that happened after that.

"It's that new girl," Mom announced, and gestured toward the door with a graceful, carefully manicured hand.

I had absolutely no idea what she was talking about.

"She's completely unacceptable," Mom said.

I could have asked her where the heck she was going with this, but I knew she'd get to the point sooner or later.

I hoped it would be sooner.

"Her work ethic is atrocious," Mom declared.

Then it hit me. She was talking about her new housekeeper.

Juanita, her former housekeeper, had worked for Mom for as long as I could remember. Aside from performing all the duties of a housekeeper, Juanita had been kind and caring. She'd always been there for me, which I had especially appreciated. Somehow, for all those years, she'd been able to put up with my mom.

Then, suddenly, a few weeks ago, Juanita disappeared. She just stopped coming to work. I'd gone to her house in Eagle Rock and looked for her—long story—but I never found her. I never discovered exactly what happened to her, where she went, or why she left—but I was pretty sure it was all Mom's fault.

"She's only worked here for a few days," I said.

Mom had already been through a number of housekeepers since Juanita left. I'm sure everyone at the employment agency was talking about her.

I know I would be.

"Maybe she just needs more time to get into a routine," I said.

Mom held out both hands and gave me a why-aren't-you-seeing-the-obvious look.

Then I realized what she was getting at. Her hands were empty.

Mom almost always had a wineglass in her hand—and, really, it should have been the rest of us knocking them back. Juanita had always made sure Mom had a glass of wine, which probably made her days here go a little smoother.

Still, Mom never drank too much. I'd never seen her drunk, thanks to her beauty queen metabolism, though I'm sure it would be a real hoot. She just liked to carry a wineglass around because she thought it made her look sophisticated.

I'm pretty sure she saw that in a magazine.

"The agency screens the housekeepers really well," I said. "I'm sure they would be happy to make any changes you want."

Mom put her hands on her hips. "Really, Haley, I'd expected more from you."

I wasn't sure how I'd gotten drawn into this, but it probably had something to do with my recent extended stay in breakup zombieland. Still, I saw no reason not to try to get out of it.

"There's nothing I can do," I said.

"Of course there is," Mom insisted. "You said you'd handle the unpleasantness of finding a suitable housekeeper."

I did?

"You assured me you wouldn't rest until you found someone to replace Juanita," she said.

This whole thing started to sounded vaguely familiar, unfortunately.

"Okay, Mom," I said. "What do you want me to do?"

"Fire her. Now."

"Now?"

"Immediately," Mom said, and pushed her chin up a bit. "I simply cannot abide such a thoughtless, self-centered, irrational person in this house."

I really had enough of my own problems to deal with at

the moment, but I couldn't refuse to help. Mom was Mom.

I felt kind of sorry for her, also, that Juanita had left and here she was trying to get to know a new housekeeper, form a bond, and make a connection with her.

"Fine, Mom, I'll fire her," I said. "What's her name?"

"I have no idea."

Honestly, where is my mind at times?

I left Mom's office and found the new housekeeper in the kitchen. She looked to be in her midtwenties. She was short, dark haired, and wearing one of those pale blue multipurpose uniforms.

"Sorry, but you're fired," I said.

Her eyes got big. "I'm fired? When?"

"Right now."

"You don't want me to stay and make dinner?" she asked.

"No."

"Or clean up something?"

"Just leave."

"Thank you!" She rushed forward and threw her arms around me. "Thank you, thank you, thank you!"

She grabbed her purse and sweater from the cabinet beside the pantry.

"I'll tell the agency it wasn't your fault," I said.

She rolled her eyes. "Don't worry about it. They know all about your mother."

I guess I should have realized that.

"No offense, but your mother is a real piece of work," she told me.

"Yeah, I know," I said.

She pointed to the door. "You want to come with me?"

It was the best thing I'd heard since I'd gotten here.

"Sure," I said.

I followed her out the door.

*   *   *

"We have a great deal of very exciting news to cover today," Jeannette announced.

I slid into a seat in the Holt's training room—my usual spot behind that big guy who worked in menswear where I could dose off, as necessary. Around me the other employees settled into the don't-bother-trying-to-get-comfortable-because-it's-impossible chairs, none of us the least bit interested in this evening's training session yet glad for the brief reprieve from our duties on the sales floor.

Not that I would have been working all that hard, but still.

At the front of the room Jeanette, the store manager, easily mustered an enthusiastic smile probably because she actually believed she was about to impart news that the rest of us—at minimum wage—would find exciting. If we all received her huge salary, quarterly bonus, and profit sharing, perhaps we would.

Not that she put all that income to good use. Jeanette, for a reason no sane person could fathom, chose to dress in the clothing Holt's carried. To be kind, let me just say that Jeanette was full-figured and in her fifties—not the easiest demographic to find stylish clothing, but she could sure as heck put her money to better use shopping elsewhere.

The Holt's clothing buyers who were, apparently, vision impaired and color-blind, somehow managed to consistently purchase the most hideous clothing on the planet. Nothing on our racks was ever the current style. The prints were all wrong, the colors were out of season, the styles were outdated. To make matters worse, though you might not think that was possible, nothing in the shoe, outerwear, or accessory departments coordinated with the clothing.

Jeanette always did a bang-up job of demonstrating how truly horrid the Holt's clothing line could be, and today was no exception. In what I could only guess was a tip of the hat to the fall season, she had on a skirt and blouse, topped with a swing coat, all in orange.

She looked like the Great Pumpkin.

Jeanette plowed ahead with her exciting news.

I drifted off.

Since, apparently, I'd promised my mom that I'd take care of finding her a new housekeeper, I really had no choice but to handle the situation—though I had put considerable thought into trying to figure a way to get out of it. I hadn't come up with anything, so I'd have to contact the agency that had sent the last girl—whatever her name was—and start the interview process.

A more pleasant thought flashed in my head—that Enchantress evening bag. Locating and purchasing the hot *it* bag of the season was something akin to a big game hunt. Certainly it wasn't for the faint of heart, the timid, or the ill-prepared. I'd have to get with Marcie soon and lay out a strategy for finding that evening bag. Then, of course, we'd have to come up with an occasion to carry it, plus buy the perfect outfit to go with it.

Then, for no apparent reason, Shuman popped into my head.

I get that a lot.

I hadn't heard from him or his girlfriend all day, as I'd expected. I'm not a worrier, usually, and I'm not big on suspense, so I was going to have to call them both again and find out just what the heck was going on. If I interrupted Shuman's vacation or his honeymoon, oh well. I needed to find out what Detective Madison was up to with Lacy Hobbs's murder investigation, and I couldn't wait forever.

The image of Lacy lying dead in her workroom floated into my head—preferable to listening to Jeanette, which says a lot about the Holt's training meetings. I couldn't help but wonder who would have wanted Lacy dead. Her bakery had been around for years, and that wouldn't have happened if her stellar clientele didn't love her work. Reputation was of supreme importance, and nobody lasted long in L.A. if the rich and famous turned on you. Plus, it was hard to imagine anyone would get so worked up about a cake that they'd murder the baker.

I guess stranger things had happened. Especially in Los Angeles.

"Haley? Haley?" Jeanette called, just as the guy seated next to me nudged me with his elbow.

I realized the room was quiet, everyone had turned toward me, and Jeanette was staring.

I was pretty sure I'd missed something.

"How is everything coming?" she asked.

I had no idea what she was talking about, so what could I say but, "Great."

"Excellent," Jeanette said. "It's a big project."

I was involved in a big project?

"Thank you for taking this on," Jeanette said.

I'd agreed to take something on? In violation of my own personal say-no-to-everything policy? Yikes! When had I done that?

Oh my God. It must have been while I was drifting through life in my breakup fog.

"Let's get out there and have a successful evening," Jeanette called, our cue that the meeting was adjourned.

I made my way out of the training room and down the hallway to the sales floor. Sandy and Bella, my Holt's BFFs, eased up beside me.

Sandy was young, red-haired, perky, and a complete idiot when it came to her loser boyfriend. He was a tattoo artist who treated her like crap. She was always making excuses for him, though I could never figure out why.

Bella, ebony to my ivory, was about my age, tall, with a

flair for hair styling. She worked at Holt's to save money for beauty school with the intention of becoming hairdresser to the stars. In the meantime, she practiced on her own hair. She seemed to have jumped onboard Jeanette's fall theme because tonight she'd fashioned her hair into a pumpkin atop her head—or maybe it was a harvest moon. Hard to tell since everything had gone 3D now.

"I still can't believe Holt's is putting on a fashion show," Sandy said.

Wow, that was a pretty lame idea, all right.

"Using only Holt's clothing," Sandy said, shaking her head.

Yikes!

"The whole thing is b.s.," Bella said.

"It might be fun," Sandy said.

She had an annoying way of always finding the good in everything.

"*Fun* would be a day off work with pay," Bella told her.

"It's a big deal," Sandy said. "A fashion show in every store, all on the same day. Maybe the clothes for the new fall line will be nice. They're all hidden in the stock room. Have you sneaked a peek?"

"I didn't want to go blind," Bella grumbled.

"The prizes look really cool," Sandy said.

"Only the prizes for the store that sells the most clothes the day of the show," Bella pointed out.

"We'll win, won't we, Haley?" Sandy asked.

I got a weird feeling.

"Haley is only the in-store fashion show coordinator," Bella told her. "Not a miracle worker."

"But Haley has a great eye for fashion," Sandy insisted.

"Nothing in this store can be called *fashion*," Bella said, then turned to me. "No offense, Haley, but not even you can come up with fifteen different looks using only Holt's clothing and accessories, send them down the runway, and make them look so good that customers in the audience will buy enough of them to make our store win the contest."

Bella might have kept talking. Sandy might have, too. I stopped listening.

Oh my God. This must have been what Jeanette said I'd agreed to take on. I was heading up a Holt's fashion show? An actual audience would see it? The store employees were depending on me to win first place—using only Holt's so-called fashion line?

How could I pull that off? *Nobody* could pull it off.

I couldn't listen to any more of this. If another sentence with the words "fashion" and "Holt's" in it was spoken, surely it would cause gridlock in the space–time continuum and the entire planet would implode.

Somehow I had to figure a way to get out of heading up this fashion show, and the best place to do that was the breakroom. I desperately needed a Snickers bar—and some M&M's. Maybe a Kit Kat—or two. And a side of Reese's Pieces.

I spun around, intent on making an all-out dash to the breakroom, and ran straight into Detective Madison.

Oh, crap.

What was he doing here? Had he come up with some evidence in Lacy Hobbs's murder, twisted it to suit his investigation, and showed up to arrest me?

Oh my God, if that happened my life would be over.

But at least I wouldn't have to head up the fashion show.

Then I noticed that Madison didn't have that gleeful I'm-going-to-get-you look in his eyes I usually saw. It was more like an I-wish-I-didn't-have-to-be-here look.

I got a yucky feeling in my stomach.

"You called Detective Shuman today," Madison said.

My yucky feeling got yuckier.

"Don't bother calling him again," he said.

No. No, no, no. This couldn't mean something had happened to Shuman. It couldn't.

"What—what happened?" I asked. "Is he okay?"

"No. He's not okay."

I'm pretty sure my heart skipped a beat. But before I could ask anything, Madison went on.

"Don't try to call Amanda Payton," he said.

How had Madison known I'd attempted to contact Amanda today? Someone in the District Attorney's office must have told him. But why?

"What's going on?" I asked.

Detective Madison hesitated, as if it took some effort to speak, then said, "Shuman is on administrative leave."

Okay, I was stunned. Detective Shuman was a good cop—a great cop. I couldn't imagine him ever doing anything that would get him suspended from the force.

Madison didn't give me a chance to ask.

"It's for his own good," he said. "Believe me, it's better for everybody that he doesn't have his shield and service weapon."

"What happened?" I asked.

Detective Madison drew a breath and let it out slowly, then said, "Four nights ago Amanda Payton was murdered. A single gunshot to the back of the head."

I felt like he'd punched me in the stomach. Breath went out of me. I couldn't think, couldn't comprehend what he'd said.

"She—she was murdered?" I managed to ask.

Detective Madison shook his head.

"She was executed."

CHAPTER 6

Holmby Hills was part of L.A.'s Golden Triangle, along with Bel Air and Beverly Hills. Back in the day, the developers decided underground utilities, tree-lined streets, and large lots for multimillion-dollar homes would ensure seclusion and exclusivity for anyone who could afford to live there. It had made unlikely neighbors out of heiresses and old-money industrialists, rock stars and Hollywood insiders—some of them living on the same street as the Playboy mansion.

I exited the 405 freeway on Sunset Boulevard and headed east. When I'd gotten to the office this morning I'd decided that if I was going to keep this job—and I was definitely keeping this job—I absolutely had to meet Sheridan Adams and try to figure out how I was possibly going to pull off this Beatles-themed party of hers—without making it look like that was the purpose of my visit, of course.

I'd made an appointment with her after mentioning Vanessa Lord's name, which, apparently, even though I was a total stranger, assured Sheridan I wasn't some psycho attempting to gain entrance to her home and steal something.

Sheridan had a lot of things worth stealing, according to the articles I'd read on the Internet, though how a burglar would find his way through what must have been a maze of rooms to get to the good stuff, I had no idea.

I mean, really, a house that had a flower-cutting room, a humidity-controlled silver storage room, a gift-wrapping room, a doll room, along with the umpteen other rooms, would surely require a GPS unit to navigate.

Sunset Boulevard wound through the hills lined with fabulous homes set on equally fabulous grounds. I passed the entrance to Bel Air and a zillion memories flashed in my mind.

Ty's grandmother, Ada, lives in Bel Air.

She's a hoot. We'd spent a lot of time together in Europe during what was supposed to be a romantic getaway with Ty. He worked for most of the trip—Ty *always* worked—so thank goodness Ada was there and I'd had someone to shop with.

I wondered if Ada knew Ty and I had broken up.

That little empty spot in my belly ached again at the thought of Ty. I pushed it away. Marcie was right. Ty and I had broken up. And that was that.

Then Shuman zoomed into my head, and that little empty spot throbbed in a whole different way. His girlfriend had been killed. I could hardly believe Amanda was gone, and I could only imagine how devastated Shuman was.

But, according to what Detective Madison had told me, Shuman wasn't content to sit at home and mourn her loss. The LAPD didn't take away a detective's shield and gun for no reason. Shuman must have been investigating Amanda's murder on his own.

I'd checked the Internet last night after I'd gotten home, hoping to find some info about Amanda's death, but I didn't discover anything. The District Attorney's office had put a lid on the incident, apparently. I'd called Shuman before I went to bed, then again this morning, but so far I hadn't heard from him.

I drove past the UCLA campus, then turned onto Beverly Glen Boulevard. I really wanted to talk to Shuman. I had to find out how he was holding up, how he was managing without Amanda.

Ty popped back into my head again, and that little ache in my belly got worse. I couldn't imagine what I'd do if something happened to Ty. For a few crazy seconds I wanted to whip my Honda around, head downtown to his office, throw my arms around him, and make sure he was okay.

I don't know what I'd do if he actually died. It was hard enough thinking he was engaged—to Sarah Covington, of all people.

I hate her.

I turned onto Wyton Drive, then made a quick right onto Mapleton. The streets here were narrow and winding, some of them steep, most of them laid out in a pattern that made no sense, just followed the slope of the hills. Residents loved their privacy. Towering trees and thick shrubs blocked out all but an occasional glimpse of a tennis court or a roofline. Massive walls and heavy gates discouraged the paparazzi, stalkers, and star-gazing tourists.

I swung into the driveway of the Adams home—mansion, actually—and announced my arrival at the call box. The gate rolled back. I parked in the circular drive and got out.

The house was roughly the size of the Superdome, a white behemoth that looked like maybe its architect had spent a lot of time in Greece. According to the article I'd found online this morning, the estate sat on several acres of manicured lawns. It had two pools, a grotto, a tennis court, a koi pond, fountains, pergolas, and more statues than the ancient Chinese Terra Cotta Warriors and Horses museum exhibit.

I'd gone with one of my black business suits this morning and teamed it with Jimmy Choo pumps, and a cherry red Marc Jacobs carryall, a take-me-seriously look I hoped would assure Sheridan Adams that I had everything under control for her party. I didn't, of course, so all the more reason to look as if I did.

Isn't that what fashion is all about?

I channeled my mom's I'm-better-than-you expression and rang the doorbell, and a servant in a white uniform let me into the foyer, which had roughly the same square footage as a Costco store. She directed me to a sitting room—my entire apartment would have fit inside it—and told me Mrs. Adams would be with me shortly. I pulled out my cell phone, took pictures, and sent them to Marcie.

"*Tell* me nothing is wrong."

Sheridan Adams, whom I recognized from this morning's Internet search, sailed into the room. The word "sailed" popped into my head because she had on what appeared to be an old-school naval uniform—white bell-bottom pants, a blue and white striped top, sneakers, and a canvas bucket hat.

I guess I shouldn't complain about how my mom dressed at home.

The article I'd read gave Sheridan's age as forty-two, but I was pretty sure she'd already crossed over into you're-seriously-old territory. She was rail thin, and all that time spent in the tanning booth had turned on her, leaving her with skin the texture of a circus elephant. Her hair was a number of shades of blond and totally fried. It stuck straight out, forming a nest, of sorts, for her hat to sit on, so I guess it was working for her.

Since she had so much money, she seemed eccentric rather than like that crazy aunt nobody ever talked about.

"*Tell* me," Sheridan insisted.

"Nothing's wrong," I said. I tried for my you-can-trust-me voice, but I don't think I pulled it off.

"*Something's* wrong," she insisted. "Muriel? Muriel?"

Sheridan turned in a circle, then shouted, "Muriel!"

"I'm right here, Mrs. Adams," a young woman said as she rushed into the room juggling an iPad, a cell phone, and a day planner. She was young, with short, dark, sensible hair and glasses that made me think of Velma in the Scooby-Doo cartoons, though I doubted she was having as much fun as the Mystery, Inc. gang.

Muriel gave me a quick smile. "Hi, I'm Mrs. Adams's personal assistant,"

I introduced myself and said, "Nothing's wrong."

"I figured that," she said quietly.

"Actually, that's why I'm here, Mrs. Adams," I said, using my there's-nothing-to-be-alarmed-about voice. "I'm working closely with Vanessa on your event and want to assure you of absolute continuity in the preparation and execution of your plans."

Okay, that was a total lie, but I didn't want her calling L.A. Affairs and complaining about me.

"What happened to—?" Sheridan pointed at Muriel.

"Jewel," she said.

"Jewel," Sheridan said. "She was Vanessa's assistant. I liked her. Where is she?"

I figured that Jewel was so fearful of having to work for Vanessa again, she was probably hiding in an abandoned bomb shelter somewhere in the Mojave Desert.

"Unfortunately, Jewel had some personal issues she had to deal with," I said. "The loss of one person will have absolutely no bearing on the success of any event. Everyone at the firm is up-to-speed on every event. That's how we do things at L.A. Affairs."

I had no idea how they did things at L.A. Affairs, but this sounded good.

Sheridan didn't look assured.

"I want to make certain you truly understand and appreciate the essence of this event," she said.

It was a Beatles-themed party. How much *essence* was involved?

"I want you to work with—" Sheridan pointed at Muriel.

"Annie and Liz," she said.

"Annie and Liz," Sheridan repeated. "They're experts on the Beatles."

I didn't need two experts on the Beatles to arrange for a caterer, but I didn't say so.

"I'll give you their contact info," Muriel said to me.

Sheridan headed for the door, then stopped and turned back. "Oh, and I want those people from the Beatles show in Las Vegas to do their act at the party."

Yikes! She wanted me to arrange for the world-renowned Cirque du Soleil dancers and acrobats to perform?

"Have them do the 'Lady Madonna' number," Sheridan said. "I love that one."

Jeez, how was I suppose to arrange that? I had no idea if the Cirque du Soleil even did private shows. So what could I say but, "Sure."

Sheridan left. Muriel was typing furiously into her iPad. I didn't want to look like I wasn't taking things seriously, so I pulled out my cell phone and sent a text message to Marcie asking about scheduling another purse party.

"I'll send you Annie and Liz's number," Muriel said. We exchanged info, then she asked, "Would you like to see the memorabilia?"

I must have looked as if I didn't know what she was talking about—because, really, I didn't—so she said, "The Beatles memorabilia that's being auctioned off at the party. The proceeds are going to The Adams Foundation."

"Yeah, that would be great," I said.

We walked across the foyer, down a hallway, up some stairs, and through another corridor. The beige carpet was thick under my Jimmy Choos. Framed prints and paintings hung on the walls. The only sound was the soft swish of cool air through the vents.

We turned right down yet another hallway, and Muriel gestured to the room on our left.

"That's the library," she said. "One of them."

I glanced inside and saw floor-to-ceiling bookshelves filled with leather-bound volumes and several oversized chairs.

We moved on and Muriel pointed again. "That's the doll room."

Hundreds of glass-eyed dolls stared at me, some in toy baby cribs, others in high chairs or seated at tiny tables, most packed together on custom-made shelves.

I gasped. Yikes!

"Yeah, I know," Muriel said. "They give me the creeps, too."

We headed down the hallway once more, and just as I was thinking I should have left a trail of bread crumbs if I had any hope of seeing daylight again, Muriel stopped in another doorway and pointed into a room.

"The whatever room," she said.

"Wow," I said, walking inside.

The room was large with built-in mahogany cabinets and shelves; a desk with a computer sat in one corner. A single window overlooked the rear lawn. A team of gardeners was clipping a tall hedge that camouflaged what I figured was an access road to the service wing, judging from the vans from a cleaning service and a plumber I spotted there. One of the pools—complete with a pool house—was nearby, and beyond that was the tennis court.

The shelves held dozens of Beatles items—lunch boxes, notebooks, book covers, all with pictures of the Fab Four on them. There were record albums, posters, art sets, bobble-heads, photos, and a model yellow submarine, some still in their original packaging.

"Mrs. Adams has been working for months to acquire them," Muriel said.

"Are these original?" I asked.

"All rare, and in mint condition," Muriel said.

Memorabilia collectors were fanatic about their favorites—Star Wars, comic books, superheroes, whatever—and would pay any price to own a desirable piece.

"These things must be worth a fortune," I said.

"Mrs. Adams expects to raise over a hundred grand," she said.

I took a final look around the room, then Muriel led the way back to the foyer.

"If anything comes up about the party just give me a call," she said. "I'm available twenty-four-seven."

I could easily see that working with Muriel would be far preferable to dealing with Sheridan.

"Thanks, I'll do that," I said, and left.

I got in my car and headed toward the freeway. My appointment with Sheridan Adams was concluded, and there was no real reason not to return to the office. Yet there was no real reason not to abuse the opportunity, either.

The freeway would have been quicker, but I decided what the heck and headed north on Beverly Glen, and wound my way into the parking lot of the Sherman Oaks mall.

I loved this mall. I mean, jeez, what's not to love? Bloomingdale's was here, and a Macy's. I figured this gave me two excellent opportunities to find the Enchantress evening bag I wanted. I only wished Marcie was here with me.

I struck out at both stores. Neither of them had the bag, which was majorly disappointing, but I put myself and Marcie—that's the kind of BFF I am—on their waiting lists.

Still, I saw no reason to rush back to the office.

It's always good to keep up on current trends, so I went to the Michael Kors store, then the Coach store. Everything looked fabulous, of course, but I was saving myself—handbag-wise—for the Enchantress.

And yet I still saw no reason to rush back to the office. I remembered a really cool jacket I'd walked past on my way to the handbag department in Macy's, so I decided to go back and take another look. I tried it on and, really, it looked fantastic on me. What could I do but buy it? Then I found an awesome pair of jeans and a sweater that would look great with the jacket, so I had to buy them, too.

By the time I made it back to the office a good chunk of the afternoon had passed with me doing very little—that benefitted L.A. Affairs, that is. I called Marcie—she loved the pics of Sheridan's house I'd sent—and we decided on an evening to go shopping.

Just because I had to—not because I really wanted to—I phoned the staffing agency about another housekeeper for Mom. The woman there—whose name I immediately forgot—suggested that in light of the recent incident—which was code for my mom being totally unreasonable and firing that other girl for no good reason—that perhaps I should interview the potential housekeepers before subjecting—my word, not hers—them to Mom. I agreed.

I managed to hide out in my office until five o'clock rolled around, then left. Since I wasn't scheduled to work at Holt's tonight, I went straight home. I was supposed to go to class tonight but decided to blow it off. Somehow, even during my time in breakup zombieland, I'd kept up on my assignments, so I figured if I could complete my college course work while in a breakup trance, actually going to class wasn't essential.

I got my Macy's shopping bags from the trunk and walked upstairs, trying to decide what to do tonight.

"Hey," someone said.

I froze.

A strange man was sitting outside my door.

CHAPTER 7

He was taller than I expected when he stood up, right at six feet. I figured him for maybe thirty, with blond hair that brushed his collar and a day's worth of stubble on his face. Nice looking, with a rugged build, though not the kind that came from hours in the gym. He had on faded jeans and a navy T-shirt that was about three washings overdue for the charity donation bag.

I didn't recognize him and he didn't look like he was there to sell something, so I wondered just what the heck he was doing here.

"Haley?" he asked. "I'm Cody Ewing."

He stepped forward and offered his hand. I don't like to shake hands with men. Their who's-got-the-strongest-grip caveman-inspired handshake was usually painful—and it ticked me off that they couldn't seem to realize I was a female and this sort of display of masculinity wasn't necessary.

I took Cody's hand with my standard I'm-a-girl-you-idiot two-fingered grasp. His touch was gentle, thankfully, and he gave me a little smile.

Hmm. Not a bad smile.

"Marcie's mom sent me," he said, and gestured to the toolbox by his feet. "I'm the handyman."

Then I remembered that Marcie had told me she'd send

somebody to get my apartment back in shape, and I totally panicked.

Oh my God, my apartment was a complete mess. Now that I was out of my breakup fog, I knew it was a disaster worthy of its own reality TV episode, and I didn't want anybody seeing it and knowing I'd actually lived that way. I couldn't have someone clean it up—until I'd cleaned it up first.

"Thanks, but now's not really a good time," I said.

"I should have called, but I lost my cell phone," he said, and gave me a yeah-I'm-a-dummy grin.

"Let's make an appointment for—" I quickly reviewed my mental calendar and said, "A couple of weeks."

Cody seemed to contemplate my suggestion for a few minutes, nodding thoughtfully, then said, "You don't want me to see your place, right? Because you think it's too messy. Right?"

How had he known that? Men didn't usually know that sort of thing.

"Have you got junk piled up shoulder-high or higher?" he asked.

"No," I said.

"Is there a path through all your stuff leading from room to room?"

"Of course not," I told him.

He leaned closer. "Did something die in there?"

"Gross!"

Now he was kind of making me mad.

"Come in. You'll see," I told him.

I unlocked my door and led the way inside. He ambled in behind me carrying his toolbox and stood in the middle of my living room looking around.

"I don't know," he said, shaking his head. "Maybe I *should* come back in a couple of weeks."

"It's not that bad," I insisted.

"I've seen worse," he said.

If he'd seen worse lately, I hoped he'd had a tetanus shot before coming to my place.

Cody grinned—wow, that was one heck of a grin he had—and said, "Go ahead and do whatever you need to do. I'll get started."

It felt kind of odd to have a strange guy working in my apartment, but what could I do?

"Want a soda or a beer or something?" I asked.

"I'm good," he said.

I left my purse and keys on the table beside my front door and headed down the hallway toward my bedroom. Some gravitational force pulled me into my second bedroom instead.

On the floor sat dozens of shopping bags bulging with items I'd purchased during my extended stay in breakup zombieland. I had vague recollections of buying all kinds of stuff to try to ease my heartache over Ty leaving. I didn't remember buying quite this much stuff.

Jeez, no wonder the bank had contacted me over and over about my checking account.

I was definitely going to do something about that tomorrow.

I set my Macy's shopping bag on the floor and just stood there for a few minutes. There were probably all kinds of fabulous clothing in those bags—I have terrific taste, even during a crisis—so maybe I was ready to check them out and put them away.

I'd tried to do that once before. It didn't work out so great.

But I was stronger now. My head was free of breakup fog.

I drew in a breath, walked to the closet, and opened the bifold doors. Since I used this bedroom for storage, the closet served as overflow for my clothes, shoes, handbags, and accessories, along with exercise equipment, an old laptop, books, and the general mishmash of things that seem to collect in a closet.

But now there was one additional item. A small, black duffel bag.

Ty's small, black duffel bag.

I'd found it there on the floor wedged between my snow boots and my bowling ball when I'd come in here a few weeks ago looking for something. Then, like now, seeing it made me think of Ty, and made that spot in my belly hurt again.

Several weeks ago Ty had been involved in a car accident—long story. He'd asked to move in here with me to recuperate, so his personal assistant had brought over some of his things. I figured Amber must have put this duffle in the closet and Ty hadn't realized it was here when he gathered his things and moved out.

I'd never really figured out what was up with Ty and that wreck he was in. The whole thing was weird. He'd cancelled his appointments on the spur of the moment one morning, ditched his totally hot Porsche for a rental, and driven north on the 14 freeway. What was even more weird was that he'd stopped at a convenience store, changed out of his suit into jeans and a polo shirt, and was headed for Palmdale when the accident happened.

He'd told me he was going there to check out a location for a new Holt's store, but I didn't believe him.

So, anyway, here I was with a duffel of Ty's personal belongings sitting for weeks now in the bottom of the closet in my second bedroom. I hadn't opened it—I hadn't even touched it. I'm sure that all his stuff inside of it smelled like he did and, well, I didn't want to make a return trip to breakup zombieland.

It hit me then that maybe Ty had left it here on purpose.

The thought zinged through me, bringing momentary joy to that achy spot in my belly that had Ty's name on it.

Maybe he thought that when I found the duffel bag I'd call him. Or maybe he intended to use it for cover so he could call me.

And what about all that other stuff he'd left in my apartment—the grill, the TV, the freezer. Did he think I'd phone him and ask what he wanted me to do with them? He'd paid for them, after all. Was that his way of wanting to talk to me again, maybe discuss our relationship, apologize for screwing up my life by leaving, for hurting me, for breaking my heart, for exiling me to breakup zombieland?

Or maybe he was really done with me, didn't care what I did with the stuff he bought, and figured it was a small price to pay to be rid of me.

Oh, crap.

I tore out of my bedroom. I needed to talk to Marcie. If I called, I knew she'd rush over. She'd talk me down, make me feel better, as only a BFF could do.

I hurried into my living room. Cody was slicing up the brown cardboard shipping containers with a box cutter. I grabbed my cell phone out of my purse and saw that I had a missed call.

It was from Shuman.

My all time favorite drink—nonalcoholic, anyway—was a mocha frappuccino available at Starbucks. My all-time favorite Starbucks was located in a little shopping center a quick four-minute—yes, I timed it—drive from my apartment. That's where I met Shuman.

After he called, I'd shooed Cody out of my apartment, thrown on jeans and a sweatshirt, and driven to meet him. I parked and jumped out of my Honda, anxious to talk to him and get the latest on what was going on, but I didn't see him. Then I spotted the only guy sitting at the outdoor café alone with a coffee and a mocha Frappuccino in front of him, and realized it was Shuman.

I hardly recognized him.

Detective Shuman was good looking, kind of tall, with brown hair and a boy-next-door smile. He didn't need that smile much in his line of work, but I'd seen it a few times and it was killer.

But tonight he looked thin and drawn, wearing a beige oxford shirt and jeans—Shuman seldom wore things that went well together—that seemed to accentuate his frailness. He sat hunched over his paper coffee cup, his arms on the table, as if the weight of Amanda's loss bore down on him so heavily he couldn't sit up straight.

"Hey," I said softly as I walked up.

A few seconds passed before he looked up, and then several more went by before he seemed to recognize me. He hadn't shaved in a while, probably since he heard about Amanda's death, and his eyes were bloodshot and red rimmed.

I sat down across from him and placed my hand atop his on the table. Shuman latched onto my hand—not too tight—and gazed into my eyes. I'd never seen anyone look so completely devastated in my entire life. Pain and sorrow radiated from him.

I guess I should just buck up, get over my breakup with Ty, and move on with life. We were, after all, both still alive.

I wanted to tell Shuman how sorry I was about Amanda, but there wasn't a word in the entire English language that could express how I felt, or one that would make things better for Shuman.

I covered his hand with my other one and we sat there for a few minutes just holding each other, then Shuman glanced away and pulled his hand free of mine.

"What's the story?" I asked.

"We're working on the theory that it was somebody she was prosecuting," he said.

"You know who it was?" I asked.

Shuman shook his head. "Several possibilities."

"You must have a gut feeling about one of them," I said.

Shuman gazed across the parking lot. "Yeah, I've got some ideas."

Unlike the other detectives investigating Amanda's murder, Shuman had the advantage of having spent his evenings, nights, and weekends with her. Surely she'd talked about her cases. She'd made casual comments, expressed worry, confessed she was scared—something that Shuman knew and had been investigating on his own, and probably not according to established LAPD procedures.

He wouldn't be on leave for no reason. More than likely he'd been looking for the creep himself.

That's what I would have been doing.

A minute passed before he looked back at me again.

"How did you find out about . . . Amanda?" he asked.

"I called your office. Whoever is covering your calls told Madison," I said. "He came by the store and told me to back off."

"Why did you call?" he asked.

"I hadn't heard from you in a while," I said. "And, well, seems I'm a murder suspect again."

Shuman's expression hardened, and he seemed to sit up a little straighter.

"The murder at the bakery," he said. "It's the only case Madison has caught since . . ."

"Madison seems to think I killed Lacy Hobbs over a cake dispute I had with her a few months ago," I said. "Which is ridiculous, of course."

"I talked to Madison," Shuman said. "He's got nothing. No clues, no leads, no witnesses. Nothing—but you."

While I appreciated Shuman asking Madison about the murder investigation I'd been thrust into, I felt a little odd thinking he'd gotten involved in my troubles when he had so many of his own. Then it occurred to me that since Shuman hadn't been able to help Amanda, maybe he wanted to help me.

"Listen to me, Haley." Shuman reached across the table and took my hand again. "Madison is in a worse mood than usual. This thing with Amanda, it's got everybody on the hunt—and wanting to bring someone down. If you've got any idea who was involved—or any way of finding out—then you'd better jump on it. Now."

Okay, this was kind of scary.

Shuman pushed out of his chair. "I've got to go."

"If you need anything—anything at all—let me know," I said. I grabbed my mocha frappuccino and walked with him to the parking lot. "Stay in touch."

Shuman nodded, got into his car, and drove away.

I slipped into my Honda and dug my cell phone out of my purse. I accessed the Internet and pulled up the Lacy Cakes Web site while I slurped down most of my frappie. They were open for business, according to the hours posted on the site. I started my car and headed for Sherman Oaks.

Okay, yeah, Shuman had scared me. I knew Madison had it in for me—he'd had it in for me for a long time now. I could see where everyone in law enforcement was majorly twisted up about Amanda's murder and wanted to take it out on anyone and everyone. Arresting me would somehow make Madison feel better about things.

No way was I going to let that happen. I had to find out who murdered Lacy Hobbs. Like Madison, I had no leads, no witnesses, no clues, and the only place I had any hope of finding them was at the bakery

I hit the 14 freeway headed south, then took the 405. Traffic was light. I exited on Burbank Boulevard and drove to Lacy Cakes. I swung into the parking lot. My headlights caught a makeshift memorial of floral bouquets and candles that someone had placed under one of the display windows.

I hopped out of the car and tried the door. It was locked. I cupped my hands against the glass and looked inside.

A dim security light burned in the back of the shop just bright enough for me to see that the furniture had been pushed together at each end of the room and all of the display cakes were gone.

Lacy Cakes was closed—permanently?

Now what was I going to do?

CHAPTER 8

"Are you ready to party?" Mindy exclaimed when I walked into the office.

This morning she had on a pink-and-white polka-dot dress. Let me just say that it wasn't working for her. Luckily, she was standing behind her desk and I couldn't see her feet, because somehow I *knew* she had on white panty hose and pink pumps.

"It's me," I said. "Haley. Remember? I work here. You don't have to say that when I walk in."

Mindy covered her lips with her palm and giggled. "Yes, of course, Haley. I know who you are."

I gave her the friendliest smile I could muster, considering I hadn't had my coffee yet, and headed for my office.

"Oh, Haley?" she called.

I turned around and saw her waving frantically at me. I walked back.

"You have clients," she said.

Mindy seemed to pick up pretty quickly on my what-the-heck-are-you-talking-about expression, because she said, "They were waiting when I opened up this morning. They said they were here to see you. They asked for you by name. 'Haley Randolph' is what they said. That's you. They're in client room number one. Waiting. For you."

Apparently, well-to-do clients intent on spending an obscene amount of money at L.A. Affairs were now waiting for me. Immediately, my Holt's customer service training kicked in.

I went to my office, dropped off my handbag—a totally awesome Gucci—grabbed one of the official leather-bound portfolios embossed with the L.A. Affairs logo, which we were required to use for each client—you always look smart carrying one of these things—and went straight to the breakroom. Several other women were there, everyone dressed to perfection. I fit right in wearing my brown business suit.

Kayla gave me a troubled look when I joined her near the coffeemaker.

"Just so you know," she said to me in a low voice, "Vanessa has been talking smack about you."

I figured she had, but hearing it still made me mad.

"She's saying that you haven't been asking her questions, and haven't been conferring with her about the clients and events," Kayla said. She rolled her eyes. "Like you're some sort of rogue event planner."

"She specifically told me not to ask her any questions," I said.

"That sounds like something she'd pull," Kayla agreed.

"She asked me to quit—the very first time we met," I said as I poured myself a cup of coffee. "She wants her other assistant to come back."

"Jewel?" Kayla uttered a short laugh. "Yeah, like that's going to happen. She only lasted three weeks working for Vanessa—which was a record. By the time she left, her hair was falling out and she'd developed a tic in her right cheek."

"They ought to get rid of Vanessa," I said, and dumped three packets of sugar into my coffee.

"As soon as she quits bringing in the big bucks—which will be never—maybe somebody will," Kayla said. "In the meantime, just watch your back."

She left, and I stirred vanilla flavoring into my coffee, silently fuming. Vanessa was setting me up. No way was I going to let her get away with that. I was going to make Sheridan Adams's Beatles party an awesome success—no matter what it took.

I left the breakroom and went to client room number one, then froze in the doorway.

Oh my God. If *this* was what it took to make the Beatles party totally rock, maybe I should rethink the whole thing.

Seated in the chairs in front of the desk were two women. Obviously, they'd both enjoyed many a good meal over the past several decades. I wasn't great at guessing a person's age much beyond the big five-oh milestone, but I knew these two women had pushed on, well beyond their somebody-please-kill-me-now-because-I-may-as-well-be-dead-anyway sixtieth birthdays.

Woodstock wasn't just a fond memory for them; they were still living it.

One of them had long hair, parted in the middle, with a beaded headband stretched across her forehead. I was pretty sure I'd seen the other woman's hairstyle on a perms-gone-wrong episode of one of those salon shows on Bravo. Both of them wore tiny, round wire-rimmed glasses with yellow lenses, tie-dyed muumuus, and necklaces with the peace sign—or maybe it was the Mercedes logo, I wasn't sure.

It took everything I had not to scream, "Styles change *for a reason.*"

Instead, I introduced myself and sat down behind the desk.

"Sheridan Adams sent us," one of them said.

Okay, so now their appearance made sense—kind of.

"You two must be the Beatles experts she mentioned," I said. "Annie and Liz?"

"No," one of them declared. She clamped her mouth shut, folded her arms across her considerable chest, and jerked her chin around.

"We're not Annie and Liz," the other woman explained.

I sincerely hoped that didn't mean there were two more women out there somewhere dressed like this that I still had to meet with.

"Well, actually, we are Annie and Liz," she went on. "But we've assumed our Beatles persona."

"From now on I will not respond unless I'm addressed as 'Eleanor,' " the other women declared.

"And I'm to be called 'Rigby,' " she said.

I looked back and forth between the two of them, and they both seemed to pick up on my you-two-old-gals-have-completely-lost-me look.

"Eleanor and Rigby," she said, gesturing between the two of them. " 'Eleanor Rigby.' It's the title of a song on their *Revolver* album."

"She doesn't understand," the one who wanted to be called Eleanor exclaimed. "We can't work with her. We can't possibly work with her. We should call Sheridan right now and tell her this girl has an inadequate background and a complete lack of understanding about the Beatles."

She wanted to get me tossed as Sheridan's event planner? Cause me to lose her account—and my job? And let Vanessa win?

It wasn't happening.

"I know a great deal about the Beatles," I told them.

I really didn't, but what else could I say?

Eleanor glared at me for a few seconds, then said, "We'll see about that. Tell me this—what was the title of their first hit single?"

Oh my God, she was giving me a quiz?

I'm not good at quizzes.

Eleanor must have realized from my expression that I

didn't know the answer because she blazed ahead and asked, "What was the name of their first movie?"

Jeez, I didn't know this was a timed test.

Before I had time to think—or come up with a good guess—Eleanor fired another question at me.

"What was the name of the television variety show they appeared on in New York?" she asked.

"I know this one," I told her. I might have yelled that.

Eleanor and Rigby stared, waiting.

"The old guy," I said, searching my memory. "The one who talked funny. Ed—Ed Sullivan."

I'm sure I yelled that.

"One out of three questions," Eleanor said, shaking her head.

"She's young," Rigby pointed out. "And she has arranged for the Cirque du Soleil people from the Love show to perform at the party."

Oh, crap. I'd forgotten all about them.

"She has lots of time to learn about the Beatles before the party," Rigby said.

I was supposed to learn the history of the Beatles?

"I'm sure she'll do better next time," Rigby said.

Next time?

"Yes, I suppose you're right," Eleanor said. She turned to me again. "But don't think this means you can slack off. Everything at Sheridan's party must be absolutely authentic—especially the music. Each tribute band should perform only songs from specific albums during each era."

There were tribute bands?

Maybe I should read the file more closely.

"You two can rest assured that I will do absolutely everything possible to ensure the success of Sheridan's party," I said in my it's-time-for-you-to-leave-now voice. "If I have any questions, I will contact you immediately."

"I'm still not satisfied you're the right one to plan Sheridan's party," Eleanor told me. "We'll talk again."

Great.

We exchanged phone numbers and I walked with them to the lobby.

"Oh! My! I love your outfits," Mindy declared.

I'm definitely going to have to have a talk with her.

As soon as Eleanor and Rigby cleared the doorway, I dashed back to my office, grabbed my things, and left. Since I had a perfectly good excuse to dig for suspects and clues in Lacy Hobbs's murder—and could combo that with keeping my job—I headed for Lacy Cakes.

The CLOSED sign still hung on the door when I swung into the parking lot. A few more flowers had been added to the memorial under the window.

I got out and peered into the bakery. Nothing had changed since last night. The display cakes were gone, and the furniture had been pushed together at each end of the room.

I knocked on the door, just in case someone was in the workroom, and waited a few minutes, but nobody came through the curtained doorway. I stood there for a couple of minutes trying to decide what to do, then the vision of Detective Madison barging into L.A. Affairs surrounded by patrol officers and arresting me flashed in my head.

I got moving.

I walked the length of the strip mall and circled around back to the service alley. It was wide enough to accommodate parking spaces, presumably for the employees. A Dumpster was positioned at the far end, and boxes and crates were stacked outside the rear entrances to some of the businesses. A delivery van idled near the liquor store.

I made my way down the alley and was surprised to see that the door to Lacy Cakes was propped open. I looked inside and spotted a woman at one of the worktables using a long serrated knife to sculpt a huge cake.

I think it was supposed to be a battleship.

"Hello?" I called.

She turned around, smiled, and waved the big knife my way.

"Hey, girl, come on in," she said.

She had on white pants, white shirt, and a Lacy Cakes apron. A bright red scarf was tied around her dark hair that matched her equally bright red lipstick. A tattoo peeked out of her sleeve and her collar. She looked to be about my age.

"Hi," I said, and walked over. "I'm Haley Randolph from L.A. Affairs."

"Oh yeah," she said. "I'm Paige Davis, Lacy's assistant—or I used to be her assistant."

I glanced at the floor beneath the worktable across the room where I'd found Lacy's body, then looked away.

"Sorry about Lacy," I said. "Must be hard for you to work here now."

"No, not really," Paige said. She eyeballed the cake and took another swipe at it with the knife.

Now it kind of looked like a Hummer.

"Things happen, you know," Paige said. "It's too bad but, well, what are you going to do?"

"Aren't you afraid to be here?" I asked. "Especially by yourself?"

She glanced around the empty room and said, "The others will be here later. We're all trying to pitch in. Besides, it's not like I have a choice."

"Why's that?" I asked.

Paige shrugged. "I just got hired a couple of weeks ago. I worked at Fairy Land Bake Shoppe, and no way can I go back there. My boss went totally berserk when he found out Lacy had hired me. He'd never take me back."

I'd left a couple of jobs that I couldn't go back to, but I don't think I ever had a boss who went berserk when I left.

"He was mad at you?" I asked.

"Yeah," Paige said. "But mostly he was mad at Lacy for

offering me more money. Said she stole me from him. It was weird."

"I saw the CLOSED sign on the front door," I said. "But you're open for business?"

"Not really," Paige said. "I'm trying to take care of some of the orders. A few customers heard about what happened to Lacy and called, so I got their orders from them. Their cakes are kind of small, so I can do them quick. Other than that, I don't have a clue."

I glanced at the office area on the other side of the workroom and saw that the fax machine and computer were missing.

"The police took everything?" I asked.

"Yeah, everything—even the message pads," Paige said. "I guess some chick complained about her cake, so the cops think she murdered Lacy."

That would be me.

Crap.

It seemed like a good time to change the subject.

"I need a cake for a party I'm planning. It was ordered a few weeks ago," I said. "It's for a Beatles-themed party."

"Cool idea," she said. "Wish I could go. I love the Beatles."

"The event will be pretty awesome," I told her. "Tribute bands, performers, a memorabilia auction."

"Super cool! Wish I could get my hands on some of that collectible stuff. I could live for months on what it's worth," Paige said. "I'd love to do the cake for you, but honestly, I don't know what's up with the business. Lacy's brother and cousin are fighting over everything."

My spirits lifted. Relatives of the deceased putting the smackdown on each other was definitely a good place to find murder clues.

"The two of them can't decide on anything," Paige said, then gestured to the curtained doorway. "Even the furniture. Belinda claimed what she wanted, then Darren saw it and got mad and pushed some of it back in his pile. It's crazy."

"I didn't know Lacy had a brother," I said.

Of course, I didn't know anything about Lacy, except that the cake she made for my mom totally sucked, but I didn't think this was the time to say so.

"They weren't close," Paige said, leaning her head right, then left, studying the cake she was sculpting. "He lives up north, some little town near San Francisco. I just met him when he showed up here after Lacy died."

"And their cousin came down with him?" I asked.

"No, she lives here," Paige said, and cut a big chunk out of the cake.

Maybe it was a frog.

"Belinda something-or-other," she said.

"I need to find out about the cake," I said, though what I really needed to find out was what was up with Darren and Belinda. "Do you have contact info for them?"

"Sure," Paige said, and pulled her cell phone from the pocket of her apron. She studied it and said, "Belinda Giles. Yeah, that's her name. And take my number too, you know, just in case."

She read off their phone numbers and I programmed them into my cell phone, then gave her my number.

"Darren is staying at the Best Western a couple of block down on Sepulveda," Paige said. "You can't miss it—he's driving our delivery van."

"Belinda must have loved that," I said, hoping to get a little more gossip.

"Yeah, those two are seriously going at it," Paige said. "I don't know where you can find Belinda. She'd been in here a few times, but honestly, I didn't know she was Lacy's cousin until she showed up after Lacy died and Darren mentioned it."

"Well, thanks for the help," I said.

"Yeah, sure. And let me know if you want me to do that Beatles cake," Paige said. "Sounds like fun."

I wondered if it would sound like fun to Belinda and Darren.

CHAPTER 9

It wasn't hard to figure out which Best Western Darren Hobbs was staying in as I cruised down Sepulveda Boulevard—the delivery van with the Lacy Cakes logo on the sides gave it away big-time.

Best Western had nice motels, but nobody—not even Best Western—thought they were catering to discerning travelers. This one looked a little worn.

I swung into the parking lot, took a slot a few spaces down from the Lacy Cakes van, and cut the engine. Paige had told me Darren's last name was Hobbs, so I figured either Lacy had never married or she was using her maiden name for some reason.

Maybe she was trying to hide something.

I hoofed it to the motel office, and the guy on duty phoned Darren's room and let him know he had a guest. I went back outside. A minute or two later, a man stepped out of room 112 on the first floor, near the Lacy Cakes van.

"Darren?" I asked, as I walked up.

"Yes," he said.

Wow, do I have mad Scooby-Doo skills or what?

Darren looked to be in his fifties, dressed in navy blue work pants and shirt, with a halfhearted comb-over ringed by a fringe of graying hair.

I introduced myself and added, "I'm sorry about your sister."

I saw no reason to mention I'd found her body.

"Thanks. I appreciate that," he said, though it didn't look as if it really made any difference to him one way or the other.

"I hate to bother you at a time like this," I said. I didn't, of course, but this sounded nicer. "I have a cake order pending with Lacy Cakes. Paige said she wants to make the cake but that I should talk to you."

"Paige told you that, huh?" he asked, and uttered a disgusted grunt. "She's anxious to keep the place going—a little *too* anxious, if you ask me."

"Why's that?" I asked.

"That's all she's talked about since I got here," Darren said. "Keeping the place open, filling the orders. Claims she can make cakes as good as Lacy."

"You don't think that's true?" I asked.

"How would I know?" Darren flung out both hands. "I just got here. I haven't seen Lacy in years. I had to leave my own business and come down here to straighten out this mess. I had to come up with money for a plane ticket and look at what I'm driving—in this traffic."

He pointed at the delivery van and shook his head. "Twelve miles to the gallon, if that."

"I thought your cousin Belinda was helping you," I said.

"Help? You call what she's doing help?" Darren's face flushed a deep red. "Sticking her nose into something that's none of her business. Coming around, making demands, telling me Lacy would want her to have her personal belongings. It's a lie. All of it."

I could see that Darren was getting angrier and angrier, and while most people would have backed off, I saw this as the best time to push forward and antagonize him further in hopes of gathering more info.

I'm pretty sure that's how all the great detectives do it.

"If Lacy and Belinda were close, wouldn't you want Belinda to have her things?" I asked.

"Close? Who said they were close? Is that what Belinda is telling everybody?" Darren demanded. He made a little snarling sound under his breath. "I doubt they'd spoken to each other in years after what happened."

Come to think of it, all the great detectives bring backup with them for occasions such as this.

I'll be sure to remember that next time.

"Lacy left home right after high school. Just walked out with no thought to what it did to our family," Darren said. "She came to Los Angeles and—and I don't know what she did for years because we seldom heard from her. Then she ends up with this bakery, and still we almost never heard from her. Broke my mother's heart. Left me to try and keep Dad's cabinet shop going, and figure a way to pay for their medications, their care."

"That was really crappy," I said.

"Darn right it was," Darren said. He huffed for a couple more minutes before his anger eased away. "Growing up, Lacy and Belinda were like sisters. Did everything together. Went everywhere together. Typical kid stuff, then typical teenage stuff. Listening to records, buying those magazines and all that other stuff, all that nonsense with the long hair. England this, British that—like all of it was so damn important. Who knows the Dave Clark Five now, anyway?"

I sure didn't, and I really hoped Eleanor and Rigby weren't going to quiz me on whatever it was.

"So what happened?" I asked.

"Something stupid," Darren said, and waved his hand as if he could wipe away whatever it was that had happened. "Belinda got tickets to some concert—won them in a radio station contest, or something—and took her boyfriend. Lacy went through the roof. They never spoke again."

Wow, that must have been an awesome concert.

"But Belinda moved to Los Angeles, like Lacy did?" I asked. "Why would she do that if they weren't friends anymore?"

"How the heck should I know?" Darren said, and flung both arms into the air. He sighed heavily. "All I know is that I've got another mess to clean up—because of Lacy."

"You could probably use some money," I said, as delicately as I can ever say anything. "The cake I need costs twelve thousand dollars, so if you—"

"Twelve grand?" Darren's eyes flew open. "For a *cake?*"

"Actually, that's probably one of the least expensive cakes Lacy made," I said. "Most of them were way more than that."

Darren muttered under his breath and shook his head. "Lacy was making that kind of money? And she couldn't send anything home to our parents? Or to me for taking care of them? Not one red cent?"

He fumed for a few more minutes, and, really, I couldn't blame him.

"I can't turn down that kind of cash," Darren said, though it didn't seem to please him in the least. "Tell that girl—what's her name?—that girl at the shop to go ahead with it."

"I'll let her know," I said.

"But I don't know what I'm going to do with the business," Darren said, his anger rising again. "So don't let her think this means she can keep working there. She already went ahead with a couple of orders without discussing them with me. You ask me, she's awful anxious to take over the place herself."

"Maybe she just needs a job," I said, remembering what she'd told me about leaving her previous employer.

Darren shook his head. "She wants to run it, and now that you're telling me the kind of money it brings in, I can see why. You ask me, it's suspicious. Makes me wonder."

It made me wonder, too. Paige claimed she'd been hired away from Fairy Land Bake Shoppe by Lacy, but how did I know if that was true? Had she seen a better opportunity at Lacy Cakes and gone for it? Had her ambition taken her further—all the way to murder?

Darren went back into his motel room and slammed the door.

I got in my Honda and left.

Since the Lacy Cakes bakery was on my way to the office—and would delay my actual arrival—I decided I'd stop in and give Paige the go-ahead for the Beatles cake Sheridan Adams wanted for her party. I parked near the entrance to the alley, grabbed the portfolio I'd brought with me from L.A. Affairs, and headed toward the rear door of the bakery.

My cell phone rang. Muriel's name appeared on the caller I.D. screen.

I froze. Oh my God, was she calling to tell me that Eleanor and Rigby had reported to Sheridan that I'd failed their Beatles trivia quiz and that I was fired? This was exactly the sort of thing someone like Sheridan would push off on her personal assistant.

Since I'm not big on suspense, I answered.

"Hi, Haley," Muriel said. "Listen, I hate to spring this on you so close to the party, but Mrs. Adams has decided she wants gift bags for all her guests."

"All two hundred of them?" I asked.

"Custom-made," Muriel said.

Where the heck was I supposed to get custom-made gift bags?

"Something that reflects the essence of the Beatles."

The Beatles had an essence?

"And she wants them filled with special, unique items," Muriel said.

Now I kind of wish she'd fired me.

Muriel seemed to read my these-people-have-way-too-much-money thoughts and said, "I'll e-mail you the details. Call me if you have any questions."

"I'll get it handled," I said.

Okay, I had no idea how I was going to pull this off, but what else could I say?

"Send me the contract amendment and I'll have her sign it," Muriel said, and we hung up.

I flipped open the portfolio and got the name and e-mail address of the woman in the L.A. Affairs' legal department who'd drawn up Sheridan's original contract. I sent her a message about the gift bags.

Lucky for me, Jewel, Vanessa's former assistant—who was probably working under an assumed name at a Taco Bell drive-through somewhere in Montana—had done a great job setting everything up, so all I had to do was pull off the gift bags and follow up on everything else—provided, of course, that Sheridan Adams wouldn't make any more requests for additions to her party.

I tucked my phone away, then closed the portfolio and went through the Lacy Cakes back door. Paige was still working on the cake—and yes, now I could see that it was definitely a frog, although why anyone would want a cake shaped like a frog I couldn't imagine. A guy was busy at the huge mixer whipping up cake batter. We exchanged head nods.

"Hey, girl, come on in," Paige called.

Darren's comment that Paige seemed *too anxious* to take over Lacy Cakes flashed in my mind. She seemed happy and carefree, yet conscientious enough to fill the orders Lacy had accepted and not let her customers down.

But looks were deceiving. I'd been fooled by appearances in the past.

I'm sure all the great detectives had made that mistake. Pretty sure.

"I talked to Darren about the cake," I said, joining her at the worktable. "He said to go ahead with it."

"Awesome," Paige said, and gave a little fist pump.

I opened the portfolio and pulled out L.A. Affairs' copy of the info on Sheridan Adams's cake that had been given to Lacy and was now in the possession of the LAPD along with all the other stuff they'd taken from the bakery as evidence. The cake was supposed to be shaped like a six-foot-long submarine.

"She wants it to be yellow," I told Paige.

"Yeah, sure. Off their *Yellow Submarine* album," she said, bobbing and swaying as if the tune was playing in her head. "One of their best songs in, like, the whole world is on that album."

I wasn't in the mood for another Beatles quiz.

"You're sure you can do this cake?" I asked. "Sheridan Adams is a huge deal."

"Oh, yeah, no problem," Paige said. "Because all you need is love. Right?"

I had no idea what she was talking about.

"So Darren's keeping the bakery open, huh?" Paige asked.

I didn't think that telling Paige her future at Lacy Cakes didn't look so hot would benefit anyone—especially me.

"He hasn't decided anything yet," I said.

Yeah, okay, that was a kind-of lie, but I needed that cake and I needed it to look perfect, and it absolutely had to be delivered on time, so what else could I say?

"I'll photocopy all this stuff and bring it back," I said. I tucked the papers into the folder again and left.

I headed back to L.A. Affairs—it was late and I didn't want to miss my lunch hour—thinking about Darren, Belinda, and Paige. So far, they were my only suspects in Lacy's murder and, really, none of them had much of a motive—that I'd uncovered, anyway.

Then I remembered the owner of Fairy Land Bake Shoppe who'd been mad about losing Paige to Lacy. I wondered if he was mad enough to kill.

Then my mom flashed in my head. She'd been unhappy with the cake Lacy had made for a charity event she was involved with—Mom had told me what it was, but honestly I wasn't listening. She'd been so upset about the way the cake had turned out, I'd had to drive over to try to calm her down.

True, Mom was a perfectionist and a demanding customer, but the charity had forked out a ton of money for the cake, and while Lacy Cakes was big on presentation, the thing ought to be edible. It wasn't.

I figured that if Mom's experience with Lacy Cakes hadn't gone so well, maybe hers wasn't the only one.

As I waited for the traffic signal to change at Sepulveda Boulevard, I put my Bluetooth in my ear and called her.

"I hope this means you've found me a housekeeper," Mom said when she picked up.

"I need to ask you about that cake you got from the Lacy Cakes bakery," I said.

Sometimes, if I hit her with a topic that's all about her, she doesn't notice that I've ignored her comment.

"Oh, that cake!"

Mom went into what everyone in the family referred to as The Great Cake Tirade that we'd all heard a couple of dozen times already. I tuned her out with practiced ease. By the time I pulled into the parking garage she took a breath. I jumped in.

"So, Mom, do you know of anyone else who wasn't pleased with their cake?" I asked.

If anyone would have this info, it would be Mom. For a reason I've never understood, women always confide in her. Among her former beauty queen, old-money, and society friends, she's considered warm—which says a lot about her circle of friends.

"I most certainly do," Mom said. "Sasha Gibson's daughter's wedding was ruined by Lacy Cakes."

I'm not exactly sure how a cake can ruin an entire wedding, but I didn't say so.

"Can you get me the daughter's phone number?" I asked.

"Are you planning a class action suit against Lacy Cakes?" Mom asked.

I'm pretty sure Mom thinks I still work for the Pike Warner law firm. She also thinks I have my bachelor's degree, and I'm certain she thinks Ty and I are still dating.

Jeez, I wish I could stop thinking about Ty.

"Yeah, Mom, that's it," I said.

"I'll call you back." Mom hung up.

I parked and took the elevator up to the third floor. My phone rang as I walked through the door of L.A. Affairs, giving me the perfect opportunity to ignore Mindy when she shouted, "Are you ready to party?" at me.

"I just spoke with Sasha and got all the information on her daughter," Mom said when I answered. "I just sent you a text."

"Great, Mom, I'll call her right away," I said.

"Unfortunately, you can't reach her," Mom said. "She was so distraught over everything she went to South America."

"South America?" I might have said that louder than I meant to, but jeez, how upset can you be over a cake?

"Yes, Sasha was surprised, too," Mom said. "It was all quite sudden. Her daughter just packed a bag and left."

I got a weird feeling.

"When was this?" I asked.

"A few days ago," Mom said.

Lacy Hobbs was murdered a few days ago.

"Now, about this lawsuit," Mom said. "When are you—"

"Sorry, Mom, you're breaking—"

I hung up—yeah, I know that's not a nice thing to do to your mom, but I had stuff to take care of.

I read the text she'd sent me as I went into my office. I sat down at my desk, accessed the Internet on my computer, and found an article from last spring in one of the local magazines that featured the runaway bride, Heather Gibson; her groom, Andrew Pritchard; and several other socially prominent couples discussing what they'd worn for their engagement photos.

Ty popped into my head. Would he and Sarah Covington be featured in one of these articles?

I forced the image out of my head.

We'd broken up—and I didn't even know for sure that it was Ty to whom Sarah was engaged—and that was that.

I focused my thoughts on my immediate problem.

Sasha's daughter might have up and vanished, but I could still get all the info I needed—provided, of course that Jack Bishop was still speaking to me.

Chapter 10

"It's b.s.," Bella said. "You ask me, it's b.s."

We were in the Holt's employee breakroom watching TV and eating snacks from the vending machines—okay, it was mostly me eating the snacks—and waiting for the last hour of our can-our-lives-get-any-worse shift to end. Bella was fixated on the poster on the wall extolling the exciting details of the upcoming Holt's fashion show. Since I was in charge of the event, I was trying to ignore it.

"They're calling it a contest," Bella grumbled. "How are we supposed to win anything? It all comes down to how many customers actually show up for the so-called fashion show, then pony up their money to buy something."

"It sounds like a crappy contest to me," I said, and picked up my second bag of M&M's.

In fact, all of Holt's contests were crappy, in my opinion. I figured that if we won anything better than the beach towel all the store employees had gotten in the last contest, we could count ourselves lucky.

"At least you'll get something good, if our store wins," Bella said.

The last prize Holt's had awarded me was a totally lame sewing machine, so I wasn't at all interested in hearing about the grand prize in this contest.

Besides, all of the Holt's employee contests were conceived and forced upon us by Sarah Covington.

I hate her.

And now she was engaged to Ty—maybe.

I ripped the end off of the M&M's bag and dumped them into my mouth.

But that's okay because Ty and I broke up.

I still hate Sarah Covington, of course.

"Hey, look at that," Bella said, and pointed to the television.

I glanced up to see a commercial for an afternoon soap opera. I knew it was a soap opera because overly dramatic music was playing and the actors were all delivering their lines as if they were newscasters reporting that a meteor was about to crash into Earth, ending all life on our planet.

"That's *her*," Bella said. "Look. It's her."

I watched as the camera zoomed in on a blond actress standing beside a fake fireplace, looking end-of-Earth worried.

"Oh my God, it *is* her," I realized.

She was that girl who used to work here and always stunk up the breakroom with those microwavable diet meals. She'd lost a hundred pounds, or something, swapped her glasses for contacts, gone blond, and quit Holt's. I'd seen her modeling in print ads, then doing a shampoo commercial. And now she was on a soap opera?

"I hate her," Bella said.

I hated her too, of course.

"I'm out of here." Bella shoved out of her chair, dumped her trash, and headed back to the sales floor. I finished off another bag of M&M's, and followed.

I'd been assigned to the boys clothing department tonight—which was the all-time most boring department in retail—and I couldn't face my final hour in the store sizing Batman briefs and Phineas and Ferb pajamas. I went into the stock room instead.

I figured that since I hadn't yet come up with a good excuse for ditching my duties as Holt's fashion show coordinator, I may as well take advantage of the situation.

The stock room was really cool. There were towering shelving units stuffed absolutely full of all kinds of fresh, new merchandise, and miles of racks that held plastic-wrapped hanging garments—although the mannequin farm by the janitor's closet was kind of creepy.

During the day, the truck team was here unloading the new merchandise from the big rigs backed up to the loading dock, and employees were busy hauling it onto the sales floor on U-boats and Z-rails, or placing it in its designated location on either the first or second floor of the stock room. In the evening few employees had reason to come back here. It was quiet except for the Holt's music track and an occasional announcement over the P.A. system.

I wound my way to the rear of the stock room near the big roll-up doors where the clothing for the Holt's fashion show had been strategically placed. There were dozens of big brown boxes that held the folded garments and accessories. The hanging items were not only wrapped in plastic but covered in tarps. Apparently, Holt's wanted to surprise the employees with the new line on the day of the fashion show.

Nobody was looking forward to *that* surprise.

A few minutes passed while I gathered my courage—and killed a little more of my shift—then lifted the tarp.

Yikes!

I jumped back. Oh my God, this stuff was horrible—no, it was beyond horrible. It was hideous—no, it was beyond hideous, whatever that was.

How the heck was I supposed to pull off a fashion show? Corporate had hired models—but how was I going to force them into these garments and make them walk down the runway?

I drew in a big breath, trying to calm myself. Just as well I wasn't interested in winning the fashion show coordinator's prize—whatever it was.

I headed back across the stock room—the boys department didn't seem so bad right now—then came to my senses and trotted up the big concrete staircase to the second floor. I didn't like coming up here—long story—but I had some personal business to attend to.

I pulled my cell phone from my back pocket—we're not supposed to keep our phones on us, but oh well—and called Shuman. I hadn't heard from him and he'd been on my mind since I saw him at Starbucks. I wanted to find out if the LAPD had made any progress in Amanda's murder, but mostly I wanted to see how Shuman was holding up. I'd never met his family or his friends, so I didn't know anyone to ask, and I sure as heck wasn't going to call Detective Madison.

Shuman's voicemail picked up. I didn't know if that meant he wasn't up to talking to me or if something else was going on. Like maybe, despite being relieved of his official duties, he was out looking for Amanda's killer himself.

Can't say that I blame him.

I left a message, then hung up and called Marcie. We talked until it was time for my shift to end—which, I know, was kind of bad, but I needed time to recover from looking directly at those awful fashion show clothes.

We discussed the purse party a girl in her office building wanted us to throw, then plotted strategy on locating that awesome Enchantress bag.

After we hung up, I went to the breakroom, clocked out, grabbed my purse—a really fantastic Coach tote—from my locker and, as was my custom, made it out the door ahead of just about everyone else.

Holt's had cut back on the parking lot lighting—they claimed they'd gone green, but I think they just wanted to save on the electric bill—so it was kind of dark. The lot was emptying out really quickly. I headed for my Honda, fishing in my bag for my keys, then stopped in my tracks.

A black Land Rover was parked next to my car—Jack Bishop's Land Rover.

I'd called him earlier today about Heather Gibson Pritchard who, according to Mom, had taken off for South America suddenly. Jack hadn't answered his phone, so I'd left a message asking him to call.

I hadn't expected to find him waiting for me after work, but there he was.

Seeing Jack's Land Rover parked next to my Honda caused my heart to beat a little faster—he's way hot.

Yeah, yeah, I know that was really bad of me because I have an official boyfriend, and—

Hang on a minute. I don't have an official boyfriend anymore.

The driver's door opened and Jack got out. He had dark hair and a square jaw that looked great sporting a day's worth of whiskers. He wore denim jeans, boots, and a henley shirt with the sleeves pushed up.

Oh, wow, he looked really hot.

I hadn't seen Jack since the night he'd come to my apartment when, I'm sure, he had something way different in mind but ended up comforting me after Ty and I broke up.

Ty? *Ty?* I'm thinking about Ty *now?*

We'd broken up. He hadn't called me—in weeks. He'd left all that stuff in my apartment—for me to clean up. He'd broken my heart and cast me into a serious breakup fog I'd only recently recovered from.

Jack was standing just a few yards in front of me looking way hot. I shouldn't have been thinking about Ty at all.

Jack crossed the parking lot to meet me. He didn't say anything, just looked at me. He smelled great.

"How are you doing?" he asked.

I couldn't help but notice he wasn't using his Barry White voice.

I have no defense against the Barry White voice.

"Great," I said, forcing a little cheer into my voice. I gestured to the store. "Just working."

Jack nodded but didn't say anything.

Jeez, was this awkward or what?

"You called," he said, oh so politely.

"Yeah, I was wondering if you could help me out with something," I said.

He didn't say anything, just stood there looking at me.

I gestured to our vehicles parked a few yards away, and said, "Do you want to get some coffee, or something?"

"Here's fine," Jack said.

Okay, this was totally weird—and completely unlike Jack.

"There's this guy named Andrew Pritchard," I said. "He's a client of Pike Warner and he works at—"

"I know where he works," Jack said.

"He got married a couple of months ago—"

"I know."

What the heck was going on? What was up with Jack?

Since I'm not big on suspense, I said, "You're being really weird. What's wrong?"

The cool thing about talking to a man was that he would give a straightforward answer to a straightforward question. None of this whining around, playing coy, or dragging it out like women did—honestly, I don't know how men stand us sometimes. Good thing we'll have sex with them, otherwise they would probably think we are just too much trouble.

"I'm treading lightly," Jack said. "Last time I saw you, you were a real mess."

"I'd just broken up with my official boyfriend," I told him.

Jack nodded. "It's only been a few weeks. You're not over it."

"Let me get this straight. Before, I wouldn't get involved with you because I was dating Ty," I said. "And now you won't get involved with me because I'm *not* dating Ty."

"You two aren't finished with each other," Jack said.

My thoughts made the jump to light speed.

Why would he say that? He hadn't seen me, so he couldn't possibly know how I was feeling. Did that mean he'd seen Ty? He was a client of Pike Warner. Had he come into the office? Seen Ty? Talked to him? Told him that breaking up with me was the biggest mistake of his life? That he was miserable? Pining away for me every waking moment? That we were meant to be together? That he wanted nothing more than to have me in his life again?

Sarah Covington—and her engagement ring—popped into my head, and I snapped back to reality.

"Ty and I," I said. "We're finished."

Jack shook his head. "It's too soon."

Okay, he was making perfect sense and, really, I should have been happy he thought enough of me not to take advantage of my situation. But this was getting kind of annoying.

"Can you at least help me out with my problem?" I asked.

Jack studied me for a minute or two, and said, "I can help you with your problem."

I guess that was the best I was going to get out of him tonight.

"So, why are you asking about Andrew Pritchard?" Jack asked.

"I need you to go see him and find out what was up with his wedding cake," I said.

Jack's brows drew together. "You want me to ask him about a *cake?*"

Obviously, Jack was concerned about having his man card revoked—or at least suspended—which I totally understood.

"Look, here's the deal," I said.

I explained to him how Lacy Cakes had reportedly ruined their wedding—I left out the part about my mom, which was always for the best—and that Lacy had been murdered around the time Andrew Pritchard's new bride suddenly bolted for South America.

"So what's this got to do with you?" Jack asked.

"It's a silly coincidence, really," I said. "I'd called Lacy Cakes a while back and complained about a cake and, because I happened to be the one who found Lacy murdered, the police think I killed her."

Jack gave me a not-again eye roll.

"I'm looking for another suspect," I told him, "since Detective Madison isn't bothering to look."

"What about his partner? Shuman?" Jack asked. "He's usually the levelheaded one."

My spirits fell.

"Things aren't going too well for Shuman," I said, and told him about Amanda's murder.

"Damn . . ." Jack murmured. "I hadn't heard anything."

"Seems everybody is keeping it quiet," I said. "I guess they're worried that if word gets out that someone from the District Attorney's office was murdered because of a prosecution, witnesses in pending cases might not be so anxious to testify."

We were both quiet for a moment because, really, what can you say about something like that?

"I'll talk to Pritchard," Jack said.

He walked to my Honda. I hit the remote and he opened my door. I stood next to him for a few seconds—he was really warm and smelled awesome—then got inside. Jack watched until I drove away.

I headed home, then decided some Chinese take-out would be just the thing to end my day. As I swung into the little shopping center near my house, my cell phone rang. I glanced at the caller ID screen and saw that Eleanor was calling.

Why was she calling me at this time of night?

Why was she calling me at all?

I didn't want to answer, but I was afraid she might tell Sheridan Adams that I wasn't available 24-7 and I'd end up getting fired from L.A. Affairs.

"Ringo Starr," Eleanor said, when I answered my phone. "What was his real last name?"

Oh, jeez, another Beatles pop quiz.

I hate my life.

"Uh, well, that's a really interesting story," I said, stalling—which I don't know why I bothered to do since I had no clue what the correct answer was. I think it's just part of my survival instinct.

"As I recall, Ringo changed his name," I said, "because, well, because—"

"You don't know, do you," Eleanor declared.

"Well, actually—"

She hung up.

Crap.

I hung up and sat there for a minute. No way was I in the mood for Chinese now. I headed home.

I was slightly annoyed with Ringo Starr for changing his name, and more than a little put out with Jack Bishop for suddenly being so sensitive. I was irritated with Detective Shuman because he hadn't called me back—which was really crappy of me, but there it was—plus, I was aggravated that I couldn't stop thinking about Ty.

Honestly, I'd had just about enough of the male species for one evening.

I swung into a parking space at my apartment complex.

Just as I got out of my car I spotted Cody Ewing climbing out of a pickup truck nearby.

"What are you doing here?" I asked. It came out sounding kind of harsh.

He shrugged and gave me a little grin. "Waiting on you."

I was in no mood.

"Yeah, I figured that," I said. "I wasn't expecting you."

"I know," he said, and nodded. "But I figured I'd come by, take a chance that it'd be okay if I put in an hour or so on your place."

I shook my head. "Tonight's not a good night."

Cody reached into his truck and pulled out a bag. "I brought ice cream."

"Really, it's not a good time," I said, though I could hear resolve weakening.

"Chocolate Fudge Brownie." He pulled the container out of the bag.

Oh my God. Ben & Jerry's—the good stuff.

Jeez, I had to let him come in now, didn't I? I couldn't be rude—after he'd gone to all the trouble of bringing ice cream.

"Okay, you can come up," I said.

Cody grabbed his toolbox out of the bed of his truck and followed me upstairs. When we reached the top, I heard tires squeal in the parking lot. I turned to see a car speeding out of the driveway.

Huh. I wonder what that was all about.

CHAPTER 11

It was a Prada day. Definitely a Prada day.

I had an important errand to run later today and only a black Prada satchel—teamed with my awesome navy blue business suit—would project the image I was going for.

I settled into my desk at L.A. Affairs with my first cup of coffee, determined to make headway on coming up with custom-made gift bags that somehow projected the image of the Beatles. I also had to figure out how I was going to fill them with items that Sheridan Adams's wealthy we've-already-got-two-of-everything guests would find special and unique. Someone on staff could probably give me some ideas, but I didn't want to ask anyone. I was sure Vanessa was still talking smack about me, and I wasn't about to let anyone think she was right.

As I sipped my coffee—waiting for the two extra packets of sugar I'd used to kick in—my brain hopped to another topic.

Lacy Hobbs's murder.

So far I wasn't exactly making great strides toward finding her killer. I had some suspects, a few weak motives, and absolutely no evidence. Obviously, I was going to have to do more digging.

I sipped my coffee and thought back to when I'd found Lacy's body in the workroom. She'd been shot point-blank in the center of her chest. Whoever had murdered her had walked into the workroom, approached her at the work-table, pulled a gun, and fired. I figured she must have known her killer, since there was no sign of a struggle and nothing had been stolen—that I knew of, anyway. I mean, jeez, what's there to steal in a bakery? So if that were the case and the murderer knew Lacy, that person must have been either really mad about something or really cold and calculating.

Heather Pritchard, the runaway bride, topped my mental really-mad suspect list. She'd decided that Lacy Cakes had ruined her wedding with the cake they'd made, and she'd probably stewed on it, relived it, and obsessed over it ever since her wedding day. Brides, after all, were a special kind of crazy.

The owner of the Fairy Land Bake Shoppe took second place on my really-mad suspect list. According to Paige he wasn't happy about losing her. Maybe he'd decided to take it out on Lacy.

As for my cold-and-calculating suspects, Paige was the only person whose name I could put on that list. Darren had suggested she was a little too anxious to take over the business. Maybe he was onto something. Maybe it had been her plan all along—get a job there, kill Lacy, and take over the business somehow.

My brain hopped to yet another topic—which was okay with me, because thinking about murder suspects was giving me a headache.

Or maybe it was all the sugar I'd dumped into my coffee.

I still had to find Mom a housekeeper—which seemed as difficult as finding Lacy's murderer, and even more unpleasant—so I pulled out my cell phone and called the employment agency. I gave my mom's name and was immediately transferred.

Mrs. Quinn, the woman who had been tasked with

dealing with my mother and was, no doubt, rethinking her entire career path, answered.

"I'd like to get this matter settled as quickly as possible," I said, after I'd introduced myself.

"We're all anxious for that as well," she said.

I know she meant that from the bottom of her heart.

"Do you have any prospective housekeepers I could interview?" I asked.

"I'm putting together a list," Mrs. Quinn said. "I should have something lined up in a few days."

"Can you at least send someone over temporarily every few days to clean?" I asked.

"Yes, I can arrange that," she said, though it didn't seem to suit her.

"Mom can't go without a housekeeper for very long," I told her.

"I understand," she replied. "But, you know, filling this position to your mother's satisfaction has proved quite a challenge for me."

She thought she had it rough? How about being her daughter?

"Try harder," I told her, which was the oh so wonderful advice I'd often gotten from Mom. I hoped Mrs. Quinn would be more anxious to rise to Mom's standards than I had been.

We hung up and, already, I'd had enough of sitting in my office. I had a great reason for leaving, so I saw no need not to take advantage of it. But first, I called the phone number for Belinda Giles that Paige had given me. To my surprise, she answered right away. I introduced myself and immediately plunged into a total lie.

"I understand you're running Lacy Cakes Bakery now," I said.

Yes, I know it's bad to tell an out-and-out lie, but come on, I had to get the dirt on what was going on with Lacy's murder, among other things.

"Paige told me you'd put in an order," Belinda said. "It'll get done."

"I'd feel a lot better about it if I could speak with you in person," I said. "The cake is for an extremely high-profile event."

Belinda was quiet for a few seconds, then said, "I can meet you, if you absolutely have to see me in person."

I didn't want her to come here, because then I wouldn't have a good excuse for leaving the office, plus I didn't want anyone here to suspect there was a problem with Sheridan Adams's party.

"I have to go to the bakery this morning," I said. "Can I meet you there?"

"I'm pretty busy today," Belinda said. "But I can run by there in about an hour."

"That will be fine," I said, though it really wasn't. No way did I want to hang out in the office for that long and be forced to do actual work—not when I had so much personal business to attend to.

We hung up. I took a chance and phoned Shuman again, and was pleased—and surprised—when he answered.

"How are you doing?" I asked.

"Better," he said.

He didn't sound better.

"Want to meet for coffee?" I asked.

"No . . . no, I don't think so," he told me.

"Come on, I owe you one," I said. "The Starbucks at the Sherman Oaks Galleria. I can be there in ten minutes."

Shuman was quiet for a while, then finally said, "Okay. I'll see you there."

He hung up.

I got some things together that I'd need later today, then left. So far, no one had said anything to me about spending so much time out of the office. I figured that everyone was just that desperate to keep me there, working as Vanessa's

assistant, or maybe it really was expected that event planners spent most of their time calling on clients and vendors.

Either way, I saw no reason not to take advantage of the
situation.

I left the building, crossed the street, and climbed the
concrete stairs to the fountain plaza at the Galleria. Water
splashed in the fountain and the sunshine was warm, making for a perfect day to be in the San Fernando Valley in
gorgeous Southern California.

The Galleria was an open-air, multistory complex of offices, retail, and entertainment space. I walked past restaurants and stores and into Starbucks. I got my favorite
drink, a mocha frappuccino, and a coffee for Shuman,
then went outside to one of the tables set up on the center
plaza. Things were kind of quiet, since it was too early for
the lunch crowd.

Just a couple of minutes later I spotted Shuman walking
toward me from the parking garage at the other end of the
complex, which made me wonder where he'd been and
what he'd been doing when I called him. He had on the
same beige oxford shirt and jeans he'd worn the last time I
saw him, and he looked kind of rumpled.

Not good.

When he sat down beside me at the table and I saw him
up close, he looked even worse. There were lines in his
face I'd never noticed before. His eyes were red. I doubted
he'd slept in days.

I didn't see any reason to ask how he was since, obviously, he wasn't doing well, so I asked, "Anything new on
the investigation?"

Shuman rested his arms on the table and cradled the cup
of coffee in both palms.

"We're sure it involved one of the cases Amanda was
prosecuting," Shuman said.

Probably one of his friends at the LAPD was feeding

him info on the sly, which I'm sure the department would not have liked. I doubted it was Detective Madison.

"It wasn't just some random..." Shuman's voice trailed off, and he pressed his palm against his forehead and turned away.

My heart ached for him. I'd known he and Amanda were crazy about each other, but I had no idea Shuman was *this* much in love with her.

I laid my hand on his forearm and he turned back to me. He drew a heavy breath and shook his head.

"I'm never going to get over this," he said softly.

"I know," I said because, really, I didn't see how he could—or how anybody could recover from losing someone they cared so much about, especially in such a violent way.

Shuman gazed at me for a moment, and I figured he appreciated that I hadn't tried to cheer him up, or tell him that Amanda was in a better place, or that everything would be all right soon.

"I've got to go," he said, and stood up.

I rose from my chair and gathered my things.

"Let me know what's happening," I said. "Let me know if you need anything."

He moved away, but I touched his shoulder and he stopped.

"Anything," I said.

Shuman nodded, grabbed his coffee, and left.

I parked near the end of the alley that ran behind Lacy Cakes and the other businesses in the strip mall and got out of my Honda. A garbage truck maneuvered past a janitorial service van, and a couple of women in white coats stood near the back door of the nail shop having a smoke.

"Hello?" I called, as I stepped inside the workroom.

The same guy I'd seen on my last visit was busy at the ovens. We exchanged another nod.

Paige stood at one of the worktables alongside a woman I'd never seen. Easily, she was in her sixties. Her complexion was sallow and she was rail thin. Of course, the clothing she wore didn't do much to help her appearance—navy blue polyester pants with an elastic waist, a flowered button-up shirt, and sneakers. I figured the woman was Belinda Giles, cousin of Darren and Lacy.

I flashed on Lacy's dead body lying on the workroom floor, her hair perfectly styled, her makeup expertly applied, her nails freshly manicured.

It appeared that life hadn't been as good to Belinda as it had to Lacy.

No wonder she wanted to keep the bakery operating.

"Hey, girl, come on in," Paige called when she saw me. She gestured to the three-tier wedding cake on the worktable in front of her. "The bride asked for a rainbow. What do you think?"

Yikes! It was a rainbow, all right.

Six different colors arched up the three tiers, then down the other side. It sure as heck wasn't something I would want to look at for decades to come in my wedding pictures, but it was okay. Paige had actually done a good job of making something that could have been truly ugly into something nice.

I wondered what kind of wedding cake Sarah Covington would want.

I hate her.

And I hate that I keep thinking about her.

"It's kind of cool," I said.

"I sent the bride and her mom a picture," Paige said, then gave me a can-you-believe-it smile. "They loved it."

The other woman stepped around Paige and offered her hand.

"Hi, I'm Belinda Giles," she said.

I took her hand; it was rough and calloused. The woman definitely needed a good moisturizer.

I introduced myself and opened the portfolio I'd brought with me from L.A. Affairs.

"Here's all the info on the cake I need," I said, and passed to Paige the spec sheet I'd promised to photocopy.

She took a quick glance and said, "Cool. I can do this. No problem."

I was really digging Paige's positive attitude, and having something go smoothly for this party would be a real plus for me. I sure as heck could use a win right now.

Paige showed it to Belinda. "I totally love this, don't you?"

Belinda got a weird look on her face, which made me wonder if she was questioning Paige's cake design skills.

There went my win.

"Can you do this? And get it ready in time?" I addressed my question to Belinda—one of the superslick ways we kind-of private detectives bring other people into the conversation.

"Of course," Belinda said.

"It's sort of short notice," I said. "Not that it's anyone's fault after, well, after what happened to Lacy."

"Let's give Paige some room to work," Belinda said, and walked out the back door into the alley. I followed.

"I don't mean to question your word," I said. "But this cake is a big deal. It absolutely has to be great, and it has to be delivered on time."

"Sheridan Adams. Yeah, I know who she is," Belinda said. "Another one of her charity events. Yellow Submarine cake. Something to do with the Beatles, right?"

I was relieved that Paige had brought Belinda up to speed on what was happening at the bakery—and with my order, specifically.

"Big parties," Belinda went on. "Lots of food, a memorabilia auction, A-list guests. I know all about it."

Belinda didn't strike me as the kind of gal who'd have the inside info on this kind of event, but maybe she'd heard

Lacy talk about them. Or maybe she read about them in *People* magazine.

"Look," Belinda said. "Your cake will get handled. Don't worry about it."

I gave her an I-don't-know shrug and said, "When I spoke with Darren, he told me he wanted to close the bakery."

Yeah, okay, that wasn't exactly what he told me. But I figured my comment would enrage Belinda and she'd blurt out something I could use to solve Lacy's murder.

"Close the bakery?" Belinda demanded. "Uh-uh. No. Never going to happen."

"Darren seemed adamant," I said. "He was pretty annoyed at having to come down here and settle Lacy's affairs."

Belinda rolled her eyes. "Everything annoys Darren."

"It sounded to me as if he had a legitimate complaint," I said. "He's got his hands full trying to take care of his parents, paying for the meds, their care, plus running his business."

"Like Darren should complain about it." Belinda huffed. "He's still got the first dime he ever made. That cabinet shop—which his dad *gave* him—makes a fortune, but he's too cheap to spend it."

Okay, this was something I hadn't heard before.

"Darren has been trying to dump his parents into a care facility for years," Belinda said. She started to fidget, like maybe she needed a cigarette. "Now that he's getting some of Lacy's life insurance money, he'll probably do it."

My spirits lifted. A huge chuck of money was definitely a motive for murder. Plus, I wasn't liking Darren so much right now.

"Lacy must have left something for you, too," I said.

"Of course she did," Belinda said, and looked away.

"Doesn't Lacy have children who'll collect the money?" I asked. "A husband or boyfriend? Someone?"

Belinda nodded toward the doorway to the workroom. "Lacy was married to this place."

"She didn't have any close friends?" I asked.

"She wasn't exactly Miss Warm-and-Fuzzy," Belinda said.

Apparently Belinda believed Lacy had left most everything to Darren, which seemed right since he was her brother, with bequeaths to her and maybe other family members. That left the bakery—an extremely lucrative business—up for grabs.

I'd gotten the impression from Darren that he expected to inherit the bakery, yet Belinda acted as if she were an heir also. Darren had complained that she was sticking her nose in where it didn't belong. Maybe, unknown to Darren, Lacy and Belinda had gotten past their teenage argument over those concert tickets—I was still going to have to find out what a Dave Clark Five was—and had grown close. I had no way of knowing the truth unless I saw Lacy's will, and that didn't seem likely.

Belinda's already hard face hardened further.

"Makes me wonder about Darren," she said. "He has a lot to gain with Lacy's death. Especially if he thinks he can sell the bakery *and* get a chunk of that insurance money."

It made me wonder about Darren, too. Had everything he told me just been for cover? Was he driving around in the bakery delivery van to make everyone think he was hard up for money?

He claimed he'd just arrived in Los Angeles, but how did I know if that was true? He could have come sooner, murdered Lacy, and spun that whole story to throw suspicion off of himself.

Belinda glanced back into the workroom, then leaned a little closer to me and lowered her voice.

"Paige seems awfully anxious to keep the business going," she said. "It makes me wonder about her."

Huh. Darren had said the same thing about Paige. Was she really out to get the bakery for herself—no matter what it took?

Belinda glanced at her watch. "I've got to go. Look, you don't need to worry about your cake. I know how things work with Sheridan Adams and her kind. It will get handled," she said, then dashed back into the workroom.

I went back to my car and took the surface streets to the 405, headed south, and exited on Wilshire Boulevard. I parked and walked toward the Golden State Bank & Trust building—the destination for which I'd selected today's impressive black Prada bag.

Last year I'd come into a whopping sum of money—long story—which I'd given away, shortly thereafter—long story—but only after I'd bought some essentials for myself, such as clothes and handbags—really fabulous handbags, of course. I'd kept some of the money and added more to it when I'd gotten back from Las Vegas—long story—not long ago.

Because I know me, I'd put those funds into a special account here at the old-money, stately, venerable GSB&T. The account was special—to me, anyway—because when I'd opened it I hadn't ordered a debit card or checks. That way I couldn't get to the money easily. If I wanted something that was out of the reach of my everyday bank account and my numerous credit cards, I'd have to go to all the trouble of coming into the bank and withdrawing the money in person.

So now, thanks to my breakup fog and all the shopping it had caused, I needed to make up the considerable shortfall my bank was hounding me about, and the only way I could manage that was if I took money out of my GSB&T account.

No way was I returning all those awesome things I purchased—whatever they were.

It was lunchtime, so lots of people were on the street. Most everyone looked sharp, dressed in really terrific business attire, carrying expensive briefcases and carryalls.

My gaze caught a man coming out of the GSB&T, and my heart jumped. Wow, he was totally gorgeous. Tall, with light brown hair, an athletic build. He had on a Tom Ford suit that fit great, and—

Oh my God. *Oh my God.*

It was Ty.

CHAPTER 12

Ty looked great—Ty always looked great—which was one of the things I always liked about him. But right now, seeing him on the sidewalk outside the GSB&T, it irked me.

Obviously, he wasn't a total mess like Shuman. Granted, Shuman's girlfriend had been murdered and I hadn't, but unlike Shuman, Ty looked pulled together, calm, and in control, just like when we were dating. It was as if, from his outward appearance anyway, our breakup hadn't affected him at all.

He glanced at his watch, then looked down the street as if he were waiting for someone, and his gaze landed on me. He froze.

My heart started to pound. My breathing got short as I stared back at him.

Was he going to come over? Talk to me?

My thoughts scattered. What would I say to him? Should I give him a big sarcastic thank-you for treating me so badly, for being such a *great* boyfriend by always putting me second? Should I tell him that I felt like a complete jackass for holding on to our relationship all that time, putting up with all the crappy things he did, trying to make it work?

Ty stood there looking at me. He didn't smile. I knew that expression on his face. He was thinking, trying to decide something. Like maybe he should just ignore me and walk away?

He headed toward me. My knees started to shake.

What should I do? Ignore him? Put my nose in the air, turn around, and leave? Hurry over to him and act like nothing had happened? Turn our conversation into a rehash of why we broke up?

Then it hit me—I couldn't do that. I couldn't—wouldn't—let him know that I'd been completely devastated by our breakup. I mean, really, telling him wouldn't do any good. And no way was I going to be one of those whiny, clingy, why-didn't-you-like-me-enough-to-stay ex-girlfriends.

I marshaled my half-beauty-queen genes, put on my everything-is-great-no-matter-what-happens expression, channeled my mom's nothing-can-upset-me attitude, and walked over to meet Ty.

"Hi, how are you doing?" I asked, putting on an it's-terrific-to-see-you grin.

Oh my God, he smelled wonderful.

"I'm okay," Ty said—he didn't have an it's-terrific-to-see-you grin. "You?"

"Awesome," I said, forcing you-broke-my-heart-but-I'm-over-it glee into my voice.

He tilted his head slightly to the right, the way I'd seen him do a zillion times when he was trying to understand something, put it in the right context.

"Really?" he asked softly.

"Really. Absolutely," I told him, stretching my it's-terrific-to-see-you grin into a look-how-great-I'm-doing smile.

Ty nodded, then said, "I understand you have a new job."

I have no idea how he knew I had a job, but I rolled with it.

"Love it," I told him. "I love the job. It's totally me. The work is fabulous, the office is terrific, my boss is fantastic."

"I'm glad," he said. "I'm really glad, Haley."

The sound of my name spoken in his mellow voice mentally zapped me back to the intimate moments we'd shared. The whispers, the giggles, the good-natured teasing.

I forced the image away.

He shifted his briefcase into his other hand, just like he used to do when I was upset, when he'd pull me against his chest and wrap his arms around me and I'd rest my head on his shoulder.

"What's new with you?" I asked, forcing renewed I'm-doing-great zeal into my voice.

Oh my God, why did I ask him that? What if he told me he was engaged to Sarah Covington? How could I stand here and listen to that? How would I not fall completely apart?

I couldn't take it anymore.

"Listen," I said, pumping up the something-bad-happened-but-I'm-not-going-to-let-it-show tone in my voice. "I've got to run."

Ty took a step toward me. "Haley—"

Tears stung my eyes.

"I've got to go," I said, and hurried away.

I rushed into the GSB&T and dashed across the lobby toward the restroom, frantic to get away. I couldn't let Ty see me crying.

Then I glanced back at the door.

Why didn't he come in and check on me? He saw I was crying.

I turned away and ran into the bathroom.

*   *   *

"I want it to pop! Sizzle! You know?"

I stared across the desk in client interview room two at Annette Bachman as she bounced on the edge of her chair. Her eyes were bulging, and her fists were clinched and raised above her head.

She was the first client assigned to me at L.A. Affairs and, clearly, she was way out in front of me on the enthusiasm scale.

I'd blown off my shift at Holt's last night—I pretty much blew off everything after seeing Ty yesterday—and stayed home. I probably could have used some company, but Marcie had a family thing to do. I thought Cody might show up and work on my apartment, but he didn't. Since he had no cell phone, I couldn't call him. So I stayed home, did my homework, and soothed myself with an Oreo cookie or two. Maybe it was more than that. Okay, it was way more than that—but at least it kept me from detouring into breakup zombieland again.

"I'm talking awesome," Annette went on. "Fabulous! Astounding! You know?"

"Yeah, I know," I said. I didn't, but I hoped that saying so might get her to move on.

Annette was in her midthirties, I guessed, with red, curly hair shaped like a triangle around her pale, round face. She had on one of those calf-length skirts, sandals, and a twin set, an outfit that screamed yeah-I'm-single-but-I-don't-know-why. So it surprised me that she was here today to discuss a birthday party for her little Minnie.

"Because, wow, you only have one third birthday, right?" Annette said. "It's got to be special! Grand! Completely and totally awesome!"

"Sure," I said. I picked up my pen. "So, what color do you want?"

Annette clamped her mouth shut for a second, then said, "Pink! No, wait, yellow! No, no. Purple! Purple would be perfect for my little Minnie—purple and pink!"

Then her shoulders slumped and her smile collapsed.

"Oh, goodness, I don't know," she said, shaking her head. "I can't decide. I'm not sure, you know? That's why I came here, so you could help me make up my mind. It's such an important day for Minnie. I want it to be perfect."

Okay, now I felt kind of bad. She was really excited about planning a terrific birthday party for her daughter, and it was, after all, my job to help her.

I felt pretty good that L.A. Affairs had assigned me my own client. Mindy had told me that Vanessa had insisted I be put in the rotation, so I figured this was a good sign.

Of course, I'd never planned a birthday party for a three-year-old, but really, how hard could it be?

"Okay, so here's what we can do," I said. "We'll pick a theme and a color palette. We'll select a venue. We'll decide on food, beverages, decorations, activities, and entertainment."

Wow, I was really on a roll with this birthday party thing.

"It sounds perfect!" Annette declared, hopping up and down on her chair again.

I picked up my pen and started making notes on the tablet in front of me.

"Let's consider having the party in your home," I said. "Since Minnie and her guests are only three, it might be easier for the other moms."

"Oh, yes, that would be perfect," Annette said.

I wrote that down and put a big star beside it because, after all, it was a fantastic idea I'd had.

"Do you have a game room, or family room you'd like to use?" I asked.

Annette frowned. "Well, I don't know. That might get a bit messy. Accidents, you know."

"Then I would recommend your backyard," I told her.

"Lovely!"

I was feeling really great about myself. Maybe I could

be good at this event-planning thing. Maybe I'd have a real career here.

"Oh, yes, the backyard would be perfect," Annette said. "That way Minnie and her guests can roll around and dig their little noses into the grass. It will be so cute!"

I got a weird feeling.

"Let's discuss refreshments," I said.

"Of course! We'll need lots of treats!" Annette declared.

My weird feeling got weirder.

"Treats?" I asked.

"I'm very particular about what Minnie eats," Annette insisted. "Everything must have high-quality, premium ingredients, with plenty of vitamins, minerals, and healthy oils."

"Healthy oils?" I asked.

"And no artificial colors or flavors," she went on. "And absolutely no animal by-products or grain fillers."

I laid my pen down.

"Do you have a picture of Minnie with you?" I asked, even though I was pretty sure I knew where this was going.

"Well, of course I do," Annette said. She dug around in her handbag and presented me with a photo.

Oh, crap.

"Minnie is a dog," I said, and somehow I didn't yell that.

"Well, of course she's a dog!" Annette said, then giggled. "And isn't she just the cutest little thing!"

I got up from the desk.

"I think that's all the info I need to get started," I said, guiding Annette out the door. "I'll get back with you soon."

"Oh, well, all right," Annette said, as I hurried her along the corridor to the reception area.

"Oh! My! I love your outfit," Mindy said.

I hate my life.

I went back to my office and saw that I'd missed a call from Mrs. Quinn at the employment agency. I phoned her and learned that she had several candidates for the position of housekeeper whom I could interview.

"I can come to your office right away," I said.

"I'll need a few hours," Mrs. Quinn said, and we hung up.

Of course, I saw no reason to wait a few hours to leave the office, especially when I had so much of my own personal business to attend to—plus a murder to solve. I gathered my things and left.

I took Ventura Boulevard to Studio City and pulled into the parking lot near Coldwater Canyon. The Fairy Land Bake Shoppe was located in a little shopping center near a health food store and a couple of mom-and-pop businesses.

Paige had told me that the owner of Fairy Land had been mad at Lacy Hobbs for offering her more money and hiring her away. Maybe he'd been mad enough to kill her.

The bakery had huge display windows that were decorated with flying fairies and magic wands, golden pixie dust, colorful mushrooms, and lovable trolls and gnomes. Featured in the windows was an array of magnificent cakes, with intricate designs and clever themes.

On the whole, this place looked a couple billion times better than Lacy Cakes. It made me wonder why Paige Davis had been so anxious to leave here and work elsewhere, even with the higher salary.

I hoped the manager of Fairy Land would tell me.

Armed with my portfolio with the L.A. Affairs logo turned out, and my this-proves-I'm-important Gucci handbag and black business suit, I walked into the bakery.

Just as the name suggested, it looked like a fairy land, with whimsical decor and baked goodies and sweets everywhere. It smelled delightful—like even if you took a bite out of the countertop, it would taste like buttercream.

My kind of place.

Several customers were at the glass display cases buying cupcakes and cookies from two young women wearing lavender aprons with fairies on the front.

"Can I help you?" one of them asked.

I passed her one of my business cards and asked, "Can I speak with August?"

She glanced at the card. "Sure," she said, and disappeared through the curtained doorway into a back room.

August, the store owner whose name I'd found on their Web site, appeared a moment later. You'd expect that a man who owned a bakery wouldn't look like someone you'd want to have your back in a bar fight, and this guy was no exception. Everything about him was average—pleasant, and average. Late forties, I guessed, and kind of round everywhere—his belly, his balding head—dressed in the I'm-average man's uniform of khaki pants and a blue shirt.

Even though he held my business card, I introduced myself. He gave me a very gentlemanly handshake.

"I'd like to speak with you about possibly doing business with L.A. Affairs," I said. "You've heard of us?"

August smiled. "I certainly have. Please, let's sit down."

He pulled out a chair for me at one of the tiny white tables near the front window, and I could see he was anxious to please. L.A. Affairs could bring him lots of business, and he knew that.

Yeah, okay, I could have felt bad about dangling the maybe-you'll-get-some-big-buck-clients-through-me carrot in front of him, but I didn't because I really was impressed with his business, so far, and would need a first-rate bakery I could rely on.

Wow, I sound like a real event planner, huh?

August jumped right in with a history of the Fairy Land Bake Shoppe, how he'd started it, when he'd started it, something about his mother, the old country, blah, blah, blah. I'd already read all of that stuff on their Web site, but I gave the impression that I was listening intently even though I was thinking about checking Nordstrom after work for that Enchantress evening bag—a skill I'd perfected in many a Holt's training session.

When I realized there was a lull in August's presentation, I instantaneously snapped back to the present—another Holt's skill I'd learned.

"I'm very impressed with your bakery," I said, glancing around. "But, August, I'm afraid I have some reservations about doing business with you."

His totally average eyebrows shot up. "Well, please, tell me what they are."

"I understand there was some bad blood between you and Lacy Cakes," I said.

August's eyes narrowed and his lips pinched together in what I took for his I'm-angry-now expression. He sat that way for a few seconds, then shook it off and said, "That is upsetting to hear."

Not exactly the hothead I'd hoped for, spewing incriminating info or confessing to Lacy's murder.

"Weren't you mad at Lacy for hiring away one of your best employees?" I asked.

"Who?" August asked, and gave the impression that he was totally lost.

"Paige Davis," I said.

Now he looked even more lost. "She didn't quit—I fired her."

Okay, this was something I hadn't expected.

August lowered his voice. "I don't usually discuss employee issues, but that girl was a problem from the day I hired her. She had all kinds of grand ideas of how I should change my shop. Make bigger cakes, charge more money, increase production."

August was definitely a slow-and-steady kind of guy, so I could see why this hadn't gone over well with him.

"Paige overstepped her authority one too many times," August said. "We were inundated with orders that she went out and got all on her own. I had to pay my staff overtime to get them done. It caused quite a commotion."

Apparently, August and I had differing visions of *commotion*.

"But she's an exceptionally talented cake designer. She's aggressive and ambitious," August told me, and gave me a rueful smile. "Can't say I'm anxious to compete with her for business when she opens her own shop."

"Do you think she'll do that?" I asked.

"Oh yes," August said. "That was her plan all along. She told me specifically when I hired her that she was here for the training and intended to move up in the world, though frankly I don't know how she could do that. Opening a bakery and running it requires quite a bit of cash."

Unless you could take over one after you murdered the owner, I thought.

Darren and Belinda had both told me that Paige seemed very anxious to keep Lacy Cakes open. They'd thought it suspicious.

I'd figured that whoever murdered Lacy had known her and that there had been a major cold factor in the way she was killed. Paige seemed to fit both of those criteria.

"Any other concerns about Fairy Land?" August asked.

"No, that's about it," I said, and rose from my chair.

He walked with me to the door and opened it for me, then passed me one of his business cards.

"If we can be of service, please let me know," August said, and gave me an average, but sincere, smile.

"Thank you. I will," I said, and headed for my car.

"Miss Randolph?" he called.

I turned back.

"Paige was right about Lacy Hobbs hiring away talent from other bakeries. She was a ruthless businesswoman," he said. "She would call on clients of other bakeries and steal them away. She would say vicious things about her competition—all lies. If anyone dared to complain about her cakes, she would start ugly rumors about them. Frankly, I'm not surprised she was murdered."

After hearing those things, I wasn't surprised, either.

CHAPTER 13

"And I need three days off during the week—the same three days, not no three when-it-suits-somebody-else days. I'm not wearing one of those ugly uniforms, either," the woman across the desk told me.

I was in the interview room at the employment agency in Encino tasked with the it's-easier-to-go-to-Mars job of finding my mom a new housekeeper. Mrs. Quinn had arranged for me to meet with three applicants.

Immediately I could see that this woman wouldn't exactly click with Mom. She was really tall, muscular, with a head of dark hair that stuck out like a lion's mane. Honestly, I think Mom might be a little afraid of her.

I was kind of afraid of her myself.

"Thank you so much for coming in," I said. "We'll be making a decision in the next few days."

"Good, 'cause I've got to know something quick," the woman said, and walked out of the room.

The next candidate walked into the room just as I picked up her application from the stack Mrs. Quinn had given me.

"Prudence Darby?" I asked and introduced myself.

She was a small, trim, compact woman who apparently thought it was still 1955, although she didn't look quite old enough to have lived back then. She wore a black wool coat with a faux-fur collar and a hat, and she clutched a huge department store handbag in both hands.

I glanced over her application as she sat down. "I see here that you've—"

"Did you read the comment at the bottom?" she asked. She spoke in a soft voice, almost in a whisper for some reason. "I'm a Christian woman. I always make that clear. I wrote it on the bottom of the form. See, right there? It says I'm a Christian woman."

"Don't worry, we're not going to feed you to the lions," I said.

Although some of the people who'd worked for Mom might feel differently.

"I don't believe in drinking alcohol," Prudence said.

I was pretty sure she'd change her mind after a few days of dealing with Mom.

"I can't work in a house where alcohol is present," she said.

I could have quizzed her on this a little more, tried to talk her into making an exception, but I didn't see the point. I thanked her for coming in and she left.

Next up was Jozelle Newcomb, a tall, attractive woman who was probably in her midforties.

Immediately I was impressed when she walked in carrying a Chanel tote and wearing a Michael Kors suit, even if it was last season's. Then I was immediately unimpressed when I looked over her application and saw that not only had she never worked as a housekeeper, she'd never worked at all.

"I see here that you haven't had any actual work experience," I said.

She burst out crying.

Oh my God. What happened?

I gave her a minute or two, hoping she'd settle down. She didn't.

I'm not good with a crier.

"Maybe this isn't the best time for your interview," I said.

She kept sobbing.

"Let's reschedule, okay?" I said.

She nodded, grabbed a handful of tissues from the box on the corner of my desk, and left.

I waited a few minutes—no way did I want to run into her again in the parking lot—then gathered my things and went to Mrs. Quinn's office down the hall.

"None of those applicants were right for the job," I said.

I felt bad for Jozelle Newcomb, who couldn't even get through the interview without crying. Obviously, she was having some major personal problems. But I couldn't imagine she'd be a good fit for the job, considering Mom could be every bit the same emotional mess as she was.

Mrs. Quinn heaved a long sigh. "I'll see what else I can come up with."

I left the building and got into my car parked in the lot around back. Honestly, I'd had about all of the personal business I could take for one day. I was considering moving my Nordstrom trip up from tonight after work to now when my cell phone rang.

My spirits fell. It was Rigby.

"Which one of the Beatles was married when the group first came to America?" she asked.

My spirits shot up again. I knew this—I actually knew the answer.

"It was . . . it was . . ." I racked my brain. "John Lennon!"

"You took too long to answer," Rigby told me, and hung up.

Crap.

This whole Beatles party was starting to get on my nerves, even though most everything was going according to plan. Muriel was taking care of the guest list, the clean-up crew, and the valets. I'd followed up on the arrangements Jewel had made for the caterer, the tribute bands, and the decorations.

The only thing I still had to do was somehow get the Cirque du Soleil dancers and acrobats from the Love show in Vegas to perform at the party, plus figure out how I was going to come up with the gift bags Sheridan had requested—as long as I passed Eleanor and Rigby's Beatles trivia quizzes and got to keep my job, of course.

I sat there for a minute trying to think of where the heck I was going to find two hundred custom-made gift bags, plus the items to put inside them.

Then I realized there was only one place to go for help—the Russian mob.

I'd met Mike Ivan a while back when I'd been in Las Vegas to assist with the opening of a new Holt's store—long story. He was from L.A. and happened to be there on business.

Mike was rumored to be in the Russian mob, though both Detective Shuman and Jack Bishop had told me they could find no hard evidence that linked him to any illegal activity. Mike always insisted he ran a legitimate import–export business and simply had the misfortune of having relatives with questionable business ethics.

Leave it to family.

We'd swapped favors, but this wasn't a relationship I wanted to get into too deep—just in case.

Mike ran his business out of the Garment District in L.A., a place I knew well since Marcie and I shopped Santee Alley for the knockoff handbags we sold at our purse parties. Among the things Mike imported was rare, expensive fabric from all around the world. I figured that if anybody could help me get Sheridan Adams's Beatle-themed gift bags made, it would be Mike.

I exited the 110 freeway on Olympic Boulevard, turned

onto Santee Street, and drove up the ramp to the parking lot Marcie and I usually used. I paid the attendant and took the stairs down to Santee Alley.

I loved Santee Alley. It was a mix of all kinds of people, all kinds of products and merchandise. Locals and tourists came here to shop in the stores with their back doors opened to the alley and with the vendors who crowded in between.

Even though Marcie and I had shopped Santee Alley for about a year now and many of the merchants knew us, that didn't mean we could walk in off the street and expect to do business with the people who ran the garment factories that filled the top floors of the old buildings in the area. Business people here were cautious. They dealt in cash. They didn't like outsiders.

When I'd left the employment agency I'd called Mike and asked if he could meet me. He was a little hesitant because last time we'd talked we'd both decided that things between us were settled, we were square—long story. But I assured him that this time it was strictly business.

I made my way out of the alley to Maple Avenue, then walked north to the textile district. Here, the exteriors of the shops were lined with huge bolts of fabric, a rainbow of every color, pattern, and texture imaginable. I turned the corner onto Ninth Street and went into the shop in which Mike had instructed me to meet him.

The place was packed with fabric—big rolls, small bolts, a few remnants. It was stacked on tables, hung on displays, and propped up in big boxes. There were bins of buttons, zippers, and all sort of other things I was clueless about.

The man sitting behind the counter eyed me sharply; they didn't get too many young white girls in here wearing business suits.

"Mike is expecting me," I said.

He gave me another long hard look, then picked up his

phone and made a call. I amused myself wandering through the store looking at fabric until Mike came out of the back room.

He didn't look like he was in the Russian mob—or even that he was related to anyone who was in the Russian mob. Thirty-five, I figured. Nice build, okay dresser, kind of good looking, a little taller than me.

Mike gave my awesome outfit a quick once-over, which was always a real morale booster, and said, "It's good to see you when you're not involved in a murder investigation, for a change."

So much for my boosted morale.

"Well . . . actually . . ."

He shook his head wearily.

"It's all a big misunderstanding," I assured him. "See, I got this new job and—"

"At the D.A.'s office?" he asked, the playfulness gone from his expression and voice.

My blood ran cold. He must have been talking about Amanda Payton, Shuman's girlfriend.

"You heard about Amanda?" I asked.

"Bad business," Mike said, looking grim.

Okay, this was weird. How come Mike had heard about Amanda's murder but Jack Bishop hadn't? Jack was wired into everything that went on in L.A.

"Actually, I don't work with Amanda," I said, since I didn't think it was a good idea to lie to someone who might really—despite protests—be involved with the Russian mob. "But I knew her. We were friends."

Mike shook his head. "Sorry to hear that. Must be tough for you."

"You should see her boyfriend," I said. "He's a complete mess. I don't know if he'll ever get over it."

He thought for a moment. "That detective. LAPD. Shuman."

I'd forgotten that Shuman had looked into Mike's alleged mob connection when I was in Las Vegas. Obviously, Mike hadn't forgotten. I wish I hadn't reminded him, but I did wonder how Mike had known that Shuman and Amanda were dating.

"Shuman is on a leave of absence from duty," I said.

Mike didn't say anything, but I was pretty sure he was thinking that Shuman was investigating Amanda's murder himself against department regulations.

I'm sure that's what Mike would have done.

I decided it was a good time to change the subject.

"So here's what I need," I said. "Gift bags. Two hundred of them that capture the essence of the Beatles."

"How much are you looking to spend?" Mike asked.

"A lot," I said. "It's for a big party and charity event Sheridan Adams is throwing. Tribute bands, a memorabilia auction. A-list guests."

"I'm sure I'll receive my invitation any day now," Mike said, and grinned. Then he was, all business again. "I'll talk to a designer I know and see what she can come up with for the bags."

"Great," I said, and passed him my business card. "Do you happen to know anybody at Cirque du Soleil in Vegas?"

Mike thought for a few seconds. "I'll get back with you."

Wow, having a friend in the maybe-or-maybe-not Russian mob could come in handy.

"This is b.s.," Bella grumbled.

We were in the stock room at Holt's going through the clothing for the upcoming so-called fashion show I was supposed to coordinate. I was totally bummed because Marcie and I had planned to go on the hunt for the fantastic Enchantress bag tonight, but I'd forgotten I was scheduled to work here.

I wasn't back in breakup fog again, I'm just really good at blocking out thoughts of Holt's.

I'd told Jeanette I could use some help styling the looks for the show, and she'd said that Bella could assist. But I didn't really need a helper—I needed a miracle.

I'd actually considered quitting my job here just so I wouldn't have to go through with the fashion show, but with my position at L.A. Affairs in question, thanks to Eleanor and Rigby and their Beatles quiz questions, not to mention Vanessa backstabbing me at every opportunity, I didn't dare resign.

"Yeah," I said, and winced. "This stuff is pretty bad."

"I'm going to end up vision impaired from looking at these crappy clothes," Bella said. "Maybe I can get disability."

We'd pulled off the tarp that covered the hanging items but left the plastic wrap on—not that it helped, really— and opened the boxes of shoes and accessories to try to assemble some looks.

Nothing went together. The buyers must have selected this stuff using a dartboard.

"There're no two things in this whole mess that are the same color, except the shoes," Bella said, "and they're ugly."

"Whoever is doing the buying for Holt's must be a complete idiot," I said, sorting through the dresses.

"You win this contest and maybe you can fix that," Bella said, as she pulled a pair of pumps from one of the boxes. "Damn. My nana wouldn't even wear these things."

"I don't see how we can possibly win the contest," I said.

"Don't ever underestimate the bad taste of a Holt's shopper," Bella said.

It flashed in my head that I should mention that to Ty, then I remembered we'd broken up.

Damn. Why do I keep thinking about him?

"How come Holt's won't give a decent prize?" Bella asked. She patted her hair. Her autumn theme continued with what appeared to be cornstalks fashioned atop her head. "Something like a year's supply of hair care products. Now that'd be a prize worth having."

"So what are the employees supposed to get?" I asked. "Not that we have a prayer of winning."

"Everybody will get a Holt's gift card," Bella said. "I don't think anybody will be too busted up if we don't win."

I figured she was right.

We spent the rest of our shift sorting through everything, matching things up, trying different accessories with dresses, pants, skirts, sweaters, and tops, and had exactly zero looks completed when it was time to go home.

"Maybe this stuff will look better tomorrow," I said, as we left the stock room.

"It can't look any worse," Bella said.

I wasn't so sure about that.

We clocked out and I headed home. When I pulled into a parking space at my apartment complex I saw Cody's pickup truck. He must have been watching for me, because he jumped out as soon as I got out of my car.

"How's it going?" he asked.

Jeez, where to start?

"Busy day," I said, since I didn't want to stand there all night filling him in on the day I'd had, and I was pretty sure he wouldn't want to hear it, anyway. "How about you?"

He walked closer. Wow, he smelled kind of good.

"Busy," he said.

He looked handsome too, with the security lighting reflecting off his blond hair. The T-shirt he wore fit tight, showing off the muscles in his chest and belly.

"I came by to explain why I haven't been here," he said.

"Do you want to come upstairs?" I asked. It came out in kind of a breathy little whisper—but I didn't mean for it to. I swear.

Cody grinned—*that* kind of grin. He eased closer. A crazy heat rolled off of him.

"I'd love to come upstairs," he said. Oh, wow, Cody had a Barry White voice. "But I can't work on your place tonight."

"Oh."

I know I sounded majorly disappointed, but what else could I do when he was talking that way?

"Maybe I should come up, anyway?" he asked.

Cody moved closer, then leaned down and kissed me.

My thoughts scattered.

Oh my God. I can't kiss Cody. I have an official boyfriend, and I'm a real stickler about—

No, wait. I don't have a boyfriend—official or otherwise.

Why can't I ever remember that?

He pulled away and gave me a how-about-it eyebrow bob.

I was tempted—really tempted. Cody was good looking, and I'd been lonely, and he seemed like a great guy. Maybe this was just what I needed to finally get over my breakup with Ty.

But I couldn't do it.

"I don't think so," I said.

"No problem." Cody smiled and eased away. "I'll be back to finish up the work in your place."

He got in his truck.

I went up to my apartment.

Chapter 14

"Good morning, good morning," Priscilla something-or-other, the office manager, called out in a pleasant singsong voice. "Let's all get settled."

I was in the conference room at L.A. Affairs for my first staff meeting. The chairs were arranged theater style, and a table at the rear of the room held coffee, juice, and pastries. Everybody looked fabulous dressed in chic business suits.

So far, I liked this way better than the meetings at Holt's.

Since there was no big-guy-from-menswear equivalent here that I could sit behind, I headed for the last row of seats.

Then I spotted Eve, one of the assistant planners I'd chatted with several times when we'd run into each other in the breakroom. Eve was a huge gossip. She was forever dishing dirt, talking smack, and running her mouth about everything and everybody in the office—so, of course, I made it a point to sit next to her.

Kayla sat down beside me and sipped her coffee. "Did you see that Vanessa is here today?"

I glanced around the room and saw her chatting with Priscilla. She looked fantastic, of course, which really irritated me.

"Brace yourself," Kayla said.

Priscilla stepped to the podium and kicked off the meeting by welcoming me, the newest employee, to the firm. At her request I stood and executed my mom's pageant wave to perfection, and everybody gave me a polite round of applause—everyone but Vanessa. I saw her lean into the woman next to her and whisper something, and I could tell from her reaction that Vanessa had said something stinky about me.

Bitch.

"I have a few announcements," Priscilla went on, consulting a tablet on the podium. "First of all, BeeBop the clown is not available for bookings. He's currently on tour."

From the reactions around the room, I got the feeling *on tour* was code for *in rehab*.

"Next, there's a list of additional vendors that will be e-mailed to everyone this afternoon," Priscilla said. "Let's all give them a try, if possible."

"We're always getting new vendors," Kayla whispered. "Mostly because the old ones get fed up working with Vanessa."

"Sadly, I must report that Lacy Cakes has been removed from our approved list," Priscilla said. "With the unfortunate and untimely death of the owner, the future of the bakery is in question, so we're holding off on placing orders there until we learn something definite."

"That Lacy Hobbs was a holy terror," Eve said quietly to me.

"How so?" I whispered back.

"It was her way or no way," Eve murmured. "If you crossed her, she never forgave you—and never forgot. You were dead to her. She'd refuse to talk to you no matter who your client was. She'd call Priscilla and demand to work with a different planner."

"And she got away with that?" I asked.

"Of course. *Everybody* wanted a Lacy Cake," Eve said. "Too bad she's dead, but good riddance."

Priscilla kept talking, but everything turned into blah, blah, blah. I kept thinking about Lacy Hobbs. Somehow she'd come from a little town near San Francisco right out of high school and built what appeared to be the most successful, highly sought after bakery in Los Angeles. But she sure as heck hadn't made any friends along the way—including people here at L.A. Affairs.

Hmm. Maybe I could find a way to blame her murder on Vanessa.

Kayla tapped me with her elbow, bringing me back to reality, and muttered, "Here we go."

I spotted Vanessa moving to the front of the room carrying a stack of postcards. She shoved them at Priscilla and took over the podium.

"I feel compelled to share these with you," Vanessa announced, as Priscilla moved down the rows passing out the postcards. "These are just another little trick I came up with to bring in more business."

I took one of the postcards as they were passed down our row. On the front was a picture of Vanessa.

"She does this at every meeting," Kayla whispered. "She's always finding some excuse to give us something with her picture on it."

"So many of you have asked me about how the Parkers' fiftieth anniversary party turned out," Vanessa said.

"Nobody has to *ask* her anything because she's always talking about herself," Kayla said.

"I'm pleased to report that after I took over the event when Suzanne wasn't about to complete it—" Vanessa said.

"Suzanne went into labor," Kayla told me.

"—everything was spectacular," Vanessa told us. "The Parkers were so thankful that I could step in and tie up all those loose ends so beautifully."

"It was the day before their party," Kayla said. "Vanessa did a walk-on and took credit for the entire event. She's always pulling something like that."

"The clients absolutely loved everything I did," Vanessa said, giving us all a look-at-me-aren't-I-fabulous-don't-you-wish-you-were-me smile.

She stood at the podium as if she expected to follow this up with a Q&A session, or at least get a round of applause, but thankfully Priscilla spoke up, though she didn't dare try to reclaim the podium.

"Thank you, Vanessa. You continue to inspire us all," she said.

I wasn't inspired, and I doubted anyone else in the room was. I figured we were all lucky that we kept down our coffee, juice, and pastries.

"Let's all have a good day," Priscilla announced, and we rose from our chairs and headed out of the conference room.

I was halfway to my office when I heard Vanessa call my name. My Holt's training kicked in immediately and I kept walking.

"Haley!" she screamed.

I heard her coming up fast behind me. I swung around, forcing her to stop. Since I was a good four inches taller than her, plus today I had on my really cool Jimmy Choos, which gave me yet another few inches, I towered over her.

The women in the hallway swerved around us and exchanged troubled looks, like they thought a bitch fight might break out or something.

I noticed Kayla standing nearby, my backup. Eve was a little farther away but taking it all in, ready to spread the word about what was going down.

Are they great BFFs or what?

Vanessa apparently didn't like the odds, because she took a half step back.

"Haley, please, you have to let me help you with the

Sheridan Adams event," she said, sounding all concerned and worried.

Oh my God, she had done a one-eighty and completely changed tactics on me.

"You told me not to ask you—"

"Please, I'm begging you," Vanessa said.

The women in the hallway had stopped and were listening.

"I'm handling the Adams' party just fine," I told her.

Vanessa pressed her lips together and shook her head. "Oh, Haley, I admire you so. You're new here and you're so inexperienced. You really have no idea what you're doing. But you're hanging in there, muddling through as best you can."

"I am not muddling!"

"Just please, promise me that you won't let your pride get the best of you," Vanessa said. "Come to me. Let me save this event while there's still time."

"What you can *save*, Vanessa, is your breath, because I know what you're doing," I told her.

She glared at me. I glared back. We progressed from stink-eye to double-stink-eye, to triple-stink-eye in a heartbeat.

Vanessa blinked first. She leaned in and hissed, "Quit now. Or else." Then she whipped around and marched off down the hall screaming, "Edie! Where are you? Edie!"

Kayla gave me a little nod. "You rock."

Yeah, maybe I did. But, jeez, Vanessa was right—I hate it when other people are right. I was barely muddling through Sheridan Adams' party prep.

I absolutely had to pull this off.

In my office, I reviewed everything that had been put in place for Sheridan's event, made calls to double-check things, and managed to calm down. Everything was in good shape with the caterer, the tribute bands, and the decorations, for now, anyway. Something could always go wrong later.

I knew Mike Ivan would come through for me on the gift bags. I still had to figure out what to do about stuffing them, plus get the Cirque du Soleil performers here somehow.

The thing that worried me most was the Yellow Submarine cake. It would be the centerpiece of the dessert buffet. It absolutely had to be ready on time, and it had to look fabulous.

Even though both Paige and Belinda had assured me the cake would be ready, I didn't feel good about it. Their promises, though well intended, wouldn't make any difference if Darren decided to give the cake an oh-well and close the bakery.

He'd made no secret of his feelings about Lacy, and that he resented having to come here and handle her affairs. I figured he'd be anxious to get back home, and that might mean cutting things short by simply selling the bakery.

I decided I'd better talk to Darren again and see where he stood on Lacy Cakes.

I sat at my desk thinking, making sure I hadn't forgotten anything about Sheridan Adams' party. I took care of a few more things, then left.

I drove to the Best Western where I'd met Darren before, but I didn't see the Lacy Cakes delivery van in the parking lot. I doubted he'd used it to tool down to Disneyland or anything, so I drove to the bakery, thinking he might be there.

I spotted the van when I pulled into the parking lot along with—yikes!—cop cars. I slid into a space near the liquor store and walked down.

The bakery's front door was propped open, and police officers in uniform were milling around. I spotted Detective Madison inside talking to Darren, and a chill ran through me. I hoped this didn't mean someone else had been murdered.

I glanced down at the floral and candle memorial someone had placed beneath the window right after Lacy died, and I hoped there wouldn't soon be another one alongside it.

I craned my neck and rose on my toes, hoping I'd see Detective Shuman here also. I really wished he could start to get over Amanda's death, and going back to work might be just the thing, but I didn't see him.

Paige was inside the bakery amid a flurry of people. She saw me through the glass and came outside. We moved a short distance away.

"What's going on?" I asked, and was almost afraid to ask more. "Did someone else get killed?"

"Oh, no, nothing like that," Paige said. "The bakery was broken into last night. I saw what had happened when I got here this morning and called the cops."

The detectives and crime scene investigators had already taken the computer, fax machine, and other office equipment when they'd been here after Lacy was murdered. What was left? Cake pans? Icing bags and decorating tips?

"You're kidding," I said.

Paige gave me an I-don't-get-it-either shrug. "Some of the baking supplies were taken, and some of the stuff Darren and Belinda had put aside for themselves."

"Oh, great," I muttered.

"Yeah," Paige said, and nodded toward the bakery display windows. "Darren isn't liking any of this."

"Is Belinda here?" I asked.

"I called her, but she didn't pick up," she said. "She's probably at work."

For some reason, it hadn't occurred to me that Belinda had a job somewhere.

"Where does she work?" I asked.

"I don't know. She's some kind of housekeeper, I think."

Mom flashed in my mind, and for about a half second I considered asking Belinda if she'd work for her, but I couldn't picture her following Mom around the house all day refilling her wineglass.

"So what do the cops think about the robbery?" I asked.

"Who knows?" Paige said. "Those uniform guys who showed up first called the detectives after I told them about Lacy getting murdered here. I guess they thought it might be connected. I don't see how. The stuff that was taken wasn't really worth much."

Breaking into a business, running the risk of getting caught and prosecuted, hardly seemed worth it for some baking supplies and used household items.

"Maybe it was kids," I said.

"Maybe," Paige agreed. "The cops think whoever broke in climbed up on the roof and got in through the ceiling. One of the drop panels in the workroom was broken and lying on the floor. That's when I first realized something was wrong."

"The door wasn't damaged?" I asked.

"Nope," Paige said. "In fact, it was locked when I got here. Thoughtful of the robbers, huh?"

So someone had found a way to access the crawl space above the bakery, dropped in through the ceiling, helped themselves to whatever they wanted, then left through the back door, making sure to lock it behind them.

Weird.

"How about the other businesses?" I asked.

"The police asked around, but I don't think any of them had their stuff stolen," Paige told me.

Weirder still.

I mean, jeez, what kind of criminals were these? They could have gotten into the liquor store and made a real haul, but didn't?

Paige seemed to read my thoughts. "Yeah, it must have been kids."

I don't think Paige read my next thought. Whoever had been here last night might have used their key to simply walk inside, knocked out a ceiling panel for cover, taken what they wanted, and left.

Paige had a key, and Darren most certainly had Lacy's key. I wondered if Belinda had one as well, or that guy I'd seen here a couple of times baking the cakes. The landlord would have a key, along with the janitorial service. And as far as I knew, only Darren and Belinda had any interest in the stuff that was taken.

Or, it really could have been kids.

"I sure hope this isn't going to make Darren decide to close the bakery," Paige said.

The uniformed officers were heading back to their patrol cars. I saw Detective Madison walk away from Darren. I didn't want him to see me here—not that I was doing anything wrong, but still.

"I need to make a quick call," I said. "I'll be right back."

It took me all of three seconds to decide the liquor store would be the best place to hide out—and not just to get away from Madison.

A little bell jangled over the door when I walked in. The place was small and crowded with merchandise. Refrigerator cases lined the rear wall. The counter was near the door, backed by racks of cigarette packs.

The man on duty stood beside a spin rack of kids' toys sealed in little plastic bags, gazing outside. He looked nice in khaki pants and a pale green shirt. He had a head full of graying hair, which surprised me since most everything else about him suggested he'd already seen his fiftieth birthday.

The impromptu memorial of artificial flowers and candles outside Lacy Cakes had been left by a casual friend or acquaintance, probably someone who worked here in the strip mall. I figured whoever it was had more than likely bought those items here in the liquor store.

"Scary, huh," I said, and nodded toward the police activity in the parking lot.

"It's not good for business, either," he said.

"Especially after what happened at the bakery," I said.

He winced. "Poor Lacy."

He seemed genuinely upset—more upset than I would have expected from a guy who happened to own a business in the same strip mall as Lacy. Then I realized that the two of them had probably known each other for years, maybe saw each other in the alley, patronized each other's businesses.

"You were friends?" I asked.

He nodded. "A little more than friends."

My spirits lifted. Surely I'd get some good info from this guy.

"This must be tough on you," I said. I offered my hand. "I'm Haley. I work for L.A. Affairs."

"Donald," he said, and we shook.

"I didn't have the opportunity to get to know Lacy very well," I said, which was really true but still kind of misleading, which was okay with me. "How long had you two known each other?"

"Two years," Donald said, and the weight of those memories seemed to cause him to slouch a little.

I could see he was truly upset about Lacy's death and probably didn't want to talk about her, but I had a murder to solve.

I mean that in the nicest way.

"You probably knew her pretty well," I said, trying to get him talking.

"Lacy didn't let a lot of people into her life," Donald said.

"Good thing she had you," I said, and smiled.

He managed a little smile also.

"And Belinda, too," I said.

"Belinda?" he asked.

"Lacy's cousin," I said. "Good thing Lacy had Belinda. She lived here in L.A. They were close."

Donald shook his head. "You must be mistaken. Lacy

wasn't close to her family. They all lived up north some-where."

Okay, that was weird. Belinda had made it sound like she and Lacy were not only cousins but best buds. Maybe Donald wasn't as close to Lacy as he'd led me to believe.

Then I remembered the story Darren had told me about Lacy turning on Belinda after the blowup they'd had over concert tickets back when they were teenagers.

"Lacy and Belinda were super close growing up, before they had a falling out over some concert tickets," I said.

Donald uttered a small chuckle. "Teenage girls. I had two older sisters, and I remember how crazy they were. Best friends one minute, fighting the next. Losing their minds over those British groups."

I had an 'N Sync flashback.

I still love Justin.

"The Rolling Stones, Herman's Hermits, Peter and Gordon," Donald said. "The Beatles, of course. All the girls were gaga over them."

"So Lacy and Belinda really weren't close?" I asked, trying to steer Donald back to a subject that would benefit me. "That's too bad. It's good to have family around."

"I don't think Lacy's family ever approved of her. When she left home she left them all behind, for the most part," Donald said, then paused for a minute. "Lacy wasn't the easiest person to get along with. She was so driven to be successful with her bakery—and I guess she achieved that, but, as the saying goes 'everything costs something.' "

Lacy's success had apparently come at the expense of not being close to her family—but from everything I'd heard about Lacy, that was probably okay with her.

I kind of knew how she felt.

The door bell jingled and a customer walked in. Donald gave me a nod and went behind the counter. I left the store.

All the police cars had cleared out of the parking lot,

and there was no sign of the white Crown Victoria Detective Madison usually drove. I wanted to talk to Darren about the future of the bakery—and, thus, the future of the Yellow Submarine cake and my job—but the Lacy Cakes delivery van he was driving was gone. I figured this wasn't the best time for the discussion, anyway. I'd catch him later.

I couldn't get my conversation with Donald out of my head. Apparently, Belinda wasn't close with Lacy, as she led me to believe. I guess Darren was right when he'd told me that she was intruding, insinuating herself into his decisions about what to do with Lacy's estate.

I'd gotten the idea from Belinda that she expected to inherit something from Lacy. Maybe she thought that the falling out they'd had all those years ago had been forgotten and Lacy would remember her in her will with either money or an interest in the bakery.

Or maybe she'd mislead me and knew that, even after all those decades had passed, Lacy still hadn't forgiven her and wouldn't leave her one thin dime. If so, her only option was to stick her nose in and hope that Darren would give her some of Lacy's possessions, or maybe even let her run the bakery for him.

Paige had said she thought Belinda worked as a housekeeper, which was really hard work. She was in her sixties now and she looked kind of rough, like maybe she had some health problems. Running a bakery—especially one as lucrative as Lacy Cakes—would definitely be a huge step up for her.

Maybe she was after money. Maybe it was the bakery she wanted.

Or maybe something else was going on.

I got in my Honda and pulled out my cell phone. Darren had made a point to tell me how he'd been saddled with all the family problems after Lacy left home, issues he was still dealing with, apparently. He'd made himself sound like the victim, which could have been true, but I couldn't help but wonder if he wasn't trying a little too hard.

I accessed the Internet, did a search of his name, and paged through a lot of links until I found something that had been posted earlier this year. It was a blog that mentioned Darren's name, his business, and a church where Darren served as a deacon.

Apparently, donations were at an all time low at the same time Darren's business had dropped off. The blogger didn't come right out and accuse Darren of skimming money from the church—only mentioned this so-called coincidence.

I sat there for a minute, thinking. Bloggers could post anything, whether or not they had evidence and facts. Just raising the question created doubt.

It sure made me think twice about Darren.

My cell phone rang. My heart jumped when I saw that it was Jack Bishop calling.

"I found you a murder suspect," he said.

Cool.

CHAPTER 15

The Perch was a rooftop restaurant in downtown L.A. I hadn't been there before, and I was pretty impressed when I stepped off the elevator.

Immediately, the Enchantress evening bag flew into my head. I was meeting Marcie later to shop for it, plus a cocktail dress for Sheridan Adams's event. This would be the perfect spot to wear both.

The place featured two outdoor fireplaces, fire pits, lots of greenery, and blooming flowers. There were seating groups of white wrought iron and wicker furniture complimented with cushions in black-and-white patterns and blue floral prints. Views of the city were breathtaking.

Then I spotted Jack—which *really* took my breath away.

He wore a charcoal gray sport coat, a shirt in a lighter shade of gray, and black slacks, definitely an upgrade from his usual private-detective mode of dress. He looked way hot.

It had been his idea to meet here after work. For a guy who'd insisted he intended to tread lightly, this place was kind of romantic. Made me wonder what Jack would do if he was treading in the other direction—which was really bad of me, I know. After all, I had an official boyfriend—

No, I don't. Damn. Why do I keep thinking that?

Jack sat at a table overlooking Pershing Square. He rose as I approached and pulled out the chair across from him.

A waiter appeared as I sat down. I ordered a glass of white wine, which I didn't intend to drink much of, since I was driving. Jack had what appeared to be bourbon on the rocks in front of him.

"Is this where you bring everybody when you have a murder suspect for them?" I asked. "Or just me?"

Jack gave me smoldering-eyes. "There're other places I'd rather take you."

Did he just use his Barry White voice? Oh my God, why was he using his totally sexy, I'm-defenseless-against-it Barry White voice? Or was I just imagining it because he's doing this treading-lightly thing?

My cell phone rang. No way would I answer it, under normal circumstances, but Jack had knocked me for a mental loop and I needed to gather myself.

I reached into my handbag—a magnificent Marc Jacobs—and got my phone.

Crap. It was Eleanor calling. I didn't even say "hello" before she hit me with my quiz question.

"What was the name of the British record company that auditioned the Beatles in January of 1962?" she asked.

I had no clue. But I couldn't afford to get any more of her questions wrong.

I covered my phone and whispered frantically to Jack, "Give me your cell phone. Quick!"

Then I spoke to Eleanor. "Oh, this one is easy. Everybody knows this one."

Jack just sat there.

"I need your phone!" I hissed.

He gave me a what's-going-on look—which I didn't have time for, not with Eleanor's I-can-get-you-fired clock ticking away.

"I need to get on the Internet," I told Jack. That might have come out sounding kind of panicky.

He puffed up slightly—which was *so* hot—like men did when they thought something was wrong.

"Who's calling you?" he asked.

"Just give me your phone!"

Jack looked as if he were about to come across the table, grab my phone, and punch out the person on the other end—somehow. It made my stomach feel kind of warm and gooey.

But no time for that now.

If I didn't give Eleanor an answer in the next few seconds she'd hang up on me again, and I didn't know how many more attempts she and Rigby would make to judge my Beatles-worthiness before she called Sheridan and told her to fire me.

"I need to find out what record company auditioned the Beatles in 1962," I told Jack in my see-you-can't-help-with-this-which-I-knew-all-along-so-just-do-what-I-asked-you-to-do voice.

"Decca Records," Jack said.

Huh?

Jack gave me a see-you-should-have-told-me-when-I-first-asked-because-I-know-things-you-don't look.

It was kind of hot.

I kept my hand over my cell phone and whispered, "Are you sure?"

He didn't even bother to answer, *that's* how confident he was.

It was way hot.

"Decca Records," I told Eleanor.

"You're correct," she said, and I wasn't sure which of us was more surprised.

"You've been reading up on the Beatles, haven't you?" Eleanor asked.

"Of course," I told her. What else could I say?

"Rigby predicted you would, but I didn't believe her," she told me.

Now I was afraid Eleanor would hit me with another question, just to see if I was telling her the truth—which I wasn't, but still. I had to head her off, and what better way to do that than to crush her with her own game.

As long as Jack could help me, of course.

"What was Ringo Starr's real last name?" I whispered to Jack. "What album was 'Eleanor Rigby' on? What was the name of their first movie? Their first single?"

"Starkey. *Revolver. A Hard Day's Night.* 'Love Me Do,' " he said.

I repeated Jack's answers into the phone.

Eleanor was quiet—stunned, I'm sure, and way impressed with me—then said, "Very good, Haley. Now we're ready to move on to the difficult questions."

Crap.

"I've got to run, but I'll talk to you again soon," I said, and hung up.

"I didn't know you were so good with Beatles history," I said to Jack.

"I'm good at a lot of things."

I don't think he meant his trivia knowledge.

The sun was disappearing toward the Pacific, so why was it getting hotter?

"Maybe I'll demonstrate the full range of my abilities someday," Jack said.

The rooftop heated up further.

Jack gestured to my cell phone I'd laid on the table beside me and said, "What was that all about?"

"It's complicated," I said.

"I like complicated," Jack said. His Barry White tone had slipped into his voice again.

Wasn't there a breeze *somewhere* in this entire city?

"It's for my job at L.A. Affairs," I said.

I guess the *affairs* portion of my explanation got his attention. He did the chest-out-nose-flair move—which got *my* attention.

"It's an event-planning company," I said.

He nodded, like maybe he was a little disappointed or I had ruined some kind of fantasy he was having. I don't know. Men can be so weird sometimes.

Then it hit me—Ty had known I had a new job, but Jack didn't. Odd.

Somewhere in the midst of my frantic Q&A with Eleanor, the waiter had brought my wine. I took a sip—I needed it, which was a good indication that this was a great time to change the subject.

"So what's up with the murder suspect you found for me?" I asked.

"Heather Gibson Pritchard, the runaway bride," Jack said, and it sounded as if he was okay with the topic switch.

"I spoke with her husband, Andrew Pritchard," Jack said. "I led him to believe I was following up on a matter involving illegal workers at Lacy Cakes. As a professional courtesy to him because he's a client of Pike Warner, I told him I'd like to speak with his wife about their wedding cake."

Jack's really good at finessing a conversation.

I probably need to work on it.

"Heather hated the cake," Jack said. "Claimed it ruined their big day."

I could see that Jack wasn't exactly onboard with the whole cake-as-a-wedding-destroyer thing, same as me, and I was pretty sure her husband felt the same way.

"I know that Heather complained to Lacy, but nothing came of it—other than that I suspect Heather might have murdered her," I said.

"Things got worse after she complained," Jack said. "Heather started hearing rumors about her wedding preparations."

"What kind of things?" I asked, leaning forward a bit.

"That she'd thrown temper tantrums, she'd cheaped out

the flowers, she'd given knockoff gifts to her bridal party, her dress had to be let out two sizes at the final fitting," Jack said. "Catty, gossipy stuff."

"Heather must have been furious," I said. I would have been.

"Heather's mom asked around and was confident that Lacy Hobbs was the source of the rumors," Jack said.

This wasn't the first time I'd heard this sort of thing about Lacy—it was a wonder she hadn't been murdered years ago.

I mean that in the nicest way, of course.

"Awful as they were, the rumors were out there. The damage had been done," I said. "So why did Heather suddenly take off for South America?"

"Andrew was a little vague on that," Jack said.

"He's protecting her?"

"Could be," Jack said. "I did some checking. Andrew Pritchard has several guns registered in his name."

It sounded as if Heather had motive for being angry at Lacy, but I'm not sure it would have driven her to murder. But the fact that there were guns in the Pritchard house and that Andrew wasn't offering up many details about Heather's sudden departure made me doubt once again that the timing of her trip was simply coincidental.

"Sounds as if you found me a murder suspect, all right," I said. "And don't worry, I won't go knocking on Andrew Pritchard's door asking more questions, or anything crazy like that."

Jack grinned. "*Crazy* is what you do best."

"I am known for it," I agreed.

Jack smiled.

Jack had a great smile.

I could get lost in that smile of his.

He seemed to realize it and shifted back into business mode, which I guess was for the best.

"I'll let you know if I hear anything else," he said.

"Great. Thanks," I said.

We just sat there for a minute looking at each other. I didn't really want to leave, but I didn't have a good reason to stay unless Jack asked me to—which he didn't.

"Well, I guess I'd better go," I said, and stood.

Jack got up and walked with me to the elevator. When it arrived he didn't get in with me, just watched while the doors closed.

My stomach jolted a little more than it should have when the elevator dropped.

I'd thought he'd asked me to meet him here because it was a cool place, kind of romantic. I thought he'd dressed up to impress me. Now I wondered if that were true. I wondered if he was meeting someone else—a date—and had squeezed me in while he was waiting.

Not a great feeling.

But Jack had never suggested that this evening would be anything but business. In fact, he'd told me right from the start that he wouldn't have anything to do with me romantically so soon after my breakup with Ty. Still, it bugged me that he might be upstairs right now, waiting for another woman to show up.

I'm not big on suspense, so I was really tempted to go back up to the rooftop, find Jack, and ask him straight out. But, for once, jumping headfirst into a situation didn't seem right.

I couldn't argue with Jack's logic or his unwillingness to put his feelings out there until he was sure Ty and I were really over—which we were. At least Ty was really over us. And me? Well . . .

Yeah, no way could I go upstairs and ask Jack what he was up to tonight.

I glanced at my watch. Marcie was probably already waiting for me at The Grove, where we planned to shop for the Enchantress bag tonight. I gave her a quick call and told her I'd be there in a few minutes, then got my car from the valet and drove over.

We'd planned to check out Nordstrom, but when Marcie saw me walk up she immediately knew something was wrong—as a BFF would.

"What happened?" she asked. Then she didn't let me answer, just took my arm. "Let's go talk."

We settled at a table at an outdoor café near the bookstore. It was dark now and a little chilly; candles flickered on the tables and patio heaters burned. All the shops and restaurants were lit up. Lots of people strolled past. The bell on the trolley clanged as it rolled by.

Since we weren't at my place where we could avail ourselves of Coronas and massive amounts of chocolate, we settled for coffee and a dessert sampler.

"I saw Ty," I told her.

Marcie gasped. "Oh my God, Haley, why didn't you tell me? Where did you see him? What happened? No wonder you're so upset."

"It wasn't today," I said, and she didn't seem mad that I hadn't confided in her when it happened—which just shows what a great BFF Marcie was. "I ran into him outside the bank."

"You just ran into him?" she asked. "You don't think he saw you and walked over? Or maybe he followed you there?"

"Followed me?" I asked. "Why?"

"Despite everything, Ty's a nice guy. I'm sure he was concerned about you after the breakup," Marcie pointed out. "Maybe he wanted to see you and make sure you were okay. Maybe he wanted to talk to you."

I shook my head. "If Ty was all that concerned about me or wanted to talk, he could have called me weeks ago."

"Maybe he was afraid calling would upset you," Marcie suggested. "A *chance* encounter would be easier for you—and him, too."

We were quiet for a minute, then Marcie asked, "How did he look?"

"Terrific," I said. It came out sounding kind of sad.

"What did you two talk about?" she asked.

"I don't know. I was just blabbing on like I was happy, like everything was great," I said. Then I remembered something Ty had asked me. "He knew I had a new job."

"How did he know about it?" she asked.

"I have no clue," I said.

"Didn't you ask him?"

I shook my head. "I was so upset I started to cry. I practically ran into the bank to get away from him."

"Maybe that was your exit cry," Marcie said. "You know, the cry that washes away the relationship and ends it for good. So you're over him now."

Marcie was almost always right about things, but I wasn't so sure about the whole exit cry thing. Neither was I sure that I was completely over Ty.

I sat there for a few minutes thinking back to when I'd seen Ty outside the GSB&T. While I'd been forcing a smile and putting on a look-at-me-I'm-happy show, he hadn't acted that way at all. Now that I thought about it, he'd seemed quiet, sort of subdued. And he had tried to tell me something when I'd bolted for the bank.

I guess Marcie read my expression, because she asked, "Do you want to talk to Ty one last time?"

"Yes." I might have moaned that.

Then I came to my senses and said, "Have you forgotten about Sarah Covington? Her engagement? To Ty?"

"I don't know for sure that she's engaged to Ty, remember? I told you I suspected it because of . . . everything," Marcie said.

"Yes, I remember," I said. I stewed for a minute, then said, "I have to know for sure if they're engaged."

"You could ask his personal assistant," Marcie said.

I'd thought about asking Amber. We'd always gotten along. She'd understand why I wanted to know, plus she wouldn't tell Ty if I asked her not to. I had that duffel bag full of Ty's things in the closet of my second bedroom. I could use it as cover to call Amber, then ask about him.

I shook my head. "I'm not going to do the ex-girlfriend stalker thing. Would you find out for me?"

"Of course," Marcie said. She was quiet for a minute, then said, "But if it turns out that Ty really is engaged to Sarah, are you going to be okay with it?"

Good question. Wish I knew the answer.

CHAPTER 16

I'd been busy all morning doing actual work for my actual job. It was no way to start a day.

I'd gotten a lot done, though. I double-checked every detail of Sheridan Adams's party and studied her file to make sure I hadn't missed anything. I hadn't.

I'd put in a call to Lyle, the owner of the company hired to do the electrical, sound, and construction at her estate on the day of the event. Jewel had already set up everything with him, which made my job easier. Kayla had told me Lyle had been a Hollywood stuntman and most of his crew also did construction on television and movie sets.

He told me that everything needed for the Cirque du Soleil dancers to perform the "Lady Madonna" number Sheridan had requested would be ready—I saw no reason to mention that I hadn't secured the actual performers yet. Lyle hadn't complained, even though it was kind of last minute. I got the feeling he was used to dealing with this sort of thing.

I spent some time on Annette Bachman's birthday party for her pooch Minnie, and sent her an e-mail suggesting a Hollywood-themed party, complete with a red carpet, a lighted archway for photos by the paparazzi—which I'd oh so cleverly termed "puparazzi"—hanging stars and banners, and a personalized miniature Oscar for everyone to take home.

I didn't know whether Annette would go for it. Maybe I'd suggested it because I had Sheridan Adams's event on my mind; at least Minnie's guests would be easier to please.

At that point, I felt as if I'd done enough for L.A. Affairs for one morning. Time to get to my own personal business.

I started by calling Mrs. Quinn at the employment agency. I needed to get this housekeeper thing finished up.

"I'm working on it every day," she assured me.

I thought about threatening to take my business elsewhere, but I suspected she'd be relieved.

"I'm anxious to get this concluded," I told her.

"As am I," she said.

I could tell by her tone that she'd never meant anything more in her entire life.

"I'll let you know the minute I have a potential candidate," Mrs. Quinn said.

I thanked her and hung up.

It wasn't quite time to head out for lunch, yet I saw no reason to linger in my office and run the risk of finding any more work to do. I went to the breakroom and was a little disappointed that no one else was there to chat with. I guess they were all at their desks working—how weird was that. I got a soda from the vending machine and flipped through *Elle* magazine until my lunch hour rolled around.

I returned to my office thinking I'd take another run at Macy's and Bloomingdale's at the Sherman Oaks mall in what was proving a very difficult hunt for the Enchantress evening bag. Marcie and I hadn't found one at Nordstrom last night, but I did buy an absolutely perfect cocktail dress to wear to Sheridan Adams's party. Even though I'd be on duty that night, I needed to fit in.

I grabbed my cell phone and saw that I had a missed call.

Yikes! It was from Detective Shuman.

I called him immediately.

"Haley, I'm—I'm glad you called back," he said when he picked up.

Shuman sounded like he was stressed out to the max.

Not good.

"Can—can you get away?" he asked.

Something major must have happened. He'd never reached out to me like this before.

"Of course," I said, using my I'm-here-for-you voice.

I don't use that one very often.

"Where can I meet you?" I asked. "Where are you?"

"I'm in Bellflower," he said.

Bellflower? What the heck was he doing in Bellflower? It was a city south of here and inland, maybe forty miles away. Of course, in L.A. forty miles translated to well over an hour's drive—if you were lucky.

I grabbed a pen from my desk drawer.

"Give me the address," I said. "I'll be there as soon as I can."

"No, no," Shuman said. "Don't come here. It's too dangerous."

My heart jumped. What the heck was Shuman up to?

"I'll meet you at—at—hang on," he said.

He went quiet. The noise in the background—traffic, I think—died. I heard a thump, like a car door had closed.

"There's a park. I forgot the name. It's north off the 118 in Simi Valley," Shuman said. "Can you find it? Can you meet me there?"

Okay, this was totally weird.

"Sure," I said, jotting down the info. "What's going on?"

"I'll call you when I get close," he told me.

"Are you okay—?"

Shuman hung up.

I didn't like the sound of this. Shuman was majorly stressed out. Something was going on.

I'd never been to Bellflower. It was probably a nice place, but like all cities it surely had its share of criminal activity. Was that what Shuman was doing there? Investigating Amanda's murder, even though the LAPD had put him on leave?

For a second I considered calling Detective Madison to see if I could find out anything, but as soon as the idea came into my head I pushed it out. Madison wouldn't help—not me, anyway—and anything I said to him might make things worse for Shuman at the department.

Of course, I could be worrying for nothing. Maybe Shuman's mom lived in Bellflower and he was just upset after visiting with her—which I totally understood. I'd have to wait to find out.

I'm not good at waiting.

I couldn't picture sitting here in my office for the next hour or until I heard from Shuman. I gathered my things and left.

I pulled into the Best Western parking lot and spotted the Lacy Cakes delivery van nosed in outside room 112. Since I had some time to kill before Shuman would get here from Bellflower, I figured another chat with Darren about the future of the bakery couldn't hurt—along with a few questions about Lacy's murder.

I parked, got out and knocked. A minute later he opened the door.

Darren looked much as he had every other time I'd seen him, dressed in work pants and a work shirt. Today the back of his hair—what there was of it—stuck straight up, like he'd been napping. I wondered what he'd been doing with his days since he'd been in town.

"Haley, isn't it?" he asked. I nodded and he stepped outside, which suited me fine because I didn't really want to be alone inside the motel room with him.

"Your cake order," he said and nodded. "Didn't Paige call you?"

A knot the size of a Prada satchel jerked in my stomach.

I guess he read the this-cannot-possibly-be-happening expression on my face because he said, "She's still doing your cake. I told her to call you just in case you heard what was going on."

I was relieved—somewhat.

"What's going on?" I asked.

"I'm closing the bakery," Darren said.

I can't say I was surprised by his decision, considering everything.

"Paige must have been disappointed," I said. "Belinda, too."

"Those two," Darren grumbled. "All this fuss over something that was never going to be theirs in the first place."

He looked as if he had more to say and had been holding it in for a while. I kept quiet—which wasn't easy for me, but that's what we sort-of-kind-of private detectives do.

"I can't run a business here from up north," Darren said, sounding agitated. "It's too far away to deal with problems. I can't be running down here every time something comes up."

"Like the break-in?" I asked.

He huffed irritably. "What if it happens again when the bakery is open for business? How much stuff could be taken? How much would that cost me?"

Belinda had told me Darren was a tightwad, and I couldn't disagree since he was still driving the delivery van instead of renting a car. Plus there was that whole thing about him possibly dipping into the church collection plate.

"Must have been expensive to get the locks changed after the burglary," I said.

"Damn right it was," Darren said. "And I'd just shelled out money to have Paige make me a key."

Hang on a second.

"You didn't have Lacy's keys?" I asked.

"I don't know what happened to them," he said, flinging out his arms. "I guess she had them on her when they took her body away. Good thing Paige had a key, otherwise I'd have had to change those locks when I got here—just like I had to change them after the break-in."

I'd suspected that the burglary was really an inside job, that Belinda or Darren had used their key to walk in, had taken some of the items they'd been arguing over, staged the break-in, and locked up after they left.

Since Lacy's keys were missing, it seemed that only Paige had a key and she'd made a copy for Darren. Had she given one to Belinda also?

And had Lacy's keys really been taken to the crime lab? Maybe her killer had grabbed them with the intention of returning to the scene and destroying evidence.

"It's just too much to fool with," Darren declared. "I'm not putting myself out so Lacy can have some sort of legacy—not after the stuff she put me through all these years."

"I understand how you feel," I said.

Darren stewed for another minute, then said, "Don't worry about your cake. Paige will make it for you. But that's it. No more. I told her not to take any more orders."

"Fair enough," I said.

"I'll be glad when all of this is over and done with," Darren mumbled, and went back inside his motel room.

A visit to Lacy Cakes seemed in order. I drove over, parked, and went around back. The door to the workroom was open, as usual, and the same guy was baking cakes when I walked in.

Paige stood at a worktable studying three round cake tiers spread out in front of her. She smiled and waved.

"Hey, girl, come over here," she called.

"Sorry about the bakery closing," I said as I joined her at the worktable.

"I guess you talked to Darren, huh?" she said. "Listen, he wanted me to call you, but I didn't because I thought you'd worry. But don't. I'm going to get your cake done and it's going to be great."

"That's good to know," I said. "But what are you going to do for a job after the bakery closes?"

"Belinda and I are going to buy it—if we can," Paige said.

Wow, I guess a lot had happened since I'd last talked to Paige.

"So Belinda didn't inherit an interest in the bakery from Lacy?" I asked.

"Darren told her he'd talked to Lacy's lawyer. Everything went to him in Lacy's will," Paige said.

"Belinda must have been upset," I said.

"Yeah, but I don't know why," Paige told me. "She and Lacy weren't all that close. Some stupid fight they had back in the day. Both of them were pretty bent over it."

I'd heard Lacy never forgave Belinda over that whole concert tickets thing, but I hadn't heard that Belinda was mad over something that Lacy had done.

"Belinda, too?" I asked.

Paige waved her hands. "She was going on and on the other day about Lacy stealing her stuff, talking trash about her, turning the family against her. I don't know. I wasn't really listening."

I could totally relate.

"We're trying to get the money together to buy the bakery," Paige said.

"Must be expensive," I said.

"You know it, girl," she said, and rolled her eyes. "I'm trying to get my dad to loan me some money. I'm not sure what Belinda is going to do."

"I guess Belinda didn't get any of Lacy's life insurance, either?" I asked.

Paige shook her head. "Not one dime."

After listening to Ty talk about opening new Holt's stores, Wallace, and Holt's International for months while we were dating, I knew any start-up required a lot of cash—even for something small like Lacy Cakes. From all appearances, Belinda wasn't exactly swimming in money, and if Paige was depending on her dad for her share of the investment, the future of the bakery didn't look so great.

But money, of course, wasn't the whole problem with opening a new business.

"Do you and Belinda really know each other that well?" I asked. "Running a shop together can be tough."

Paige shrugged. "I talked to her some when she came in to see Lacy. We hit it off pretty well."

"Does Belinda know anything about baking?" I asked.

"Not really, but it doesn't matter. I'll make the cakes and she'll do everything else," Paige said. "Besides, it's not like I have a choice. It's partner with Belinda or hit the streets."

Lacy Cakes had a fantastic reputation and an established clientele, so if Paige and Belinda could keep the place going it would be a gold mine for them. I could see why they were willing to take the chance.

"I hope it works out," I said. "And thanks for taking care of my cake."

"No problem," she said.

I walked back to my car, figuring that Shuman should call me any time now. I drove to the Subway down the block, went inside, and bought sandwiches, chips, and sodas, and with the help of my GPS I headed for the park in Simi Valley. Just as I transitioned onto the westbound 118, he called and said he was about fifteen minutes away.

I exited the freeway and drove north through a residential neighborhood, then turned into the parking lot. Not a lot of cars were there. I spotted two moms with toddlers in the grassy field off to my right. No sign of Shuman.

I got out and opened my trunk. All kinds of things accumulated in there. I scrounged around and found a pair of flats that I had no memory of buying—maybe one of my breakup fog purchases that never made it into my second bedroom—along with a quilt my dad had insisted I keep in there when he'd given me a roadside emergency kit not long ago, after my car had broken down on the way to Las Vegas—long story.

I changed my shoes, grabbed the quilt and Subway bags, and set up lunch on a nearby picnic table beneath several tall, shady trees. Just as I was spreading the quilt over the bench—no way was I roughing it while wearing my awesome gray business suit—Shuman walked up.

Yikes! I hardly recognized him.

He had on black pants, T-shirt, a hoodie, and CAT boots. A black baseball cap was pulled low on his forehead, almost touching his wraparound sunglasses. What little of his face I could see was covered with a full beard.

This wasn't the Shuman I knew. Not at all.

I was scared. Scared about what he was doing, what he might do, and what it might turn him into.

I was kind of scared for myself as well, thinking what I might do to keep that from happening.

"I brought lunch," I said.

He didn't sit down. Instead he threw both arms around me and pulled me full against his chest. He buried his nose in my hair and held on as if his life depended on it. I wrapped my arms around his waist.

We stayed like that for a long time, then slowly Shuman released me and stepped back.

"Thanks for coming, Haley, for meeting me," he said. "I—I just . . . I just needed . . ."

"I'm glad you called me," I said, and I truly meant it—which was totally unlike me but there it was.

"I had to—" Shuman pressed his lips together, then forced himself to go on. "I had to tell somebody what really happened with Amanda."

CHAPTER 17

Shuman was about to lose it big-time.

"Sit down," I said. "We'll eat, then talk."

He didn't say anything, but allowed me to guide him around the picnic table. He dropped onto the bench. By the time I unrolled our sandwiches, opened bags of chips, and screwed the tops off our bottles of soda he'd pulled himself together. He ate everything; I didn't have much of an appetite.

"Let's walk," Shuman said.

We dumped our trash and strolled into the park. The gently rolling meadow was shaded by tall trees. A little stream meandered over rocks worn smooth by the water. Birds chirped.

I realized why Shuman had wanted to meet here. It was quiet, peaceful. Whatever he intended to tell me about Amanda was too painful to talk about in a public place.

"Amanda and I broke up," Shuman said.

I froze and touched his arm, stopping him next to me. This was the very last thing I expected to hear him say.

"It was what she wanted," Shuman said. He gulped hard. "And I—I went along with it."

"I don't get it," I said. "You two seemed so solid."

"That's what I thought, too," he said. "We had some

differences, but I was okay with everything. I mean, I could live with them. You know?"

I knew exactly.

"She was so special in so many ways," Shuman said. "My days could be grim sometimes, and she was always my bright spot."

We started walking again.

"I guess she wasn't okay with some of our differences," Shuman said. "She wanted to work in Boston. She asked me if I'd go with her. I didn't want to leave my job here. So she said maybe we should end things."

I pictured the two of them having that last conversation, saying those things to each other, making that decision. It made my heart hurt.

"That must have been a tough decision for you two. Really painful," I said. "But I guess it was the right thing to do."

"*No.*"

The word exploded out of Shuman. He laid his hands on my shoulders and leaned closer.

"No, Haley, it was wrong, all wrong," he told me. "I shouldn't have gone along with what she wanted. I should have fought for our relationship, for us. But I didn't fight her on it. I was stunned and hurt, and she seemed so sure it was the best thing. I let it happen, Haley. I just stood there and let it happen—and look how it turned out. Look what happened to her."

"Are you blaming yourself for Amanda's murder?" I asked.

He dropped his hands from my shoulders and shook his head. "If I haven't agreed to the breakup, I might have been there that night. I might have stopped it."

I shook my head. "No. You can't think that way."

"Maybe she could have stopped it," Shuman said. "I keep thinking that she might have been distracted, not pay-

ing attention to her surroundings because she was thinking about me, wondering why I'd agreed to ending our relationship, why I'd let her go so easily."

"This isn't your fault," I told him.

"I could have stopped it. I could have saved her."

"You don't know that," I said.

He gazed off across the park, his jaw clenched, his lips
pressed together.

"There's only one way to make it right," he said.

If I had any doubt about Shuman's intention to find
Amanda's killer, the look on his face and the tone of his
voice erased it.

"I know who did it," he said. "LAPD knows. They've
got an eyewitness, surveillance tape, fingerprints, DNA.
Everything. There's no doubt."

"Who is it?" I asked.

"Adolfo Renaldi," Shuman said. "Amanda was prosecuting his brother Lorenzo. A couple of real scumbags.
Into everything. Ruthless."

"If the LAPD knows who he is, why haven't they arrested him?" I asked.

"They can't find him."

"Are you having any better luck?" I asked.

He didn't say anything, so I guess I had my answer.

I'd figured that a friend of Shuman's inside the department was feeding him info on the investigation and that he
hadn't backed off the case just because they'd taken his authority to do so. Looked like I was right about both.

"They'll find him," I said. "The whole department must
be looking for him. Sooner or later, they'll find him."

"And then what?" Shuman asked. "Put him in jail so
some defense lawyer can get him off on a technicality? So
his attorneys can drag his case out for years? So he can live
like a king in his palace if he ever does go to prison?"

I couldn't disagree with him, because I knew he was

right. All of those things could happen—they'd happened in the past to other criminals. Our justice system was really great, but it wasn't perfect.

Not everybody got the justice they deserved.

Shuman straightened his shoulders and drew in a breath.

"I can't let this go," he said. "I won't, until I make it right."

"I understand," I said because, really, I did.

All the way back to the office I couldn't stop thinking about Shuman. That look on his face, the tone in his voice when he spoke about how he should have fought for his relationship with Amanda.

Maybe I should have done the same with Ty.

I settled behind my desk in my office and saw that I had an e-mail from Annette. She liked my idea for the Hollywood birthday party for Minnie but wondered if I had any other suggestions.

Like there are *that many* themes for a dog's birthday party.

I came up with a garden party birthday celebration for Minnie, with big hats for all her guests, flowers, a wishing well, and doggie treats that resembled tea cakes.

I slumped on my desk and clicked Send. I was planning a birthday party for a dog. Was this any way to spend my day?

Maybe this event planner thing wasn't for me, after all.

Then I pulled myself together—as I almost always do—and decided it was time to tackle my major obstacle with Sheridan Adams's Beatles party: getting the Cirque du Soleil dancers to perform. I looked up the Love show in Las Vegas on the Internet, found a phone number, and after being transferred around a dozen times, reached the theater manager.

I wasn't sure she was even listening to what I was saying—just waiting for me to take a breath so she could
transfer me to someone else—until I said, "And it's a charity event at the home of Talbot and Sheridan Adams.
There will—"

"Talbot Adams? *The* Talbot Adams? The producer and
director?" she asked. "At his *home?*"

"Yes, along with two hundred A-list guests," I said.

"How exciting for you," she gushed. "What a fabulous
job you have."

I saw no need to mention that I was also planning Minnie the dog's birthday party.

"Of course we can work something out," she said.

I got her e-mail address and composed the message with
all the details while she was yammering on about the Beatles, Talbot Adams, "Lady Madonna," and blah, blah,
blah.

I snapped back to reality in time to hear her ask for
Sheridan Adams's e-mail address. No way was I going to
give that out, so I gave her contact info for Muriel, which
seemed to suit her just as well. I thanked her and hung up.

Huh. That was easier than I thought it would be, thanks
to my dropping Talbot Adams's name.

I didn't think playing on someone else's celebrity was
really the thing to do in life—unless it benefited me, of
course.

I got on the Internet again and found the names of companies that specialized in creating celebrity gift bags for
the Oscars, the Emmys, and other high-profile award cere-
monies. One of them, Distinctive Gifting, jumped out at
me. I remembered hearing my mom talk about the fabulous swag they'd provided for an event she'd attended
with some of her ex-beauty-queen friends, so I decided to
call them.

"This is Haley Randolph from L.A. Affairs," I said,

using Mom's I'm-better-than-you voice. "I'm calling regarding an event for Talbot and Sheridan Adams."

"One moment, please," the receptionist said.

Two clicks and a few seconds later, a woman picked up.

"Well, hello, Miss Randolph." She had a kind of Jamaican accent thing going. "This is Tiberia Marsh. It's always good to hear from L.A. Affairs. I don't believe we've met. Are you new with the firm?"

"Somewhat," I said.

I saw no reason to explain that this was my first event.

"And you're handling Talbot and Sheridan's party? My, but you must be very well respected at L.A. Affairs," she said.

I saw no reason to mention that my job was dangling by a thread that Vanessa couldn't wait to snip.

"I'm always pleased to work with your firm," Tiberia said. "Just tell me what you need and it will be yours."

So far, I was loving Tiberia—even though I suspected she'd made up her own first name.

I gave her the info about Sheridan's Beatles-themed party and explained that I'd ordered the bags so all she had to do was provide the luxury items for people who probably didn't really need them.

"Sorry it's sort of last minute," I said.

Tiberia chuckled. "Everything Sheridan does is last minute. We're used to it, as I'm sure L.A. Affairs is."

Okay, that was weird. L.A. Affairs had worked with Distinctive Gifting on Sheridan's parties in the past?

"Don't worry, I know exactly what will make Sheridan and her guests happy," Tiberia said. "I'll handle everything."

"Great," I said, and we hung up.

Whew! I was really relieved that Tiberia had taken over the whole gift bag thing, but it bugged me that I hadn't known to call her in the first place. I wondered why it hadn't been noted in Sheridan Adams's file.

Just to be sure I hadn't overlooked it I flipped through the file and reviewed the vendors listed for all the parties and events L.A. Affairs had handled for Sheridan. No mention of Distinctive Gifting.

Then it hit me—oh my God, Vanessa must have taken it out on purpose. Just to make things harder on me, to make me look incompetent in front of Sheridan, to try to get me fired.

Bitch.

I was ready to storm down the hall and confront Vanessa when my cell phone rang. Mike Ivan's name appeared on my caller ID screen.

"I've got a sample of the gift bag you wanted," he said when I answered. "I can bring it over, if you want."

Since I didn't think it was a good idea to have a maybe-connected-to-the-Russian-mob guy show up at L.A. Affairs, plus I didn't like to miss a chance to get out of the office, I said, "I can come by your place."

"I'll be here all afternoon," he said.

We hung up. I got my things and left.

There was no quick way to get anywhere in Los Angeles at this time of day, so I settled on the 101 freeway, then went south on the 110. I crept along the surface streets to my favorite parking lot on Santee Street, then hoofed it a block to the fabric store on Ninth Street, where I'd met Mike before.

The same guy who'd given me stink-eye the last time I was there sat behind the counter. He gave me stink-eye again.

I spotted Mike at the rear of the store. He was on his cell phone. We made eye contact, and a few seconds later he hung up. As I walked over he disappeared into the stock room, then came out again carrying a brown box.

"What do you think?" he asked, pulling off the lid.

I moved aside the plastic wrap and picked up the sample tote bag his designer friend had made. It was black with a red heart that had "all you need is love" stitched across it in a colorful pattern that I think was called psychedelic back in the day. The lining—crucial to the success of any handbag—had the same pattern. The fabric felt great, and the design was awesome.

"It's perfect," I said, and put it back in the box. "Sheridan will love it."

Mike nodded. "I can get them to you in a couple of days."

A two day turnaround time for the hundreds of bags I needed was quick, even for one of the factories housed in the upper floors of the nearby buildings. I guess Mike was putting a rush on it for me.

"What's going on with your friend's murder? That detective's girlfriend?" he asked.

Mike and I had discussed Amanda's death the last time I was here, and I was a bit surprised that he brought it up again. Yet it didn't seem like a casual question. Mike looked troubled.

I got a weird feeling.

"The LAPD knows who murdered her," I said. "They're—"

"Who?" Mike demanded.

My weird feeling got weirder.

Jeez, maybe I was wrong to connect with Mike again—no matter how desperate I was for gift bags so I could keep my job. I didn't know if the identity of Amanda's killer was confidential—Shuman hadn't asked me to keep it to myself—but I guess he didn't figure on me discussing the murder with a maybe-maybe-not guy from the Russian mob.

I couldn't exactly refuse to give Mike the guy's name. I just wish I knew what he planned to do with it.

Maybe I was better off not knowing.

"Some guy named Adolfo—"

"Renaldi." Mike bristled. His chest expanded and his shoulders straightened—which was usually a really hot look on men, but this time it kind of frightened me.

"Are they sure it was him?" Mike asked.

"They've got DNA, fingerprints, surveillance footage, even an eyewitness," I said. "Do you know this guy?"

"Lorenzo's brother." Mike shook his head. "Scum. The worse kind of scum. The whole family ought to be taken off the streets."

"The LAPD is trying to find the guy," I said. "No luck—yet."

Mike grunted as if that was what he expected from the police department.

"What about that detective? Shuman?" he asked.

"He's taking Amanda's death hard, really hard," I said. "He's working the case, but not officially."

Mike nodded, and by the look on his face I could see he didn't disagree with Shuman's actions.

"I'll call you when the bags are ready," Mike said, and disappeared into the stock room.

I headed back to the parking lot. While I stood on the corner at Maple and Olympic waiting for the light to change, I pulled out my cell phone and Googled Adolfo Renaldi's name.

Yikes! The guy, along with his family, was mentioned in a number of news reports linking them to all sorts of crimes in the Long Beach area.

I crossed the street thinking about Mike. He owned an import–export company. He did business at the port in Long Beach.

Maybe his interest in Amanda's murder went beyond that of a concerned citizen.

By the time I got my car and crawled up the freeway with the zillion other commuters, it was too late to go

back to the office. I texted Muriel—which was okay because traffic was at a complete standstill—and let her
know that the gift bags and the swag were handled, and
that the theater manager from the Beatles Love show in
Vegas would contact her.

By the time I got to my apartment, I had just enough
time to run in and change clothes for my shift at Holt's. I
jumped out of my car and spotted Cody sitting in his
pickup truck.

Oh my God. Cody. I'd forgotten all about him—and
that he'd kissed me.

Jeez, what's happening to my life?

He got out and ambled over.

"Sorry, tonight's not a good night for you to work on
my apartment," I said.

Cody glanced around the parking lot, then said, "Do
you have a boyfriend?"

"Yes—no. No, I don't have a boyfriend," I said.

He leaned around me and gazed at I don't know what,
then turned the other way and did the same thing.

"What's going on?" I asked.

"Remember the last time I was here?" he asked.

"Of course," I said.

The night I'd met him in the parking lot and we'd
kissed.

I saw no reason to mention that I'd totally forgotten
about it until now.

"After you went upstairs, some guy came up and told
me to stay away from you," he said.

"What?"

Cody nodded. "He said to leave you alone. You were
going through some things and I'd better back off."

"*What?*"

"I'm not looking for any trouble," Cody said. "You'll
have to find somebody else to fix up your place."

He got back in his pickup truck and drove away. I stood in the parking lot staring after him.

Oh my God, had I turned into some sort of pariah?

Ty had broken up with me, Jack was treading lightly, Shuman was consumed by the death of his girlfriend—whom he'd actually broken up with—and Cody turned tail at the first sign of a problem.

Only . . . why was there a problem? Who would have approached Cody in my parking lot and told him to back off?

Jack Bishop.

It had to be him.

I guess that had been him a few nights before, speeding out of the parking lot when Cody and I had gone upstairs to my apartment. He'd been hanging out, watching for me, spying on me?

Who could it have been but Jack?

I didn't know whether to be mad—or flattered.

CHAPTER 18

"In two Beatles films ice-cream cones can be seen," Rigby said. "Name the films."

Eleanor had told me my quiz questions would get more difficult, but this was ridiculous.

I was in the drive-through at Starbucks because my afternoon definitely needed a boost. My name had come back to the top of the list in the L.A. Affairs' rotation, so I was headed to Altadena to consult with a client. Mindy had been vague about just what sort of event this would be. I just hoped it wouldn't be another doggie birthday party.

"All the Beatles movies were really great," I said, hoping that somehow the right answer would come to me.

Nothing came to me.

"Everybody has a favorite," I said. "Which is your favorite?"

Rigby hung up.

Crap.

I was going to have to buy either a second cell phone so I could look up the answers to Eleanor and Rigby's questions on the Internet while I stalled them or a Beatles trivia book—and then actually read it and learn the material.

I hate my life.

But thankfully Starbucks was here for me. I got my mocha frappuccino and headed east on the 134.

Traffic was light—plus my frappie gave me a great brain boost—so I settled into the drive to Altadena and let my thoughts wander. Immediately, murder came to mind.

This thing with Shuman being on leave from the LAPD was putting a crimp in my investigation of Lacy Hobbs's murder. If he was on the job I could tell him about Heather Pritchard, the runaway bride who'd complained about the wedding cake Lacy had made for her, and he could investigate her supposedly impromptu trip to South America.

But since he wasn't available—not that I blamed him, of course—I was on my own. The only thing I could think to do was talk to Heather's mother, Sasha, and hope that she'd let something incriminating slip.

I didn't really think that would happen, though. Sasha would be protective of her daughter.

Just like my mom would be of me.

Jeez, I hope she'd be protective.

Anyway, I hadn't found any new info about August, the guy who owned Fairy Land bakery. Though I'm sure he was glad to no longer have Lacy Cakes as competition, I didn't see any real motive for him to kill her. I figured I could mark him off my suspect list until I found evidence that would implicate him.

Belinda seemed to have more reason to want Lacy killed than anyone else—but it didn't seem like that much of a reason at all. Some old argument from back in the day, a squabble over concert tickets and, apparently, years of Lacy talking trash about her to their family didn't seem like much of a motive to walk into the workroom at the bakery, pull out a gun, and open fire.

I mean, jeez, if Belinda was going to murder Lacy, why do it now? All that stuff had been going on for years.

Darren came into my thoughts as I transitioned onto the

210. He'd resented Lacy for decades. She'd left him to manage their parents and the family business, and if what he'd said was true, she'd had little contact with them. He'd been really ticked off when he learned how much she was making at the bakery but hadn't sent any of it home.

Maybe he'd had enough of Lacy's callous disregard for the family. I had no way of knowing when he'd actually arrived in L.A.—it could have been days before Lacy was murdered—or whether it was true that he didn't really know what kind of income Lacy made from her cakes. Maybe he'd found out. Maybe he'd figured that either he or his parents would be named in her will. Maybe the years of resentment had gotten the best of him.

Paige popped into my mind. I couldn't help but think that starting work at Lacy Cakes just a short time before Lacy was murdered wasn't a coincidence—especially after she'd told me that she was trying to buy the bakery. She'd downplayed borrowing the money from her dad, so I wondered if it was a lie. For all I knew she had plenty of money. She probably hadn't wanted to start a bakery from nothing and spend years building a reputation when it was so much easier to step into Lacy Cakes, the most successful one in L.A.

She'd told me she and Belinda were going to be partners in the business, which made me wonder if maybe they'd been partners in Lacy's murder.

I took the Lake Avenue exit off the 210 and drove north, then hung a right on Poppyfields Drive. This was an older, upscale neighborhood of really nice homes with mature trees and well-tended landscaping. I squeezed through the narrow street and parked, got my official L.A. Affairs portfolio, climbed the steep sloping driveway, and rang the doorbell.

"Back here!" someone called. "We're back here!"

I followed a pathway to the tall wooden gate at the side of the house and pushed it open. A woman dressed in jeans and a T-shirt waved me closer. I figured her for about thirty-five, with blond curly hair that she had, apparently, neglected to brush today.

Then I realized why. Beyond her in the yard, four children—all under the age of five, I guessed—ran around, yelling and screaming for no apparent reason. Two dogs—a little black-and-white one and an even smaller brown one—were barking and chasing the kids.

"You must be Haley from the party company," the woman said. "I'm Maeve."

"Nice to meet you," I said, even though it wasn't.

"And these are my little darlings," Maeve declared, sweeping her hand toward the children and dogs. "I want to have the party out here."

I was afraid of that.

"So the party is for . . . ?" I asked.

"Daphne and Demetria. They're turning four," she announced.

"Are they two of the kids, or the dogs?" I asked.

She threw back her head and laughed like people did when they didn't often have adults around to talk to.

"My daughters—twins." She gave me a proud smile and paused, waiting for me to say something about how fabulous I thought her kids were.

I couldn't think of anything.

"So, what did you have in mind for the party?" I asked.

Maeve started talking and I made notes, but only a few of her words penetrated the screaming and barking. The kids spotted us and ran over, circling us at a run. The dogs followed, yapping and jumping up and down. One of the little girls fell and started a whole different kind of screaming. Maeve scooped her up and kept talking.

I couldn't take it anymore.

"That's everything I need to get started," I shouted.

"It is?" she shouted back.

Jeez, she'd already told me she wanted clowns, pony

rides, a bounce house, and a magician. What else could she need for the kids' party?

"I'll be in touch," I yelled, and headed for the gate.

I was tempted ask her if I could use her bathroom so I could tie my own tubes, but I just wanted to get the heck out of there.

I got in my Honda and drove away.

How come I wasn't assigned a really cool party with fabulous food, a great band, and some hot guys?

I wasn't loving this whole event planner thing. But I had to work somewhere. Even with my job at L.A. Affairs and at Holt's, I'd managed to keep up on my college courses—even though I'd ditched class a lot lately—but my degree was years away. I didn't know how long I could hold out at L.A. Affairs. I'd have to figure out something.

Since it was time for my lunch hour—not really, but oh well—I drove to Colorado Boulevard in Pasadena and parked behind Vroman's Bookstore. I'd already failed Rigby's Beatles pop quiz today and I couldn't afford to get another question wrong.

I went inside and—wow—the place was huge. Two stories with books absolutely everywhere. All kinds of other cool stuff, too. I asked the guy at the counter, and he took me to the shelves that held books about the Beatles.

Yikes! There were zillions of them. I didn't have time to look at each of them, so I grabbed the one with the thickest spine—if it was the biggest it should have the most info, right?—paid for it and left.

Jeez, this book was heavy, I realized as I crossed the parking lot. It would probably take a really long time to read.

I got out my cell phone, did a search, and downloaded everything I could find about the Beatles on iTunes and YouTube. I ordered all of the movies and documentaries made about them. I figured I could watch them all at the office—it was work related, technically—and use the book for a quick reference if I needed it when Eleanor or Rigby called with a pop quiz question.

Just as I was getting in my car thinking I could hit Macy's down the street for the Enchantress evening bag—I absolutely had to have it to go with the gorgeous cocktail dress I'd bought for Sheridan's party—my cell phone rang. I was relieved to see that Marcie was calling. This hadn't exactly been the best day of my life and I was anxious to talk to my BFF. She always made things better.

"Bad news," Marcie said, when I answered.

Crap.

"My uncle died," she told me.

Okay, now I felt like a complete jerk.

"Sorry to hear that," I told her.

"Don't be," Marcie said. "I never met him. Mom wants to go to the funeral and, well, you know how family things can be, so she doesn't want to go alone. Dad can't take time off from work. I'm going with her. To Maine."

"How long will you be gone?" I asked.

"A week at least. We're leaving tonight," Marcie said.

She paused, and I knew something more was coming.

"So I won't be able to track down Sarah Covington and find out if she's engaged to Ty," Marcie said.

My spirits fell. I'd really counted on her to handle that for me. I couldn't stand not knowing, but no way could I ask Sarah or Ty myself.

"It's okay," I said. "Family comes first."

I didn't really think that, but it sounded nicer.

"Call Amber, Ty's assistant," Marcie said.

Marcie was usually right about things, but I didn't know if I could do that.

"I'll think about it," I told her, and we hung up.

Damn. Was I having a crappy day or what?

I didn't see how my day could get any worse. Then my cell phone rang.

Mrs. Quinn's name appeared on the caller ID screen,

and my spirits lifted. She had no doubt found several candidates for Mom's housekeeper position, all of whom were perfectly suited for the job. Thank goodness this was one problem I would be done with.

"Good news?" I asked, when I answered my phone.

"Not exactly," she replied.

Not exactly didn't mean bad news, did it?

"Word has gotten out about your mother," Mrs. Quinn said. "No one will work for her."

Not one housekeeper—not that I blamed them, of course—would work for her? There had to be *someone* who would do it.

"I'll just call another agency," I said.

"It won't matter," Mrs. Quinn said. "Your mother has been blacklisted."

Oh my God, this could not be happening. Mom absolutely had to have a housekeeper.

And what if she found out she'd been blacklisted? I—along with everyone else in the family—would never hear the end of it. She might completely lose it, take off to some exotic country, stay for ages, I'd never see her—

Okay, hang on a minute.

I let the idea play around in my head for a while—which was really bad of me, I know—and then came to my senses. No matter what she was like, she was still my mom. I would have to find her a housekeeper somehow.

"I can keep the temporary housekeepers at your mother's home for a while longer," Mrs. Quinn said. "But I'm having to change them out every other day now. I only have a few more who are willing to go there."

"I'll figure out something," I said.

"Good luck," Mrs. Quinn said, and graciously left the you'll-need-it unspoken.

Oh, crap. Now what was I going to do?

*   *   *

"This is b.s.," Bella said. "You ask me, this is all b.s."

I didn't disagree.

We were leaving the Holt's breakroom where we'd both just clocked in for our evening shifts. Near the customer service booth, all the merchandise was being moved and workmen were busy setting up the curtained walkway that would connect the stock room to the stage and runway for the upcoming fashion show—or something like that. I don't know. I wasn't really paying attention when Jeanette explained it.

"I can't believe Holt's found actual models—women with real fashion sense—to put these clothes on and parade down the runway in front of people," Bella said.

"Holt's must be paying them a fortune," I said.

We made our way through the roped-off work area and went through the double doors into the stock room. The clothes for the fashion show were where we'd left them; none of them had magically morphed into something remotely stylish.

"I say we put on blindfolds and starting picking up clothes, shoes, and accessories," Bella said, shaking her head. "At least we won't get nauseated from actually having to look at everything."

"Haley? Bella?"

I spotted Jeanette walking toward us.

Speaking of nauseated . . .

Her ode to the fall season continued with a skirt and jacket of mustard yellow and burnt orange plaid chenille.

She looked like a seventies bath mat.

"How is everything going?" Jeanette asked, standing next to us and studying the hanging dresses.

No matter how awful the so-called fashions were, this was better than being out on the sales floor—which just shows how I feel about waiting on customers—so I decided to take the route that would most benefit *me*.

"It's . . . okay," I said.

Yeah, all right, that wasn't exactly a rousing show of enthusiasm for the fashion show, but it was the best I could muster.

I don't think Jeanette noticed.

She was busy pulling dresses off the rack, holding them in front of her, and digging through the boxes of costume jewelry.

"I love fashion," Jeanette said, draping a coral-colored plastic necklace over the hanger that held an orange and teal striped dress.

Yikes!

Bella and I nearly bolted for the stock room exit, but managed to stand still.

Then I had a brilliant idea.

"You know, Jeanette, you really do have an eye for color," I said.

I could hardly get the words out. But, really, Jeanette was a dedicated Holt's shopper. She actually liked this stuff. Maybe I could get her to assemble the looks I'd need for the runway show so I wouldn't have to do it.

Jeanette was way ahead of me.

I hate it when that happens.

She dropped the necklace back in the box and hung the dress on the rack.

"I know you two girls will put on a fabulous show," she said. "Everyone at the store is counting on you to win this contest for us."

I knew I should say something positive about the contest.

I couldn't think of anything.

"And don't forget about the grand prize for the fashion show coordinator," Jeanette said. She gave me a knowing smile—which was kind of creepy—and said, "You know, Corporate had initially announced the grand prize would be a set of our best cookware, but you-know-who changed it."

My heart jumped. She must have been referring to Ty.

I'd wondered if the gossip at the corporate office had reached the stores and Jeanette had found out that Ty and I had broken up. Apparently, Jeanette was as clueless about company rumors as she was about fashion.

"At the last minute it was announced that the fashion show coordinator would receive a different prize," Jeanette said. "A month-long internship as a stylist at the corporate headquarters."

A stylist? At corporate headquarters? That's where Ty worked.

Oh my God, if I won the fashion show contest that would mean I'd be in the same building with Ty? I might see him—every day? Pass him in the hall? See him in the breakroom? Maybe even sit in on meetings with him?

Jeanette kept talking, but it all turned into blah, blah, blah.

Had I actually volunteered to be the store's fashion show coordinator? I'd been in my breakup fog at the time, so now I couldn't be sure.

Maybe Jeanette assigned it to me. Why would she do that? She knew Ty and I were dating, so maybe she was playing cupid and trying to get us together at the corporate office.

She couldn't have been trying to get me out of her store for a month, could she?

It hit me then that maybe I should go all-out to try to win the contest. If I worked at the corporate office with Ty for a whole month, maybe we'd realize we had a lot in common, like the stores, the merchandise, ways to increase sales. Maybe we'd get back together.

Then something else hit me.

Maybe I should go all-out and try to lose the contest. If I worked at the corporate office I'd see Sarah Covington. She'd be all over Ty and I'd have to watch. And—oh my God—what if they really were engaged?

I knew in my heart I wouldn't be able to bear up seeing the two of them together.

Then yet another thing hit me.

There was no way to deliberately throw the contest. The clothing was hideous. No matter what horrible outfits I sent down the runway, Holt's customers would buy them.

Jeez, how had I gotten into this mess?

And why would Ty have changed the contest's grand prize?

CHAPTER 19

"Haley, Mrs. Adams needs to see you," Muriel said when I answered my cell phone.

I'd just gotten into my car—looking way hot in one of my black business suits that I'd jazzed up with a bold Betsey Johnson bag—and was heading to L.A. Affairs. I was surprised to hear from her so early in the morning.

Then I realized that—wow—Sheridan probably wanted to tell me what a great job I was doing on her Beatles party. I was doing pretty darn good on Eleanor and Rigby's pop quizzes. Plus I'd kept Muriel updated on everything, and she'd surely told Sheridan that I'd gotten fabulous gift bags, filled with even-though-you-don't-need-any-free-stuff-you're-going-to-love-this swag, and that the Cirque du Soleil performers were a lock.

"Sure," I said. "I can come by this afternoon."

I couldn't wait to throw this in Vanessa's face.

"First thing this morning would be better," Muriel said.

Maybe I'd get Edie to announce my triumph at our next staff meeting.

"Just let me run by at L.A. Affairs and I'll be there," I said.

I should definitely get something printed with my picture on it and make sure Vanessa got a dozen of them.

"You should come now," Muriel said. "Like right this minute."

Sheridan wanted to see me immediately? Maybe she'd planned a light brunch for us and we'd sit on one of her many patios while her servants attended us so she could go on and on about what a fabulous event planner I was—far superior to Vanessa—and vow to give me all her future business.

Cool.

"I'm on my way," I said, and hung up.

This was so awesome. My day was off to a great start—even the freeway traffic cooperated with me. I listened to the radio, sang along, did a little seat-dancing, and pulled into the driveway of Sheridan's Holmby Hills home in record time.

I parked and saw the front door swing open. Sheridan Adams herself stood in the doorway. She must *really* be thrilled with my work if she'd waited by the door for me to arrive, then opened it herself, sans servants.

Sheridan had a bit of an Effie Trinket thing going this morning. Her totally fried-out hair had a pink hue, for some reason, and had been whipped into a severe updo. She was dressed in a pencil skirt and jacket—both in an extremely unflattering shade of magenta—and wore four-inch heels and a choker of fresh flowers.

I got out of my car and morphed my face into Mom's I'm-fabulous-but-I-have-to-appear-humble-right-now expression.

"Good morning," I said, as I walked to the door. "It's so nice to—"

"What have you *done?*" she shrieked.

I froze and braced myself, ready to bob and weave in case she came at me like a spider monkey.

"It's ruined—*ruined!*" Sheridan clenched her fists and waved them in the air. "The entire party is *ruined!*"

She stomped her feet and let out a scream that I was sure could be heard all the way in Bel Air. For a minute, I thought she might have a stroke—not that I really cared—and then a servant appeared beside her.

"And it's your fault!" Sheridan yelled. She pointed her finger at me, as if she were putting a curse on me. *"Your fault!"*

The servant gently urged Sheridan back into the house.

Oh my God, what had just happened? How could the party be ruined—because of *me?*

I'm not big on suspense, so I wanted to march into the house and find out what the heck was going on. Had Sheridan simply lost her mind? Or had something really happened?

Muriel appeared in the doorway looking calm and composed, as if this were just another day at work.

"Would you come inside, Haley?" she asked.

I followed Muriel into the sitting room. I had to admire the way she let Sheridan Adams's hissy fit roll off her back.

No way could I be a personal assistant.

"Thank you for coming," Muriel said. We sat down in facing chairs. "There was a break-in last night. Here. An item was stolen."

My first thought was that, jeez, there was so much stuff in this house, how had anyone noticed that something had been taken—especially so quickly.

Then I realized I hadn't seen police cars in the driveway when I'd pulled up.

"Have the police left already?" I asked. "Did they get fingerprints? Shoe prints? DNA? Was there surveillance footage?"

Muriel shook her head. "No police. Mrs. Adams wants to keep this quiet."

It wasn't unusual that the rich and famous wanted to maintain their privacy. Advertising a burglary and announcing what was taken would likely alert other thieves to the location, the wealth, and the apparent lack of security.

"The video feed has already been reviewed," Muriel said. "The entrances to the estate are under constant surveillance, but the cameras don't cover every inch of the grounds. There are no interior cameras, of course. The exterior of the house has spot coverage."

"What did they see?" I asked.

"Only the usual," Muriel said. "The servants coming and going, a delivery from the florist, the cleaning service, the plumber, the pool people."

"What was taken?" I asked.

"Bobbleheads," Muriel said. "The Beatles bobbleheads donated for the charity auction at the party."

Okay, that was weird.

"Bobbleheads?" I asked, and I couldn't keep the are-you-kidding-me tone out of my voice—not that I tried very hard. "Somebody actually went to the trouble to break in, risk getting caught and prosecuted, maybe even going to jail, for a set of bobbleheads?"

"They're rare and in mint condition," Muriel pointed out.

I remembered seeing them on the shelves with all the other Beatles memorabilia that would be auctioned off at the party. It was a complete set of all four Beatles, maybe eight inches tall, painted with identical blue suits, white shirts, and dark neckties, each of them standing on a small platform. Their oversized bobbing heads were covered with long—well, long for the early sixties—brown painted-on hair, and a pretty good representation of each Beatle's facial features. They were in what looked like their original packaging, a box with cellophane panels that displayed each bobblehead.

"I'm sure the bobbleheads would have done well at the auction," I said.

"Ten grand—at least," she said.

"But what's up with Sheridan?" I asked. "I mean, I can understand why she'd be upset that somebody broke into her home, but she looked like she was about to lose her mind."

"All the items for the charity auction came from friends of Talbot and Sheridan, or people attempting to curry favor with them, or—if you can believe it—people whom the Adamses were trying to impress with their philanthropic endeavors," Muriel said. "The bobbleheads were donated by someone linked to British royalty."

"Oh. Wow," I said.

"Yeah," Muriel agreed. "If the bobbleheads aren't seen at the party, if they're not part of the auction, the repercussions will be staggering."

We both sat there for a moment letting everything sink in, then I said, "I'm not clear on why Sheridan thinks any of this is my fault."

"You were supposed to hire extra security for the collectibles," she said.

I was?

"L.A. Affairs put it in the contract," she said.

They did?

"So, really, it is your fault," she said.

Oh, crap.

How could that have happened? If it was in the contract for L.A. Affairs to hire security personnel, why hadn't Jewel—who was probably now being addressed as Sister Jewel at a convent in the Himalayas—done it?

All I could figure was that she must have left the company before she could see that it was handled. So why hadn't Vanessa followed up and—

Damn. Vanessa must have taken the info out of the file before she gave it to me—just like she'd done with Distinctive Gifting.

If she'd deliberately taken the security company requirement out of the file to make me look bad, she'd succeeded, all right.

Not that I intended to let her get away with it.

I'd have to get the bobbleheads back myself.

Immediately, my brain launched into detective mode.

The Adams home was huge, and it was a maze inside. How would a thief know the bobbleheads were in the house? In that particular room?

Of all the memorabilia there, why take just the bobbleheads? Whoever had stolen them must have known their significance.

It sounded like an inside job. But there were dozens of servants and service people who had access to the house, who were routinely coming and going. I'd have to investigate them all. Somehow.

"I'll find them," I said.

Muriel shook her head. "You don't have to do that."

"I want to," I insisted. "I'm kind of good at this sort of thing. Really."

"No, you don't understand," Muriel said. "You don't have to find them. We already know where they are, sort of. Mrs. Adams got a ransom demand for them this morning."

Okay, that blew me away.

Somebody actually expected Sheridan Adams to fork out money for the return of the bobbleheads? Was there a black market for Beatles memorabilia somewhere that I didn't know about? Or were all the collectors slightly crazy?

I wonder if John, Paul, George, and Ringo ever anticipated this.

"I've already contacted a couple of private security agencies to deliver the ransom money," Muriel said.

"Sheridan is actually going to pay?" I asked.

"She won't risk the scandal," Muriel said. "Believe me, her reputation is worth way more than the twenty-grand—"

"Twenty thousand dollars?" I might have shouted that.

"Yes."

"For Beatles bobbleheads?" I'm sure I shouted that.

"I know. It's twice what they're worth. But Mrs. Adams is more than willing to pay it to get them back." Muriel shrugged. "Besides, she's got a great accountant. He'll figure some way to write it off."

It seemed that Sheridan Adams had everything worked out, tied up nice and neat in a pretty little package—one that left me hung out to dry.

No way was I letting that happen.

"I'll do it," I said. "I'll deliver the ransom and get the bobbleheads back."

Muriel looked surprised, then shook her head.

I spoke again before she could tell me "no."

"I can do this. I've have experience with murder investigations," I said.

She drew back a little. "You do?"

"Yes—but always in a good way," I said.

"I don't know . . ."

I could see that she didn't want to go along with this, but I had to do it. I had to redeem myself.

So what could I do but drag Jack Bishop into it with me?

"I've got a partner," I said. "He's a licensed private detective with years of experience."

"Really?" she asked.

She wasn't convinced so I had to hit her with something really big.

"He works for the Pike Warner law firm," I said.

Everybody knew about the Pike Warner law firm. Talbot and Sheridan Adams were probably represented by them.

"I didn't realize Pike Warner handled this sort of thing," Muriel admitted. "I guess I should have called them first."

Now she looked a little worried about her own job.

"I can make this happen," I said, using my somebody-is-going-down voice.

"If you don't get those bobbleheads back, Mrs. Adams will bury you," Muriel said. "You and L.A. Affairs. The company will be lucky to book a D-list kids' dance recital after-party."

I wouldn't mind if Vanessa lost her job, but I sure as heck didn't want the whole company to go down. Besides, nobody would ever know Vanessa had gutted the file and sabotaged the party. Everyone would blame me.

"I'll find the bobbleheads and get them back in time for the party," I told her. "I swear."

"Okay," Muriel said, then hesitated a moment and said again, "Okay, if you're sure."

"I'm sure," I said.

"The cash is being delivered to the house any minute," Muriel said. "The person who called this morning said we'd hear back later today with instructions."

"I'll be ready," I said, and stood up.

Muriel rose. "I'll let you know as soon as I hear something."

I headed for the door, but she touched my shoulder, stopping me.

"Let's just keep this between the two of us," Muriel said. "For now."

I could see she was worried that letting me handle the ransom would blow up in her face, and honestly I didn't blame her.

"As long as Sheridan knows it was me who got them back," I said.

"Of course," Muriel agreed.

I left the house, got in my car, and drove away.

Yeah, okay, I'd had second thoughts about this whole event planner thing, but no way was I going to get fired—

and I sure as heck wasn't going to let Sheridan Adams blab all over Los Angeles and ruin L.A. Affairs.

I was going to deliver that ransom money and get back those Beatles bobbleheads.

And Jack was going to help me.

Whether he liked it or not.

Chapter 20

I had to act natural. Be calm. Cool and collected. I couldn't let anyone at L.A. Affairs know—or even suspect—there was a problem with Sheridan Adams's event.

I'd called Jack Bishop the second I cleared Sheridan's driveway to discuss the situation with him. His voicemail had picked up, so I told him to call me back immediately.

I swung into the parking garage at L.A. Affairs determined not to give the tiniest hint that anything was up. I would go through my morning just as I always did and mentally prepare myself to make the ransom drop when the call came in from Muriel.

I pulled into a parking spot and hopped out of my car, trying to draw on the beauty queen genes I'd inherited from my mom—such as they were—and channel her there's-no-way-the-judges-could-hate-me-but-I'm-going-to-pretend-everything-is-okay-just-in-case expression. I slammed my car door and turned to walk away, then froze at the sight of a man standing at the rear of my car, blocking my path.

My heart did its this-doesn't-look-good flip-flop.

He was tall and burly, fortyish, with old-school black hair, wearing jeans and a leather jacket. He didn't look happy.

My heart amped up its flip-flop to a trot.

I glanced around, anxious to see someone else in the parking garage, or maybe a security guard.

Nobody.

"You Haley Randolph?" he asked.

He sounded like he was from New York. I didn't know if New Yorkers were really angry all the time or if their accent just made them sound like it.

"That's me," I said. I tried to come across all brave and bold, but I don't think I pulled it off.

He just stared at me, like maybe he was deciding if my body would fit into his trunk.

"I've got to get to work," I said, and backed away.

"Mike sent me," he told me.

Mike Ivan had sent this guy? He'd never done that before. Mike had always showed up in person.

Oh my God, what did that mean?

I searched my brain trying to remember if I'd done something to make Mike mad, something he might have misinterpreted or misunderstood.

I couldn't come up with anything.

I didn't know whether to be relieved or more frightened.

"I got something for you," the guy said, nodding to a black Lexus SUV parked nearby. "From Mike."

Of course. The Beatles gift bags for Sheridan's party. Whew!

Jeez, why had I gotten so upset? Mike had always been great to me. He insisted he wasn't in the Russian mob or involved in any sort of criminal activity, so why had I thought that him sending this guy meant trouble?

"Great," I said.

"I'll put them in your car," he said, and headed for the SUV.

Mike had told me it would take a couple of days to manufacture the bags, but he'd gotten them finished ahead of schedule. I made a mental note to call and thank him.

I popped my trunk and rearranged the stuff that was

back there. The guy brought over four brown cardboard boxes and fitted two inside, then put the others in my backseat.

"Thanks," I said, hitting the remote to lock my doors.

The guy just stood there for a while staring at me. I wondered if I was supposed to give him a tip or something. Then he pulled a small white envelope from his jacket pocket and held it up.

"From Mike?" I asked, thinking it was the invoice for the bags.

He pulled it back. "Not from Mike. From nobody."

My heart jumped.

"You got that?" the guy asked, leaning forward slightly. "From nobody."

I tried to answer, but all I managed was a quick nod.

I guess that was enough. The guy slapped the envelope down on the trunk of my car, got in his SUV, and left.

I scanned the parking garage to make sure no one had seen what had gone down, then picked up the envelope and opened it.

Inside was a slip of paper with an address on it.

Okay, that was weird.

Why the heck would Mike give me a street address, of all things, and have it delivered by that scary guy who insisted it wasn't from Mike?

I looked at the address again and tried to figure out why a place in Bellflower would—oh my God.

Bellflower.

The address was in Bellflower, the city I suspected Detective Shuman had been searching for Adolfo Renaldi, the guy the LAPD was sure had murdered Amanda. Mike had known Adolfo and his brother, too. He'd mentioned them—no, he'd specifically asked about them—when I'd last seen him.

I shoved the slip of paper into the envelope, dropped it in my handbag, and headed for the elevator.

This address had to be the location where Adolfo Renaldi was hiding. Somehow Mike had found him.

Mike had seemed sympathetic toward Detective Shuman when we'd talked about Amanda's murder in the fabric store. He seemed to understand what Shuman was going through—which made me realize how little I actually knew about Mike. Maybe he'd also lost someone he loved to violence.

I'd gotten the feeling that, in a way, Mike admired Shuman for hunting down Amanda's killer, especially since he wasn't supposed to. In my heart I knew that Mike would have handled it the same way.

Of course, Mike hadn't hesitated to tell me exactly what he thought of the Renaldi brothers and their whole family. It was possible Mike had an ulterior motive for giving me the address. Obviously, there was no love lost between them. I didn't know the extent of their involvement with each other—which suited me fine. I figured I was better off not knowing.

I took the elevator up to the third floor, ignored Mindy's greeting—no way was I ready to party at the moment—and went to my office. I sat at my desk, thinking.

Mike had found Adolfo Renaldi's location.

And now he'd passed it on to me.

For a few minutes I considered calling Detective Madison and telling him where he could find Renaldi. I envisioned the entire LAPD mobilizing, S.W.A.T. rolling out, helicopters launching, dozens of officers converging on the Bellflower address.

But I wasn't sure Madison would believe me. He'd probably want me to come to headquarters so he could question me. He might think I was somehow involved with Amanda's murder. At the very least, he'd expect me to give up Mike Ivan as the source of the info—which I would never do, of course.

If we got past all of that and the LAPD took Renaldi

alive, would a smart defense attorney get him released on bail, as Detective Shuman had suggested? How many years would pass before he even went to trial? Plus, there was no guarantee that Renaldi would be convicted. Witnesses could disappear. Evidence might go missing. It had happened before.

I sat at my desk staring off at nothing and thinking that maybe I could call in an anonymous tip to the police. But I had no way of knowing how long it would take for the info to reach the right people. With the entire LAPD searching for him, Renaldi might be jumping around, staying for only a short time at different places. I had to move fast.

And that meant my only other choice was to tell Shuman.

I got out of my desk chair and walked to the window. I stood looking down at the traffic on Sepulveda Boulevard and let the idea swirl around in my head for a while.

If I gave Shuman the address, if I told him where to find the dirtbag who murdered Amanda, I was pretty sure I knew how he'd handle it.

Then another horrible thought came to me. What if I gave this info to Shuman, he acted on it, and he got hurt or killed. How would I live with that?

But if Shuman were in my position, what would he do? What would I want him to do?

He was my friend. So really, it wasn't much of a choice at all.

I couldn't stay in the office for long, not with Vanessa mad-dogging me every time I passed her in the hallway and my living in constant fear that my name would come up in the rotation again and I would be assigned another kid's or dog's birthday party—I still wasn't sure which was worse—so I had to get out of there as quickly as I could.

That, unfortunately, meant I first had to do some actual work.

I checked L.A. Affairs' list of approved vendors and hired a security firm for the Beatles memorabilia at Sheridan Adams's house, then called Muriel.

"Any word from the kidnapper?" I asked when she picked up.

I didn't know what else to call the culprit. "Bobbleheadnapper" seemed a little lengthy to me.

"Not yet," Muriel said in a low voice. "Things are superintense around here."

I figured that was code for Sheridan-is-still-running-around-the-house-screaming-like-the-crazy-woman-she-is.

"I hired a security firm. I'll text you the info," I said. "They can start this evening."

"Good. I'll let you know when I hear something," Muriel said, and we hung up.

I sat at my desk and texted her, then found myself more than a little annoyed that I hadn't yet heard back from Jack. I really wanted to talk to him before I had to deliver the ransom money—there were probably some stealthy private detective moves he could share with me. I figured he must have been doing something important—which was probably also way cool—if he hadn't returned my call. I found myself a little envious.

I wonder if Jack would like a partner.

The idea swirled around in my head for a minute or two, which made me even more anxious to escape my office.

I checked my e-mail and cringed when I saw that Annette had sent me a message. I forced myself to open it and saw that she was asking for a different idea for her puppy Minnie's birthday celebration—just how she knew Minnie wasn't loving my Hollywood or garden party suggestions I don't know. I replied with the first thing that popped into my head—a Star Wars theme.

If Minnie loved the idea I would definitely have to use the Force to figure out how to pull it off.

Then I saw that Maeve had also e-mailed me about food and beverages for the birthday party for her twin girls. I dashed off a quick reply stating that the only way I could see getting through the event was with a full bar and a dozen hot-looking guys who would tend bar without their shirts on.

Then I came to my senses and deleted the message.

"Enough . . ." I mumbled.

I got my things and left the office.

I called Tiberia Marsh on my cell phone as I took the 405 south.

"The gift bags are finished already?" she asked. "How wonderful. I can't wait to see them."

"I'm headed your way now," I said.

"Of course. Please, come," she told me.

All I could figure was that Distinctive Gifting must be a fabulous place to work, because Tiberia was always up-beat and in a great mood.

Jeez, I wonder what that would be like.

I exited west on Santa Monica Boulevard, then cut over to Melrose Avenue and found the Distinctive Gifting office among a row of upscale businesses. I pulled into their driveway and parked behind the building. A large van was backed up to a service entrance and a couple of men with dollies were carting boxes inside.

I gave Tiberia a call and told her I'd arrived. A minute later a tall, super-slender, dark-skinned woman walked out the rear door. She had on a long sheath dress in deep pur-ple, jeweled sandals, and lots of chunky accessories. Her thick black hair stood straight out. The look gave her a chic, sophisticated appeal.

"Haley, I'm delighted to meet you," Tiberia said, and threw her arms around me.

She motioned to one of the men unloading the truck. He

wheeled a dolly over, stacked my boxes on it, and took them away.

"Come inside," Tiberia said. "Let me show you what I've assembled for your gift bags so far."

My day definitely needed a boost, so I said, "I'd love to."

The interior of Distinctive Gifting was as elegant, serene, and sophisticated as Tiberia herself. Everything was decorated in soft whites and cool blues.

She led the way down a corridor and unlocked a door with the key she pulled from her pocket.

"My treasure trove," Tiberia said, as I followed her inside.

"Wow . . ." I said. I might have moaned that.

I felt like I'd walked into Neiman Marcus—only better because it was all free.

Hundreds of items were stacked on shelves—jewelry, bottles of champagne, beauty products, cell phones, fragrances. There were vouchers for resorts, hotels, and memberships at celebrity spas. Designer brands, exclusive destinations, exquisite items, affordable only to the wealthy and elite.

Everything was fabulous—totally fabulous.

An image popped into my head.

"Do you happen to have the Enchantress evening bag here?" I asked. I'm sure I moaned that.

Tiberia gave me a knowing smile. "Ah, Haley, you are a woman of discriminating taste. But, alas, I have no Enchantress."

Darn it. I was having no luck at all getting an Enchantress in time for Sheridan's party.

"I suppose I could settle for one of the gift bags," I said, and gave Tiberia an I'm-really-serious-but-I-want-you-to-think-I'm-kidding smile.

"All these beautiful items. How could you not want

them?" she said. "Perhaps Sheridan will present you with one for the fabulous job you're doing on her event?"

My spirits lifted—a little. Sheridan wasn't happy with me right now, but after I recovered her Beatles bobble-heads surely she'd feel differently.

"More items are on their way," Tiberia said as we left the room. "I'll send you a complete list when I have everything."

I thanked her and headed outside.

I'd left my totally fabulous Betsey Johnson bag in my car, so when I got in I checked my cell phone. Damn. Jack had called and I'd missed him. I tried to reach him, but my call went to his voice mail.

We couldn't keep playing phone tag. I needed to talk with him before Muriel called with instructions on the ransom demand. I hadn't wanted to leave him a message spelling out the situation, but if I didn't get to actually speak with him soon, I'd have to.

I started my car and was backing out of the parking spot when my phone rang. Thanks God, Jack was calling me again.

"In what West German city did the Beatles perform in the fall of 1960?" Crap. It was Eleanor with another quiz question.

I'd read the Beatles book I'd bought—well, okay, I'd skimmed it—and I'd watched some of the stuff I'd down-loaded, but I had no clue what she was talking about. So what could I do but say, "Jeez, Eleanor, you'd said your questions would get harder but this one is so simple. The Beatles performed in—"

I hung up.

What else could I do? I was already in enough trouble with Sheridan. I didn't need Eleanor ratting me out about not knowing the answer to her who-really-cares-anyway question.

I pulled back into the parking space, accessed the Internet, then called Eleanor back.

"Hamburg," I said, and hung up again.

I'm not sure my answer really counted since I didn't answer it on the spot, but this would have to do.

My day definitely needed a boost—a big one. I headed west and took Pacific Coast Highway north. This was one of my favorite places to clear my head and put things into perspective. The view was spectacular along this stretch of PCH. High, rugged hills dotted with fabulous homes on my right, and the blue waters of the Pacific on my left, sparkling in the sunlight.

Ty floated into my head. Not long ago he'd offered to buy a beach house, if I'd move in with him. He'd sweetened the deal with a convertible and tons of new shorts, tops, bathing suits, cover-ups, sundresses, sandals, and flip-flops—okay, the clothes were my idea, but he'd have definitely been okay with them.

Now everything was different—real different. Ty was engaged—maybe. My heart started to hurt just thinking about it.

I'm not big on suspense, usually, but I hadn't wanted to confront Ty and ask him outright. I'd put it off on Marcie, and that hadn't worked out either. There was nothing left to do but handle the situation myself.

I accessed the address book on my cell phone and called Amber, Ty's personal assistant. Yeah, okay, this wasn't exactly the boldest move I could have made, but it was the only one I could manage.

Amber answered right away.

"Hi, Haley, I'm really glad to hear from you," she said. "How are you?"

She sounded as if she was genuinely glad to hear from me. We'd always gotten along, and I didn't want that to change by putting her in a difficult position with Ty by asking a lot of personal questions about him.

"Is Ty engaged?" I asked.

Damn. I hadn't meant to say that—not so soon in the conversation, anyway.

"Engaged? Are you kidding? Mr. Gloom and Doom?" Amber asked. "No way."

I almost ran my car off the highway.

"Oh my God, he's not engaged?" I am pretty sure I yelled that.

"Why would you think that?" Amber asked.

"Sarah Covington is engaged. Since she'd been all over Ty all the time, I figured they were a couple," I said.

"I haven't heard anything about Sarah getting engaged," Amber said.

"A friend of mine got a visual on her wearing a diamond ring," I told her.

"Ty hasn't been acting like he's engaged," she said. "But he has been really weird lately."

Ty was stable, sensible, cautious, predictable. *Weird* for him could mean he'd taken an alternate route home from the office.

"Weird how?" I asked.

"Secretive. He used to tell me everything, now not so much," Amber said.

"What's he keeping secret?" I asked. "Any idea?"

"It started back when he was in the car accident, remember?" Amber said.

I remembered how the hospital had called because Ty wanted me to pick him up from the emergency room. I remembered how scared I was thinking he'd been hurt, how relieved I'd felt when I saw him and knew he was okay.

"And a couple of days ago," Amber said, "he had me hire actresses. Twenty of them."

Okay, that was definitely weird.

"Maybe he wanted them for show. Maybe he was having a party or something?" I didn't like the idea, but it was all I could think of.

"A party with hot chicks? Ty?" Amber asked.

True, Ty wasn't the party animal that some people—okay, me—were, but I'd seen flashes of a wild guy lurking inside him. He'd had to take over the helm of the family business when his dad had a heart attack, even though I don't think he really wanted to. Five generations of the Holt's chain were riding on his shoulders. He wouldn't let the family down.

"Besides, if he was throwing a party—or any sort of social event—he would have asked me to plan it for him," Amber said. "I can tell you for a fact that he's not having fun at anything. He's working twelve to fifteen hours a day, nearly every day."

"That's not good," I said.

"I'm worried about him," Amber said. "I wish you two would get back together."

I really didn't know how to respond, so I just said, "Thanks for letting me know what's going on."

"I'll ask around about Sarah and see what's up with her engagement," Amber promised, and we hung up.

I'd decided to drive out to PCH to clear my thoughts, but now all I could think about was Ty and the things I liked about him.

He always did the right thing. He was very thoughtful, extremely generous, and sensitive without being a ticket-stub-saver kind of guy. He was aggressive in business, but not ruthless, more like a chess master plotting, strategizing, looking ahead a half-dozen moves, maneuvering to get what he wanted.

Memories bounced around in my head. The image of his crooked grin I saw during our special moments, the feel of his arms around me, the way he smelled after a shower. They all settled around my heart.

I missed him.

Why hadn't I fought for us?

CHAPTER 21

I called Holt's with my touch-of-the-stomach-flu excuse, a personal favorite of mine, and said I wouldn't be in for my shift tonight. I didn't get any push-back, but I didn't expect to. I mean, really, what were they going to do? Working there was already the ultimate punishment.

I wasn't concerned that the outfits for the fashion show still had to be put together. Everything was so hideous I could just pick things at random the day of the show and send them down the runway, and nobody in the we-love-a-flashing-blue-light-special audience would know the difference.

My real concern was being available to make the ransom drop tonight and retrieving the Beatles bobbleheads when Muriel called with the kidnapper's instructions.

I glanced at my watch as I sat in my office. Nearly five. Why hadn't I heard from Muriel yet?

And why hadn't Jack called me back? Yeah, okay, he worked for the Pike Warner law firm, plus handled cases on the side, but I am, after all, *me*.

I couldn't take it anymore. I got my cell phone and called Muriel.

"Nothing yet," she said softly when she answered.

"What's up with that?"

All kinds of this-would-be-awful-if-it-happened scenarios pinged around in my head: what if the kidnapper was holding out for more money; what if the bobbleheads had somehow been damaged or destroyed; what if the kidnapper was shopping them around for more money elsewhere.

"It was supposed to be tonight. We haven't heard a word. I don't know what's going on," Muriel said. "I'm really worried that something will go wrong when you make the ransom payment. What if you don't find the right person, or make a mistake doing the exchange? What if you do something wrong and we don't get the bobbleheads back?"

Muriel sounded really tense and majorly stressed—not that I blamed her, of course—but I didn't want her to cave and blab to Sheridan that I was handling the ransom drop, then hire a real security firm to take over.

"The delay in hearing from the kidnapper is normal," I said.

I didn't know if it was or not, but this sounded good.

"It is?" she asked, and I heard a tiny glimmer of hope in her voice.

"It's just a ploy, a tactic to make you worry more, make you anxious to cooperate," I said.

It could have been true, couldn't it? I mean, that's what happened on those TV crime dramas.

"I've got a professional private detective—my partner—standing by ready to mobilize," I said.

I didn't, of course, but what else could I say?

And where was Jack, anyway?

"Stay calm," I said, "and call me the minute you hear from them."

"I will," Muriel promised, and we hung up.

I hopped out of my desk chair and launched into total-panic mode.

Oh my God, why hadn't the kidnapper called? What would I do if this whole thing went sideways? What if I botched the ransom exchange? What if I got the bobbleheads back and Sheridan was still so upset that she shot off her mouth to all her high-profile friends and put L.A. Affairs out of business?

I really needed to talk to Jack. I couldn't imagine what he'd been doing all afternoon that he hadn't returned my call. Was he really working? Or was he playing me? Was this part of his whole idiotic *treading lightly* idea?

I absolutely *had* to talk to him. I absolutely *had* to get him to return my call.

Maybe I should leave him a message and offer to have sex with him. Maybe *that* would get him to return my call.

But I'd been mooning over Ty all afternoon, so I couldn't have sex with Jack—okay, well, maybe I could. Yes, I definitely could. No. It wouldn't be right. Having sex with Jack would reduce our relationship to nothing but a hot, sweaty, prolonged—surely—physical encounter. What would that do to our friendship? What would—

My cell phone rang. Jack's name appeared on the caller ID screen.

"Why haven't you called me?" I'm positive I screamed that.

He didn't answer—not that I gave him an opportunity.

"I've been trying to reach you *forever!* I've left you a zillion messages!" My voice was really high-pitched now, and I was squeezing my cell phone so tight I thought my SIM card might shoot out.

"I was even considering having sex with you!" People in the hallway outside my office might have heard that.

"I'll be right over," Jack said.

"No! I'm not having sex with you now!"

"Do you have a fever?" he asked.

"What?"

"Have you recently hit your head on something?" Jack asked, sounding way too calm to suit me at the moment. "Because I'm sensing some erratic brain activity."

"Something major is going down," I said. "I need to talk to you. Now. Can you meet me at Starbucks at the Galleria?"

"I'm on my way," Jack said. "And if you change your mind about the sex, surprise me when I get there."

I drove to the Galleria and left my car in the parking garage. Even though it was just across the street from my office, I wanted to have my car close by when Muriel called.

I took the walkway to the center plaza where the restaurants were located. It was in shadows, thanks to the setting sun and the tall buildings. A lot of people were out—tourists in Disneyland T-shirts, couples, men and women with briefcases and messenger bags who'd just gotten off work.

I didn't see Jack. He hadn't mentioned where he was or how long it would take him to get here, so I didn't know how long I'd have to wait. Yet I saw no reason to deprive myself of my favorite drink in the entire world. I went inside Starbucks and got a mocha Frappuccino and a coffee, then found a table on the plaza and sat down. I was only three sips in when I spotted Jack walking toward me from the parking garage.

Whatever he'd been doing when he'd finally called me at my office required that he be in stealth mode.

Jack looked great in stealth mode.

He had on black everything—pants, shirt, jacket. I looked great in black, too. We'd make great partners.

Jack took the chair across from me. "Something major is going down?"

The table I'd selected for our meeting was situated away from the other customers to ensure our conversation wasn't overheard. I glanced around because it seemed the covert thing to do, then leaned toward Jack.

He smelled fabulous.

Maybe we wouldn't make great partners. I think I might get distracted a lot.

"I'm making a ransom payment tonight," I said quietly.

Jack's brows drew together and he straightened his shoulders like he was ready to come out swinging—at what, I don't know. Then he dragged his chair close to mine and said, "Talk to me."

"I'm planning a major event for Sheridan Adams. It includes a charity auction of collectible memorabilia," I said. "The set of Beatles bobbleheads was stolen from her house, so I have to deliver the twenty-grand ransom and get them back."

Jack shook his head. "Tell her call the police."

"She won't," I said.

"Tell her to hire a professional. It's too dangerous," he said, and looked as if Sheridan was crazy for getting me involved.

"I volunteered," I said.

Now he looked as if I were the crazy one.

I get that a lot.

"There was a mix-up at the office," I said. "I didn't hire security for the memorabilia. Sheridan is blaming me. If I don't get the bobbleheads back she'll get me fired—not that it will really matter, because she'll tell everybody what happened and put L.A. Affairs out of business."

Jack shook his head. "It's too dangerous."

"It's the only way I can make it right," I said.

"No. No, you're not doing it," he told me.

"I need you to talk me through the ransom exchange," I told him. "Just give me some tips."

His expression darkened and he leaned into me.

"People who resort to kidnapping aren't what you'd call stable," he told me. "You could get hurt. Do you understand that?"

"Then lend me a gun," I said.

Jack rolled his eyes and sat back in his chair.

"It's just for one evening," I said.

"No."

"A few hours."

"No." Jack shook his head. "Absolutely not."

I appreciated that he was concerned about my safety, but now he was kind of getting on my nerves.

"Look, Jack, I'm doing this," I told him, "whether you help me or not."

He leaned into me until we were eye to eye. "No, you're not."

We glared at each other—which, under other circumstances would have been totally hot—but no way was I backing down.

"It's not your call," I said.

"I'm making it my call," he told me.

"It's none of your business."

"You made it my business," he said.

He was right about that—which totally annoyed me.

"Look, Jack, you can't pick and choose when you want to be involved with what I'm doing," I said.

Yeah, okay, I knew that didn't really make sense, so what could I do but keep talking?

"Like the thing in the parking lot at my apartment," I told him. "You can't tell me you're treading lightly, then threaten a guy you see kissing me."

His jaw tightened. He drew himself up. His breathing got heavy.

"You kissed a guy?" he demanded.

Oh my God. What was going on?

"I'm treading lightly, doing the decent thing, giving you time to get over your breakup," Jack said. "And you kissed a guy? In your *parking lot?*"

"He was nobody," I told him

"You kissed *nobody?*"

Yikes! I'd never seen Jack so riled up.

"It was nothing," I insisted. "I'd forgotten all about it."

Jack leaned in, even closer this time. "When I kiss you, you won't forget it."

I figured that was true—but I wasn't going to say so.

This seemed like an excellent time to change the subject.

"So here's the thing," I said. "I'm supposed to deliver the ransom money tonight, but the kidnapper hasn't called with the instructions like they said they would. Why would they do that?"

Jack fumed for another minute, then shifted into private detective mode again.

"It could mean anything, but there's nothing you can do about it. It's their game. Just be ready when the call comes in," he said. "Get there as early as you can. Keep your eyes open. Watch for anybody who looks like they don't belong. It might be a partner. And don't—don't—turn over the money until you see the bobbleheads."

"Got it," I said.

Jack finally took a sip of the coffee I'd bought for him.

"Who do you suspect took the bobbleheads?" he asked.

I'd been so consumed with getting them back I hadn't put any more thought into who had taken them.

"They were stolen from the room in Sheridan's house where all the collectibles for the charity auction were stored. The room isn't easily accessible," I said. "Probably an inside job."

Jack nodded. "Who would benefit from the theft? From the ransom money?"

"Everybody who works in Sheridan's home," I said. "There are lots of workers in the house and on the grounds who could use the money."

Muriel flashed in my mind. I could easily see where she might have her fill of dealing with Sheridan Adams and use the ransom money to escape and start over somewhere else, but I couldn't imagine Muriel actually pulling it off.

"Who knew the memorabilia would be auctioned off?" Jack asked.

"Most everyone on Sheridan's staff, and anyone at L.A. Affairs who'd seen the file on the event," I said.

Vanessa flashed in my head. What if she'd gone to Sheridan's house and somehow stolen the bobbleheads? Just to make me look bad and get me fired?

It would be so cool if I could blame everything on her.

"Who else knew?" Jack asked.

I thought for a minute or two and realized—oh my God—I'd actually told a number of people about the memorabilia and the auction.

"I might have mentioned it to a couple of people," I said.

I'd told Mike Ivan about the auction because we'd been discussing the gift bags Sheridan wanted.

I saw no reason to mention a maybe-connected-to-the-Russian-mob guy to Jack.

"I remember talking about the party with Paige at Lacy Cakes," I said. "She's making the Yellow Submarine cake for the event."

"Who else?" Jack asked.

"Belinda Giles," I said. "She's trying to buy the bakery with Paige."

"Who else knew?" he asked.

"There's the guy at the bakery who bakes the cakes. He might have overheard our conversation," I said. "And maybe the guy who runs a rival bakery. I can't remember if I mentioned it to him."

Jack just looked at me.

"And Darren, Belinda's cousin," I said. "That's all I can think of."

Jack nodded. "And you?"

Yeah, I knew about them too—which was another great reason for the police not to get involved with the theft and ransom demand.

"And you're sure this is the real deal?" Jack asked. "Not a hoax?"

I sat there stunned. It had never occurred to me that it wasn't the real thing.

"These Hollywood people—the ultra-wealthy, celebrities—will do anything for publicity," Jack said. "Get involved with them and you might find yourself the target of unwanted attention."

Yikes! I hadn't thought of that.

I considered the whole thing for a minute or two, then shook my head.

"This is real," I said.

Jack rose from his chair. "Call me when you hear from the kidnapper with the time and location," he said.

I hoped that meant he'd come with me, but he didn't say so.

Jack left. I sat there thinking, sipping on my mocha Frappuccino.

I'd gotten enough info to handle the ransom money delivery, and Jack had made me think a little harder about the theft itself. But that wasn't what was on my mind.

He'd been completely outraged when I'd mentioned Cody kissing me in the parking lot. Obviously, he hadn't witnessed it, hadn't warned Cody off.

So if Jack hadn't done it, who had?

CHAPTER 22

"What was the first Beatles album that was issued as a two-record set?" Rigby asked.

I knew this one, sort of.

I sat down at my desk in my office, grabbed the Beatles book I'd bought, and frantically flipped through the pages. I knew I'd read about that album somewhere in this book.

"That was a great album, wasn't it?" I asked, stalling.

I couldn't be sure, but I think she was humming the theme music played during the *Jeopardy!* final round.

I didn't need this stress. Not today.

"One of my favorite albums," Rigby said. "Do you know the answer?"

"Of course. Everyone knows this one," I said and—thank God—found the page I was looking for. "It was titled *The Beatles*, but everyone called it *The White Album*."

"Very good, Haley," Rigby said.

I collapsed onto my desk.

"I'll talk with you again soon," she said, and hung up.

I clutched my cell phone in my hand—I didn't dare put it down since I still hadn't heard from Muriel about the ransom—and stared out of my office window at the Galleria across the street. I'd spoken with Muriel several times today, but she had nothing to report. It was midafternoon now, and both of us had frayed nerves.

I might find a gun from somewhere and shoot that kidnapper at the ransom exchange just for making me worry so much.

My cell phone rang. I shot out of my chair and answered it.

"This situation is intolerable."

Oh my God. It was Mom—which just shows how totally frazzled I was over this ransom thing if I hadn't checked my caller ID screen first.

I sank into my chair again.

"I don't know how much longer I should be expected to go on under these circumstances," Mom said.

Note—I hadn't even said "hello."

"The temporary housekeepers the agency is sending simply are not working out," Mom said. "When am I going to get someone permanent?"

I couldn't tell her over the phone that she'd been blacklisted by all the employment agencies in Los Angeles and that there was little chance she'd ever have a permanent, full-time housekeeper again. I'd have to tell her in person—something I wasn't usually crazy about doing, but right now it was a good excuse to get out of the office.

"I'm coming by to see you," I said.

"Do you have good news?" she asked.

"I have news," I told her—which wasn't exactly a lie.

We hung up, I got my things, and I left.

I kept my Bluetooth in my ear as I drove east on the 101 toward Mom's house, ready to dive across five lanes of traffic and cut off every vehicle on the freeway if Muriel called. I still didn't know what, exactly, I'd tell Mom about the whole housekeeper situation. I hoped something would come to me when I got there.

My cell phone rang. Immediately I switched to high-alert mode, then realized it was Amber.

"Sorry I don't have better news for you," she said.

I hate it when a conversation starts off that way.

"I asked around and found out that Sarah Covington is definitely engaged," Amber said.

Oh, great. Just what I needed to hear.

I gathered my courage and asked, "To Ty?"

Maybe I should have waited until I pulled off the freeway to ask that question in case she said "yes."

"I couldn't find out," Amber said. "Everybody is being really quiet about it."

Okay, that was weird.

"Maybe it's Ty," I said, and had a little difficulty actually speaking the words aloud. "Maybe they're keeping it quiet because they work together."

"I don't think so," Amber said. "But he's still acting really odd, so I can't be sure what's up with him."

A scary thought blossomed in my head.

"He's not sick, is he?" I asked.

Personal assistants knew the good, the bad, and the ugly about their bosses—medical conditions, prescriptions, vices, spouse/lover birthday, peculiar eccentricities—and Amber usually handled all those things for Ty. But she'd told me that at times he'd been a bit secretive.

"Sick in the head," Amber said. "I don't know what's up with him. Now he's got me buying Holt's gift cards. Dozens of them. He's spent a fortune on them."

"Do you think he's donating them to charity?" I asked.

"Maybe. But donations are usually handled through the corporation," Amber said. "He's working almost around the clock on acquiring another chain of department stores, so maybe he's not thinking clearly."

I doubted that. Ty thought in his sleep.

"If I hear anything else I'll let you know," Amber said.

"Thanks," I said, and we hung up.

I didn't know what to make of Ty's behavior. Just as well I had Mom to focus on for a while.

I drove to her house. Today's temporary housekeeper, a young woman in a blue uniform, met me at the door. I hadn't figured out exactly what I'd say to Mom about the whole you've-been-blacklisted situation, so I decided to take a run at getting this housekeeper to stay on permanently.

It was worth a try.

"Hi," I said in my I'm-super-nice voice as I gestured through the house. "I'm Haley, her daughter."

"Sorry to hear that," she mumbled.

By the time we'd walked together to the kitchen, she'd looked at her watch three times, no doubt counting down the minutes until she could leave.

I guess my I'm-super-nice voice needs some work.

I found Mom in the family room seated on the chaise dressed in her usual former-beauty-queen's-interpretation-of-loungewear attire of a dress and four-inch heels—both Prada—with her makeup and nails done and her hair styled in an updo.

I could see that she was really feeling the effects of not having a housekeeper because she was actually holding a pen and writing on a tablet herself.

"What are you doing next Saturday?" Mom asked.

"I'm busy all day and evening," I said.

I had no idea what I was doing next Saturday, but this was safer.

"I'm having a dinner party and I want you to come," she said, sounding surprisingly happy. "And Ty too, of course."

I'd never gotten around to telling Mom that Ty and I had broken up.

I never got around to telling Mom a lot of things.

I saw no reason to start now.

"You're having a dinner party?" I asked. "What about the housekeeper situation?"

No way Mom would cook or clean for her own dinner party.

"You've handled that," she said, smiling brightly. "By next Saturday I'll have had plenty of time to get the new housekeeper into my routine."

I didn't know which was worse—telling her I still didn't have a housekeeper for her or that Ty and I had broken up.

I took the easy route.

"Well, actually, Mom," I said. "Ty and I aren't together anymore."

"What?" She gasped. "You're—what?"

I couldn't bring myself to say the words again, so I just shrugged.

"Oh, Haley, honey, that's terrible," Mom said.

She got off the chaise and hurried to me, wrapped her arms around me, and gave me a hug.

Wow, that was nice. Maybe I should have told her we'd broken up a long time ago.

She stepped back. "What happened, sweetie?"

"We decided we weren't really right for each other," I said, thinking it better that I kept it simple before Mom got distracted with her dinner party again.

"Nonsense," she declared. "You two are perfect for each other."

"No, not really," I said.

"Of course you were," Mom insisted. "Those Cameron men are boring to the bone, every one of them. All they do is work, work, work. They need exciting women like you in their lives."

Now I kind of wished she'd start talking about her dinner party again. Talking about Ty made my heart hurt.

"I guess Ty didn't feel that way," I said.

"Did he say he didn't love you?" Mom asked.

Now she wants to be a concerned mother?

"No, but he never actually said he *did* love me," I said.

"What's not to love?" Mom asked, waving her carefully manicured hands toward me. "You're pretty, you're smart, you're fun, you're interesting, you're extremely competent and capable."

Breaking up with Ty was almost worth it to hear my mom say those things.

"He's just being a typical man," Mom said. "He'll come to his senses."

I shook my head. "I don't think so, Mom."

"I've seen you two together," she said. "I've seen the way you look at him and the way he looks at you. I know love when I see it."

"It doesn't matter," I said. "We're done."

"You know, sometimes it takes losing someone to make you realize how much you care for that person. You see how important they are. You realize that the little things don't matter," Mom said. "It's normal to disagree over the small things because you already agree on the big, important things."

Okay, where was my real mom?

Mom gave me another hug. "Now, I want you to check your calendar for next Saturday and my dinner party. And I'll need my new housekeeper to start right away."

Oh, crap.

I don't know how Mom had taken my simple comment that I needed to talk with her about a housekeeper and spun it into believing I'd found one for her.

Such were the mysterious workings of an ex–beauty queen's mind, I guess.

But I couldn't deal with it right now, not after that conversation about Ty.

So what could I say but, "Sure, Mom. No problem."

I got in my car and left.

I headed west on the 210 not really thinking much about

where I was going. My head was filled with the things Mom had said about relationships.

It was scary to think she might be right about something—especially something as important as this—but I knew she was.

Some people were just right for each other. Some relationships worked without an obvious, apparent reason. Were Ty and I one of those couples? I was sure other people had looked at us and wondered what we saw in each other, why we were together—I'd wondered that myself a time or two.

But maybe there wasn't a reason. Maybe there wasn't anything that could be pointed to with a definite look-that's-it kind of thing. Maybe some relationships were just meant to be.

Maybe that applied to Mom and her housekeeper also.

I cut across three lanes of traffic and headed south on the 2 to Eagle Rock.

Much as I didn't want to, I had to go to work at Holt's. I'd blown off my shift last night and I couldn't do it again. I still hadn't heard from Muriel about the ransom exchange, but I kept my cell phone in my pocket so I could blast out of there the minute she called with the instructions.

Bella and I were in the stock room putting looks together for the fashion show—or trying to—sorting through boxes of shoes and accessories.

She pulled a pair of whose-big-idea-were-these canvas turquoise and orange pumps out of a box.

"Damn. This stuff gets scarier and scarier," Bella said. "I thought doing this show would be cool because I wouldn't have to work on the sales floor. But all the nausea medication I'm needing is costing me a fortune."

"The best accessories for Holt's clothing are a can of

lighter fluid and a pack of matches," I said, "but I haven't found them in any of the boxes."

"Keep digging," Bella told me.

"Haley?" a woman called.

Immediately I recognized the voice of Jeanette, the store manager. I didn't know how I would hold up if she wanted to talk about how great the Holt's clothing line was again.

I kept my back to her and pretended to sort through the necklaces—a move I'd practiced numerous time with customers on the sales floor—but Jeanette wasn't to be put off.

"I need to see you in my office, Haley," Jeanette said.

Bella and I exchanged a what-now look before I turned to Jeanette. I had no idea why she wanted to see me in her office, but I was pretty sure it wasn't for something that would be good—for me.

"I'm kind of busy right now, Jeanette," I said.

"This can't wait," she said, and headed toward the stock room door.

A zillion things flashed in my head.

Had she finally learned that Ty and I had broken up and was now exiling me to the ad-set team on night shift? Cutting my hours—or worse, giving me more hours? Putting me in charge of something—as if this fashion show wasn't punishment enough?

Bella gave me a let-me-know-if-you-need-backup eyebrow bob—as a BFF would—and I followed Jeanette out of the stock room.

We walked down the hallway and she stopped outside of her office.

"Someone is here to see you," she said, gesturing inside.

My heart jumped.

Was it Ty? Had he come to see me? Was he using something about the store as an excuse to talk to me?

The scenario flashed in my head. Me walking into the office. Ty standing there looking handsome but troubled. His expression stating that, without me, his life is meaningless. Us sharing a long, lingering look. Then both of us rushing together, hugging each other, kissing, saying that we're sorry, that we can't live without each other. Me telling him how Mom had said we were meant for each other—no, wait, I'll leave out the part about Mom, it's kind of a mood killer—me telling him how I missed him and—

"Haley?" Jeanette said.

I snapped back to reality and hurried inside her office.

Detective Madison stood behind Jeanette's desk.

Talk about a mood killer.

Then it hit me—was Madison here to arrest me for the murder of Lacy Hobbs? Last time I'd talked to Shuman about the case, he'd said Madison hadn't come up with any leads, evidence, or suspects. All he had was *me*. Had he finally decided that was enough?

But Detective Madison didn't have that overjoyed, gleeful look on his face that I'd expect to see if he'd actually come to arrest me. There were no patrol officers with him, and whomever he'd partnered with in Shuman's absence wasn't there, either.

I had no idea why he was there, but I'd learned—the hard way—to keep my mouth shut around homicide detectives, especially Madison.

But he didn't seem all that anxious to get the conversation rolling, either. A couple of minutes passed while we were locked into some sort of who's-going-to-speak-first confrontation. Madison broke first.

"When was the last time you spoke with Detective Shuman?" he asked.

He'd said the words softly, but I felt as if he'd blasted them at me with a laser cannon.

Shuman. Oh my God. *Shuman.*

"Why? What's wrong? What happened?" I asked, blasting him right back with my questions.

"Nothing," Madison said. "Maybe nothing."

"Is he okay?" I asked.

"I haven't heard from him," Madison said. "He's missing."

I guess I shouldn't have been surprised that Madison had kept in contact with Shuman. They were, after all, partners.

So now it looked as if he were the person I'd suspected was feeding Shuman info on the investigation into Amanda's murder. By the worried look on Madison's face I could see that he wasn't sure he'd done the right thing.

I knew how he felt.

When Mike Ivan had given me the location of Amanda's murderer I'd mentally wrestled with what to do with the info. Give it to Shuman? Or not?

Now, knowing that he'd gone missing, which meant there was a possibility that he could be injured somewhere—or worse—I could be asking myself the same question.

But I wasn't.

I'd made my decision and I would to stick by it. I couldn't second-guess myself. I had to believe that what I'd done was the right thing. I couldn't back out now. I was confident it was what Shuman wanted. It was his call. I would have to trust in him to handle things.

That's what friends did.

"I saw him a few days ago," I told Madison.

"Did he tell you . . . anything?" he asked.

Madison knew Shuman and I were friends. That's why he'd come here. I figured he must be pretty desperate—or worried—to ask me for help.

"We talked about Amanda, mostly," I said, which wasn't a total lie.

"How did he seem?" Detective Madison asked.

I mentally debated for a moment, then decided it was time for a total lie.

"Better," I said. "He seemed like he was coming to terms with everything."

Madison nodded thoughtfully, then said, "If you hear from him, let me know."

I nodded, and Madison left. I lingered in Jeanette's office for a couple of minutes, then went back to the stock room. Out of habit, I pulled my cell phone from my pants pocket.

Yikes! I'd missed a call—from Muriel!

I must have been so caught up in thinking about Shuman and talking to Madison, I hadn't felt it vibrate.

I called Muriel, and immediately she picked up.

"We got the call." She sounded breathless and majorly stressed. "It was one of those computer voices. Creepy."

"What's the deal?" I asked.

"You have to meet the kidnapper at nine tonight," she said.

I glanced at my watch. That was only a little over an hour from now. Not much time.

"Where?" I asked.

"At Hollywood and Highland," Muriel said. "Wear red, lots of red, so you can be spotted."

"What am I supposed to do with the money?" I asked.

"Give it to Janice," she said.

"Janice? Who's Janice?" I asked.

"I have no idea."

Oh, crap.

CHAPTER 23

I swung into the parking structure at the Hollywood & Highland Center, circled down the ramp, and found an empty space near the escalators. I'd made it down here from Holt's in record time—with some help.

After I'd hung up with Muriel, I told Bella I had to leave immediately. She was good with it. Since I'd been told to wear red and I didn't have time to go home, I'd grabbed a red hoodie, scarf, and knit hat from the juniors section of the stock room—it wasn't stealing, technically, because I'd bring them back tomorrow. Besides, what else could I do? Bella said she'd clock out for me—she rolls with *anything*— and I left the store by the rear door.

I'd told Muriel to meet me at a convenience store near the Lankershim Avenue exit off the 101. She'd been waiting locked inside her car, cradling the duffel bag of cash in her arms, when I pulled up. She tossed me the bag through our open windows, and I took off again.

Now that I'd arrived, I stayed seated in my Honda and glanced around—although I'm not sure what I expected to see. The parking garage was nearly filled with vehicles, but few people were there. With all the shops, stores, and restaurants still open, everyone was enjoying the nightlife.

I got out of my car, zipped into my hoodie, wrapped the scarf around my neck, and pulled on the knit hat.

Jeez, I really hope nothing goes bad tonight. No way did I want to have my mug shot taken in this getup.

I took another look around the parking garage, thinking I might spot Jack. I'd called him with the ransom info when I left Holt's, as he'd asked me to do, but he hadn't answered. I hoped he'd listened to the voicemail I'd left. He hadn't said he'd come help and I hadn't asked him to. Still, I wished he'd show up or at least call. Maybe he could help me figure out who Janice was and just how the heck I was supposed to find her.

I circled my car and pulled the black duffel Muriel had given me off of the passenger seat. Surprisingly, twenty grand didn't weigh all that much. Or maybe I was just pumped up. I took the escalator up to Level 2 and walked out to the central courtyard.

I'd been to the Hollywood & Highland Center many times. It was a hot spot for tourists, locals—everybody. The multistory complex held all sorts of shops and restaurants, dozens of kiosks, a spa, a bowling alley, and lots of places for photo ops, plus outdoor seating and a view of the Hollywood sign.

The place was huge. I hadn't been told where I was supposed to meet the kidnapper who called herself Janice, so I strolled around the courtyard for a while. Nobody approached me. I saw no one who looked suspicious—other than myself, a young woman alone, dressed in a hideous outfit, carrying a duffel bag for no apparent reason.

I took a peek at my watch. Nearly nine.

I fought off total panic.

How the heck was I supposed to find the kidnapper and deliver the ransom? Was I expected to just stand around and wait?

I'm not good at waiting.

I took the long, wide staircase down to Hollywood Boulevard.

The street was alive with bumper-to-bumper traffic and droves of people. The marquee of Disney's old school El Capitan Theater blazed. The bronze stars of the Walk of Fame shimmered with reflected light.

To my right was the Dolby Theater, and a couple of blocks farther the huge Hotel Roosevelt sign shone atop the building. In between was Grauman's Chinese Theatre and the footprints of stars cast in cement. To my left toward Highland Avenue was Ripley's Believe It or Not! Museum with a dinosaur's head coming out of the roof, and nearby was the Hollywood Museum.

The crowd was thick, and the H&H complex was immense. How the heck was the kidnapper going to find me—even though I was wearing red? I wasn't sure whomever it was knew to look for a female. I hadn't been instructed where to stand. We could wander around this place for hours and keep missing each other.

How was I supposed to find the kidnapper when all I had to go on was a first name? Janice? Who was that? Was somebody going to walk by carrying a sign that read JAN-ICE like limo drivers did at the airport?

I couldn't stand still waiting for something to happen. I headed toward Highland Avenue, maneuvering my way through the crowd and—froze.

On the corner stood Superman and Marilyn. Nearby were Iron Man, Darth Vader, and Batman. Harry Potter, Elvis, and Cher were positioned a little farther up the block. Dozens of tourist crowded around the celebrity and superhero look-alikes, smiling, joking, and having their pictures taken.

Oh my God—I'd seen these guys a zillion times. Why hadn't I thought about them before? That's how I'd find the kidnapper. All I had to do was look for a famous Janice.

I moved closer to the building near the stairs that led down to the underground Metrolink station where I could keep watch. The costumed impersonators were really working it, waving tourists over, mugging for their cameras, flirting, posing for whatever tip was offered.

Another Batman rounded the corner, and I wondered if there would be trouble. The look-alikes—or, rather, the actors in the costumes—were territorial. They staked out the best spots and didn't want another costumed character nearby distracting the tourists and taking their tips. Arguments and fights had broken out.

Great. That's all I needed. A throwdown that brought the police.

But this new Batman didn't seem to want trouble. He moved slowly down the street, taking in the traffic, the lights, the people, looking for a good spot on the sidewalk where he could draw a crowd of his own.

I glanced at my watch. A couple of minutes past nine. Janice should appear any minute now.

My heart rate picked up, and the twenty grand in the duffel bag seemed to get heavier.

My thoughts raced.

Maybe I should have insisted Jack come with me—even though he hadn't volunteered. Maybe I should have offered to pay him. Or have sex with him.

Jeez, why did I keep thinking about having sex with Jack? I couldn't have sex with Jack. Not when I still thought so much about Ty. Jack was right. We shouldn't get involved—not until this thing with Ty was settled.

Still, I hadn't had sex in a while. Would it be wrong—totally completely wrong—if we did? Jeez, didn't anybody have empty, meaningless sex anymore? Couldn't we just—

Oh my God, there was Janis Joplin.

A woman with a mop of long, thick, curly hair was headed my way from Highland Avenue. She had on a huge, wide-brimmed floppy hat and tiny round glasses with rose-colored lenses, a long tie-dyed top with bell sleeves, and purple elephant-leg pants; she'd styled the costume with a zillion necklaces and bracelets.

She looked totally retro except for the Coach bag I recognized from three years ago, a yikes-what's-this-thing tote covered in fuchsia flower blossoms, and a black duffel bag, which I hoped held Sheridan Adams's Beatles bobbleheads.

Thoughts pinged around in my head, things Jack had told me—kidnappers were unstable, make sure to see the bobbleheads before handing over the money, and . . . something else. He'd told me something else that had seemed important at the time. What was it?

I stepped away from the building and faced Janis Joplin so she'd be sure to see me. Even though I couldn't make out her features clearly, I sensed that she'd spotted me. She shifted direction slightly and walked straight toward me.

Jeez, I wish I could remember that last thing Jack told me to watch out for.

Janis walked closer. My heart pounded.

She drew nearer. My gaze moved to her duffel bag. Inside was my job, the future of L.A. Affairs, Sheridan Adams's Beatles charity auction.

My palms started to sweat. I drew a breath, forcing myself to calm down.

Janis stopped. Our gazes held for about two seconds, then she whipped around and headed back toward Highland Avenue.

Oh, no! What happened? She wasn't supposed to leave. We were supposed to—

My duffel ripped off of my arm. I held on to the strap, whirled around, and came face-to-face with Batman.

A partner. *That's* what Jack said I should watch out for.

No way was I letting Janis Joplin's partner take the money while she got away with the bobbleheads.

I held on for all I was worth and dug in my heels, locked in a tug of war with Batman.

"Let go, Haley," he said.

That voice. I knew that voice.

Oh my God, it was Jack—in the Batman costume.

"Stay here," he told me.

The duffel slipped through my fingers. Jack took off down the street after Janis, his cape flying behind him.

I just stood there, too stunned to move.

What the heck had happened? Why had Janis Joplin left? What was Jack doing here? And was that bulge in his tights a gun?

I dodged through the crowd, stopped at Highland Avenue, and peeked around the corner. A block away near the entrance to the parking garage, Batman and Janis Joplin faced each other and were peering into the open duffel bags held between them.

Batman reached inside Janis's bag and pulled out the cardboard display box containing the Beatles bobble-heads. He checked it over, then put it back inside. He handed his duffel to Janis and took hers. She locked her arms around it and disappeared into the parking garage.

Rage burst inside me. Janis Joplin was getting away. She'd taken what didn't belong to her, ransomed it, created havoc in my life, Muriel's life, Sheridan's life, all of which nearly resulted in me losing my job and L.A. Affairs going out of business. No way was I going to just stand there and let her get away.

Jack headed in my direction, the duffel tucked under his arm. I took off down the sidewalk and cut around him, headed for the parking garage. He caught my arm and pulled me up short.

"Let go," I said, yanking away from him.

Jack held on. "We have to get out of here."

"No!"

He headed for the corner, pulling me along with him, and leaned down.

"She knew you, Haley. That's why she took off," he told me. "Who was she?"

"What?" I asked, stumbling along beside him.

"She recognized you. She must have. There was no other reason for her to bolt," he said.

My head spun. I thought back, trying to remember what little I'd seen of her face.

"I—I have no idea who she was," I said.

Jack kept his hand locked around my arm as we turned the corner onto Hollywood Boulevard. A few people on the sidewalk glanced our way. If any of them had noticed the struggle we'd had over the duffel a few minutes ago, they didn't say anything.

"You need to get out of here," Jack said. "Where are you parked?"

He was looking around, taking in the crowd, watching for trouble—which I hadn't even thought about.

Jeez, my private detective skills need a lot of work.

Worried now that Janis Joplin might still have a partner nearby who would try to take the bobbleheads back, I hurried alongside Jack up the stairs to the central court-yard, then down the escalators to the parking garage.

"Do you think she has an accomplice here somewhere?" I asked.

The Caped Crusader and I were getting a lot of looks now.

"Doubtful," Jack said.

Wish I could have worn a Catwoman costume.

"This wasn't a professional operation," he said.

At my car, I popped the trunk and Jack put the duffel inside, then opened my door and hustled me in behind the wheel. I started the engine and buzzed the window down.

"Watch behind you to make sure you're not followed. Go straight to Sheridan's," Jack said. "Call her. Tell her you're on the way. Don't get out of the car until you recognize someone standing in the doorway."

"Got it," I said.

I put the car in reverse and backed up a little, then hit the brakes.

"How did you get into that costume and down here so quick?" I asked.

He shrugged. "I was in the Batcave when you called."

I grinned and backed out of the spot, then drove away.

I exited the parking garage and crept along Highland Avenue as it curved around to the entrance to the 101. Once I'd merged into traffic, I put in my Bluetooth and called Muriel.

"Got them," I said, when she answered.

All I heard was a little mewling sound, which I took to mean she was both happy and relieved.

"I'm on my way to Sheridan's house," I said. "Meet me there. Tell the security guard on duty to let me through the gate. Stand in the open doorway. I'm not getting out of the car until I make sure everything is safe."

"I understand," she said. "Wow, Haley, you really are good at this."

I saw no need to tell her that I might have blown the whole thing if it hadn't been for Jack.

"See you soon," I said, and we hung up.

Keeping Jack's other advice in mind, I checked my rearview mirror in case Janis Joplin and a possible partner might be somehow following me. But since it was dark and all I could see were headlights, it was hard to tell if a vehicle was tailing me. I changed lanes frequently, sped up and slowed down—well, mostly I sped up—just in case.

I tried to focus on the traffic but the whole ransom exchange kept playing over and over in my head.

I thought I'd handled everything pretty well. I'd followed the kidnapper's instructions, gotten everything I needed, made it to the appointed spot, and I'd even figured out who to make the ransom exchange with.

But if Jack hadn't been there when the whole thing went bad, I don't know what I'd have done.

I glanced in my side mirror and changed lanes again, pulling in front of a pickup truck.

Of course, there had been no way I could possibly know that the kidnapper would take off without making the exchange. Jack had claimed that Janis Joplin recognized me. He'd thought that if she knew me, I'd know her. But I had no clue who she was.

Or maybe I did.

I hung in the lane behind the pickup, thinking back. In my mind I played the whole encounter over slowly. Seeing Janis Joplin as she turned the corner. Realizing she was the kidnapper. The relief I'd felt that I'd found her.

A couple of miles passed. I checked my mirrors and glanced over my shoulder, and eased into the next lane behind a green janitorial service van.

Mentally I pictured the kidnapper. I'd been so overwhelmed at realizing just who Janis was that all I'd noticed was her costume. The floppy hat, the mass of long curly hair, and the round glasses had all disguised her features. Yet something about her—other than that ratty old Coach tote—had seemed familiar.

Miles passed. I transitioned south onto the 405. I ran dozens of people and places through my head, hoping something would match up—like that facial recognition software casinos use when they target cheaters.

Had I seen her at Holt's? At a restaurant? In my classes at the College of the Canyons? Was she connected to L.A. Affairs? Maybe she'd been at—

A face exploded in my head, like the mushroom cloud from a nuclear bomb.

Oh my God—could I be right? Was I remembering her correctly?

I ran everything through my head again—her height, weight, build, age, chin, jaw, nose, forehead—and knew I wasn't mistaken.

But how could it be? It didn't make sense.

Why—and how—would Belinda Giles steal the Beatles bobbleheads?

*   *   *

I was still fired up when I pulled into the parking lot of my favorite Starbucks in Santa Clarita. Jack had called to make sure I'd gotten the bobbleheads to Sheridan okay, and we'd agreed to meet here.

When I'd pulled into Sheridan's driveway, the guard for the private security firm I'd hired had waved me through the gate. Muriel had been watching from a window and came out of the house. She hadn't asked for details on the exchange or if I'd gleaned any clue about who had stolen the bobbleheads in the first place. She seemed relieved and glad the ordeal was over—and that she'd get to keep her job.

She wanted me to come inside, but after hearing that she would have to wake Sheridan with the news of the bobbleheads' return I decided I could definitely pass on seeing Sheridan in her PJs or whatever she slept in. I fig-ured I could talk to her about the whole ransom thing at the party tomorrow.

I spotted Jack's black Land Rover parked nearby, then saw him seated at an umbrella table looking more like Bruce Wayne—if Bruce Wayne had been a Navy S.E.A.L.—than Batman, in jeans and a black T-shirt.

I walked over. Just seeing Jack made my blood boil—but not for the usual reasons.

My outrage over recognizing Belinda and knowing what she'd done must have shown on my face. Jack sprang out of the chair.

"Forget it," he told me.

His know-it-all tone irked me—even though he did, in fact, know it all when it came to security work.

But no way was I going to forget what I knew.

"I know who it was," I told him.

"I figured you'd remember," he said.

"I can't stand by and do nothing." I might have said that kind of loud.

"Yes, you can."

"I won't let her get away with it." I'm pretty sure I shouted that.

"Yes, you will."

Jack sounded way calm—which annoyed me further.

"It's not right." I definitely yelled that.

The couple seated at a nearby table turned to look at us. Jack touched my shoulder.

"Sit down," he said quietly.

I didn't want to sit down. I didn't want to hear anything Jack had to say. I wanted to call the police and rat out Belinda big-time. I wanted to see her arrested, tried, jailed, and made to pay for stealing those bobbleheads and putting Sheridan, Muriel, and me through this whole thing.

"You want justice," Jack said. "I understand that."

Okay, that made me feel better—but only enough that I sat down at the table. Plus, Jack had a mocha Frappuccino waiting for me.

He took the chair next to me and sipped the coffee he'd bought for himself. He didn't say anything. I gulped down some of my Frappie; the chocolate, caffeine, and sugar calmed me, which was weird but there it was.

"It was Belinda Giles," I said. "I met her at Lacy Cakes. She's Lacy Hobbs's cousin."

"The owner who was murdered," Jack said.

I could see that his mind was racing, trying to make a connection.

"I don't get it," I said. "I don't know how Belinda could have stolen the bobbleheads from Sheridan's estate, and I don't see how it could have anything to do with Lacy's murder."

"I don't put much stock in coincidence," Jack said.

I didn't either, but so far I couldn't come up with anything that linked the two crimes—although I wished it could be Darren, somehow, since I didn't especially like him.

Jack sipped his coffee and I worked on my Frappie for a minute or two, then he said, "You can't go near Belinda."

My anger spiked and I was ready to blast Jack with what I thought of his advice, but he cut me off.

"Your suspicion about her connection to the bakery owner's murder will show. So will the fact that you recognized her at the ransom exchange," he said.

"Good," I said. "She should be worried that I intend to go to the cops."

"Belinda believes you didn't recognize her," Jack said. "If she thought that disguise of hers had failed, she'd have never stopped for me and made the exchange."

I just looked at him, unsure of where he was going with this.

"If Belinda knew you'd recognized her, and if she's connected to Lacy Hobbs's murder," Jack said, "she might try to kill you to keep you quiet."

Oh. I hadn't thought about that.

I calmed down, thinking over what he'd said.

It made perfect sense—but didn't make me feel any better about Belinda.

"I can't stand it that she's going to get away with this," I said.

"I know," Jack said. "You want justice."

"Damn right I do," I said.

"You're not in law enforcement, Haley," he said. "And neither am I."

"But—"

"*Private* investigation," Jack said. "Private. That means doing what you're hired to do, what your client wants you to do."

I shook my head. "No, I can't pretend I don't know what I know—and do nothing about it—just to make Sheridan Adams happy."

"Sometimes there's no justice in this kind of work. No

good guys. No win," Jack said. "You have to do what you do, know what you know, and let it go."

I fumed for a few more minutes. My head understood what Jack was saying but the rest of me was fighting it big-time.

Maybe private investigation work wasn't for me after all.

CHAPTER 24

It was early, but Mom would be up—something about how the sunlight produced a delicate blush to the skin as the UV rays crested the eastern horizon.

I don't know. I wasn't really listening.

Anyway, I had a lot going today, the Holt's fashion show—which would finish up before noon—and Sheridan Adams's event, where I would spend the rest of the day and evening until the party ended. I had to be on hand to handle any problems that might arise.

I might have to rethink the whole event planner job. Being a party *guest* seemed like a heck of a lot more fun.

Mom was the quickest—though certainly not the easiest—item I could check off my list this morning, so I went to her house first.

The temporary housekeeper—a really young blonde who was texting a desperate request to be reinstated at dental hygienist school when she let me in the house—pointed to the patio doors. I spotted Mom seated at an umbrella table poolside, flipping through a magazine.

"Hi, sweetie," she said when I walked outside.

Mom tended to get distracted—especially when the new issue of *Vogue* arrived—so I came right to the point.

"I found the perfect housekeeper for you," I said.

Mom perked up. She actually closed the magazine and

turned to me—which I appreciated because I'd gone to a heck of a lot of trouble, and then some, to accomplish this.

"She'll do everything you want done, exactly as you want it done," I said. "She's flexible with her daily schedule and her days off. She's an excellent cook. She knows all your favorite dishes. She can start immediately."

An I'm-a-pageant-queen smile bloomed on Mom's face.

"Oh, Haley, that's wonderful," she said. "Where did you find her? Who is she?"

I drew a breath and braced myself.

"It's Juanita," I said.

Mom's you're-my-favorite smile vanished. Her lips curled into a very unpageant-like snarl.

I cut her off.

"Juanita is the only person who can be your housekeeper," I said.

After the last time I was at Mom's house I knew there was only one real option available. I'd driven to Juanita's house in Eagle Rock and talked with her. Just as I'd suspected, the entire incident that caused Juanita to leave in the first place was Mom's fault.

After much discussion, I'd convinced her to return to work for Mom. It wasn't easy.

Nothing concerning Mom is easy.

"She left without a word," Mom said. "She disappeared. I was completely abandoned."

"Juanita explained the whole thing to me," I said. "It was a family emergency. Her daughter who is pregnant was having problems."

What Juanita really told me was that after sharing that troubling news with Mom, her only comment was to ask Juanita what she planned to serve for dessert that night.

I saw no need to mention that.

Mom pressed her lips together and stewed for a moment, then said, "Well, it has been extremely difficult here without her."

At this point, I would usually keep quiet and wait for Mom to mentally process everything.

I didn't have that kind of time.

"So you're good with it?" I asked.

"Everything will be like it was?" she asked. "Nothing will change?"

Nothing except for the substantial salary increase I'd had to promise Juanita to get her to come back. Plus paid holidays, a membership to a spa, annual passes to Disneyland, and the new car I still had to discuss with Mom's accountant.

Anyway, the important thing was that Juanita had agreed to work for Mom once more. Now I had to make sure Mom didn't drive her away again.

"You might want to inquire about Juanita's family once in a while," I said. "Show some interest in her personal life, and not expect her to just come here and work for you."

Okay, now Mom looked totally lost.

Jeez, what was I thinking?

I decided to move on.

"It's all settled," I announced. "Juanita will be here this afternoon."

Mom nodded thoughtfully and said, "You're right, Haley. Some people are meant to be together no matter what. You can't explain it and it's useless to fight it, so you may as well accept it."

Ty popped into my head.

My heart began to ache, so I pushed him out.

Mom opened her magazine again, so I figured I should get away while I could. I left the house, got into my car, and headed for Sherman Oaks.

As I cruised down the 2 past Glendale, I plugged in my Bluetooth and called Detective Shuman. I hadn't heard from him in a while and wondered if Detective Madison had, but no way was I going to call him and ask.

I was starting to get an icky feeling in my stomach about Shuman.

His voicemail picked up. I left a message asking him to call me.

As I transitioned west onto the 134 I ran the mental checklist of everything I had to do today. The fashion show at Holt's would begin in a couple of hours, but it didn't require much effort on my part—mostly I had to show up and make sure the models didn't mutiny after they got there and saw the clothing they'd have to wear down the runway.

Maybe I should have hired security for that event, too.

I exited the freeway and drove to the Lacy Cakes bakery. The CLOSED sign still hung on the front door, so I walked around back. Their delivery van was parked near the rear entrance.

Belinda popped into my head. The image of her in that Janis Joplin costume had been floating around in my brain nonstop. I still couldn't figure out how she'd gotten involved with the Beatles bobbleheads kidnapping.

A lot of people knew about the charity auction and the memorabilia, but how many of them knew the collectibles were inside Sheridan's house, in that particular room?

I also couldn't figure out why the bobbleheads, of all things, had been taken. There were many other items, most worth at least as much as the bobbleheads, maybe more. And a lot of those things were smaller, much easier to conceal.

Someone must have known their significance, their link to British royalty Muriel had told me about. I doubted that fact was common knowledge. Sheridan would have wanted to make that announcement herself at the party.

All I could figure was that Jack had been right. Someone else—a partner—had been involved in the theft and the ransom demand. Belinda didn't seem like the criminal type to me, so I wondered if she'd gotten caught up in the scheme by the partner—but who could that have been?

The rear door to Lacy Cakes was propped open, and the delicious scent of baked goods floated out. I stepped inside and saw that same guy at the oven and Paige at the worktable. In front of her was the Yellow Submarine cake for tonight's event.

If I was going to pretend I didn't know Belinda had been involved in stealing the bobbleheads, as Jack had insisted, how could I go into Lacy Cakes to place orders for L.A. Affairs? How could I let Paige go into business with Belinda knowing what I know?

And how was I going to live with myself?

"Hey, girl," Paige called. "Come on in. Take a look. What do you think?"

I walked over. The cake was about six feet long and three feet high, covered in bright yellow fondant, surrounded by what I guessed was some kind of blue sugar work to represent the sea.

"It looks fantastic," I said, and mentally heaved a sigh of relief.

"I'll take it to the party in a while," Paige said. "The finishing touches will go on after I get there."

I nodded toward the parking lot out back and said, "I see you have the delivery van."

"Yeah, Darren dropped it off this morning," Paige said. "He went back home."

I figured that could mean only one thing.

"So he sold the bakery?" I asked.

"Yeah," Paige said, smiling broadly. "To Belinda and me. She called me last night with the news."

So Belinda had put the ransom money to good use, apparently.

The robbery at the bakery flashed in my mind. It had come on the heels of Darren saying he was selling the place and keeping everything for himself—and that Belinda was getting nothing from Lacy in her will.

Oh my God—could Belinda have robbed the bakery? I didn't see why not since she'd been involved with the Beatles bobbleheads theft and ransom.

Okay, hang on a second.

Darren had returned the Lacy Cakes delivery van this morning, then left town—or so he'd claimed. But was he really involved in the bobbleheads theft?

Had he used the delivery van to gain access to the Adams estate and somehow stolen the Beatles bobbleheads, then drawn Belinda into the ransom scheme with him? Had he broken into the bakery and faked the robbery to throw suspicion on her? Was all of this some plan of his to make Belinda look guilty so she wouldn't challenge Lacy's will?

Or was something else going on with them?

Paige yammered on about plans for the bakery, but all I could think about was Belinda and Darren. I still didn't see how either of them could have pulled off the theft of the bobbleheads from inside Sheridan's estate. I was missing something. But what?

And did any of this connect to Lacy's murder?

When I got to Holt's, the place was in chaos—but that was okay with me. Having caused a great deal of chaos in my life, I was okay working in it.

Show prep had taken over the stock room. A large section of it had been curtained off for the models—all fifteen of them—to change into our so-called fashions. Since none of them had "super" in front of their job title, mirrors, tables, and chairs from Holt's inventory had been set up for them to put on their own makeup.

Their hair was something else entirely.

Bella had taken over one of the stations and was styling the models' hair herself.

In keeping with the fall fashion show theme, she'd created a stunning array of autumn icons atop each models head—pumpkins, cornstalks, a harvest moon—and had embellished them with sunflowers to complete each look.

Bella has absolutely got to get into beauty school soon.

"Wow, that's really something," I said, and walked over.

She expertly twisted the model's red hair into a—oh my God, I think that's a crow—and gave me a broad smile.

"You just wait until I get my training done and get my hands on all those celebrities," Bella said. "The red carpet will never be the same."

She hit the model's hair with enough spray to freeze the space shuttle on the launch pad, then said, "You're done. Go get your makeup."

The model smiled and moved on.

All I could figure was that these girls were desperate for money.

Bella patted the chair. "Hop in, Haley, you're next."

Yikes!

"I got an idea for a scarecrow," Bella said.

I didn't really want my hair twisted into the shape of a scarecrow—or anything else, for that matter—but Bella was my friend, so I decided, what the heck?

"Better make it quick," I said. "The show is starting soon."

She glanced at her watch and said, "Damn. You're right. Don't worry, though, I'll save it for Halloween."

Bella and I moved to the racks where we'd assembled each runway look and started handing them out to the models. There was a lot of chatter and some laughter. I guess the girls were happy to have the work, regardless of the circumstances.

"Do you think customers are going to buy any of this stuff?" Bella asked, as she handed a fuchsia and purple plaid pantsuit to one of the models.

I figured this campaign to launch their fall clothing line had cost Holt's a fortune, so I was sure they'd advertised the heck out of it. I hoped, for Ty's sake, it would be a success.

"Knowing our customers, they'll buy two of everything," I said, and thrust a navy blue dress with orange cap sleeves and patch pockets at the next model who walked by.

"We'll sell lots of stuff," Bella predicted. "Everybody in the audience will be looking at my hairstyles, not the clothes."

"How's it going?" Jeanette asked as she walked up. She eyed the emerald green and burnt orange polka-dot dress Bella was holding. "That is a smart-looking dress. I would wear that with those turquoise and orange pumps we just got in. What do you think?"

I thought I might get sick.

"We're kind of busy here, Jeanette," I said. "Did you need something?"

I know that was sort of rude, but handling all these dust-rags-in-the-making was starting to get to me.

"We've got a packed house," Jeanette said, smiling proudly. "Our store could very well win this contest."

I'm sure the potential boost to her quarterly bonus was living large in her head, but I didn't say so.

"And you know what *that* means," Jeanette said in a singsong voice.

It would mean that I'd be the fashion coordinator who would work at the Holt's corporate office—which I didn't even want to think about right now.

"Ten minutes until the show starts," she said, glancing at her watch.

She went into a spiel about how she'd do the welcome speech—which turned into blah, blah, blah—then left.

"That's the last one," Bella said, as a model wearing a

mustard yellow swing coat covered with crocheted red, orange, and brown leaves left the dressing area.

"Let's line up," I said, motioning the models toward the stock room doors.

The order in which models walked the runway at the major fashion events was crucial, but here at Holt's I went with smallest to tallest.

I stood back and assessed the looks Bella and I had put together. Considering what we'd had to work with, I decided it could have been worse.

Things can always be worse.

The mumble of the audience assembled outside on the sales floor grew louder, and I wondered why Jeanette hadn't started the show yet. I slipped out of the stock room and walked through the screened-off area the workmen had built to keep the audience from seeing the fashions before they hit the runway—maybe corporate had feared a sneak peek might result in a stampede that would injure customers and bring on lawsuits.

I stepped up onto the little stage that had been built and peeked out. Wow, Jeanette hadn't been kidding—the place was packed.

The workmen had set up two rows of chairs facing the runway, and every seat was taken. People were standing behind them, three deep. Most of them were young women dressed in really nice clothes. Jeez, what were they doing in Holt's?

I spotted Jeanette heading toward the stage just as my cell phone vibrated in my pocket. I whipped it out and saw that Rigby was calling.

Jeez, not now. I didn't have time for a Beatles quiz question. The show would start any minute.

But I didn't dare not answer. Sheridan's event was tonight and I didn't want to hear about a missed question after I arrived.

I hit the green button as I hurried back into the stock room.

"What was the location of the Beatles last official concert?" Rigby asked before I could even say hello.

All the models were lined up in their Holt's clothing. Bella busied herself tweaking their hairstyles. Jeanette's voice boomed over the P.A. system.

There was a last concert? An official one, at that?

Oh my God, I didn't know the answer—and there was no way to look it up. I didn't have the Beatles book with me, and there was no time to borrow a phone and access the Internet.

I covered my phone with my hand and said, "Do any of you know where the Beatles performed their last official concert?"

All the models—even Bella—gave me a what-planet-are-you-*really*-from look, then said in unison, "Candlestick Park in San Francisco."

Jeez, did absolutely everybody know extensive Beatles trivia but me?

No time for that now.

"San Francisco," I said to Rigby. "Candlestick Park."

"You're correct," she announced, and hung up.

A round of applause boomed from the sales floor.

"Time to go," Bella said, and led the models out of the stockroom.

I didn't go with them. I just stood there, thinking.

San Francisco. Darren and Lacy were from a little town near there. So was Belinda. They'd all grown up there together. Lacy and Belinda had been closer than most cousins—best friends, really—until they'd had a fight because Belinda had won concert tickets and taken her boyfriend instead of Lacy.

A connect-the-dots moment hit me.

Could they have been Beatles concert tickets? But not just any Beatles concert—their very last concert ever?

My mind raced recalling things I'd been told, things I'd learned about Lacy, Belinda, and Darren. Accusations of stealing, telling lies, trying to turn the family against each other.

And now, it seemed, I could add murder to the list.

CHAPTER 25

I drove into the Adams estate and crawled along with a slow-moving line of delivery vans and service trucks. The start of the party was still hours away, but work had been in progress here since dawn. I'd spoken with Muriel a number of times and, so far, party prep was on schedule.

Two guards from the security firm I'd hired were stationed at the checkpoint wearing navy blue uniforms and dark glasses; one of them held an iPad. I eased forward and buzzed down my window.

"Haley Randolph," I said using my I-hired-you-so-I'd-like-preferential-treatment voice.

I didn't get any.

"ID," he said.

I passed him my driver's license. He checked my photo, looked hard at me, consulted his iPad, then handed back my identification.

"Enjoy the party," he said.

I drove around to the mansion's service wing. The sun was bright overhead in a cloudless Southern California sky. I could see dozens of workers spread out across the estate's extensive grounds.

Jewel had done almost all of the planning for the event, but I'd followed up on everything a number of times. I could see why Vanessa wanted her back. The valets she'd hired were all dressed in psychedelic vests and wearing sixties-era Beatles wigs.

Not sure I'd have thought of that.

I was directed to a parking space on the first floor of the expansive garage and nosed my Honda in between a Webber's Florist van and an Angel's Catering truck. I spotted an Ever Clean Janitorial Service truck parked a couple of rows back, and delivery vans from Lacy Cakes and Party On were nearby.

More vehicles pulled in. Workers poured out of them wheeling dollies and pushing carts.

I put in my Bluetooth and got out my portfolio—just so I'd look as busy as everyone else—and got the garment bag and tote with tonight's outfit in it from my trunk.

As I headed toward the entrance of the service wing, I spotted Muriel. She had an iPad in one hand, an old school organizer in the other, and a Bluetooth in her ear.

"How's it going?" I asked as I walked over.

"No problems, so far," Muriel said.

Since she'd been involved with planning all sorts of events for Sheridan for a long time now, I figured her idea of no-problems and my idea of no-problems might not be the same. Still, I was pumped, ready to take on whatever situation presented itself.

I'm really good at telling other people what to do.

"Let me show you where you can put your things," Muriel said.

She led the way into the service wing through double doors. On my right was a gargantuan commercial kitchen. Multiple stainless steel, industrial-grade appliances filled the space, along with worktables and an army of chefs. The room was warm and something smelled really good.

"The Beatles collectibles are all together in a storage room," Muriel said.

We passed another huge room, this one with a dozen florists turning a mountain of flowers and greenery into gorgeous floral arrangements.

"There are two security guards posted outside the door," she went on. "Nobody but Sheridan or me will be let in until it's time to move them to the auction site on the grounds."

It didn't seem likely to me that, with all the security in place, anyone would attempt to steal the bobbleheads—or any other pieces of the memorabilia—before or during the party, but I could see where Muriel wouldn't want to take a chance.

We climbed the stairs and continued down a hallway. It was obvious this was where the servants were housed. The carpet wasn't quite as thick as in the main house, and the wall art wasn't exactly "art," yet it was still nicer than my apartment.

Muriel stopped in front of a door halfway down the hall, checked her iPad, and pulled a key from her pocket.

"This room is yours for the duration. You can change in here for the party tonight," she said, passing me the key. "Oh, and Sheridan wants to see you right away."

Muriel tapped her Bluetooth to answer a call, and I went inside. The room contained simple furnishings—bed, nightstand, chest—and had an adjoining bathroom. I hung my cocktail dress in the closet.

The Enchantress evening bag popped into my head. It would have looked perfect with my dress, but the Judith Leiber I'd brought with me was more than adequate.

Muriel took two more calls as we left the service wing. I pulled out my cell phone and texted Marcie so I'd look important.

The grounds of the estate were in total chaos, just as the Holt's stock room had been—only here, most everyone was dressed better.

Construction workers and sound and lighting guys were everywhere. The caterer and florists had already started setting up. Hammers, saws, power tools, shouts, and a zillion cell phone conversations added to the cacophony. Sliced-up packing boxes and sheets of plastic were strewn all around.

I pulled the event diagram from my portfolio and saw that the wide pathway—"The Long and Winding Road"—that would take guests from one event area to another was already in place. Workers were ripping the protective covering off the white wicker furniture that, along with hundreds of flowers and plants all blooming in white, would make up the Lady Madonna serenity garden.

The giant aquarium for the Octopus's Garden was being filled. The fish pond had been assembled nearby, and landscapers were surrounding it with lush ferns, shrubs, bright flowering plants, and palm trees.

Tonight, after dark, everything would be lit with accent, spot, and twinkle lights, and the two Beatles tribute bands—one that would cover songs from the sixties, the other the seventies—would play almost nonstop.

Muriel walked over, nodding and mumbling, then hit the button on her Bluetooth and said, "Mrs. Adams is ready for you now."

I followed Muriel across the grounds, not really knowing what to expect. I figured Sheridan would either be really grateful that I'd gotten back the bobbleheads and recommend me for a promotion at L.A. Affairs or be really grateful but angry that I'd gotten them stolen in the first place and recommend that I be fired.

From what I'd seen of Sheridan so far, I figured it could go either way.

We found her near one of the swimming pools where tables and chairs were being set up.

Sheridan had on a neon pink and red print caftan that, I

swear, looked as if it had come from Holt's and a matching turban that I figured the store was destined to carry sooner or later.

"Oh, yes, there you are—" She pointed at Muriel.

"Haley," she said.

"Haley," Sheridan repeated. "So you own a detective agency."

Where the heck had she gotten that idea?

Muriel gave me a please-let-it-go look, so I figured Sheridan had misunderstood what Muriel had told her about me—or maybe Muriel had embellished my credentials a bit to stay out of trouble with her boss.

Sheridan leaned in a little. "And you're working undercover at L.A. Affairs, aren't you."

Sheridan must have read too many of her husband's movie scripts, but I decided it was better to just let this go also.

"I'm glad everything turned out well," I said.

I wondered if Sheridan had given any thought to who might have stolen the Beatles bobbleheads. Did she suspect an inside job?

I didn't think so. Sheridan seemed to live in her own private zombieland. She probably thought everyone she employed loved her and wouldn't possibly steal from her.

"I won't forget what you've done," Sheridan said.

Jeez, I really hope she meant that in a good way.

"A reliable, discreet security firm isn't easy to come by," Sheridan said.

Something shiny must have caught her attention because she wandered away, Muriel trailing after her.

Sheridan thought I owned a private detective firm? And I was working undercover?

Cool.

I headed across the grounds again consulting the event diagram so everyone would think I was working, but really the idea of a detective agency was playing around in my head—even though I was still having trouble coming to terms with the whole Belinda-ransom thing.

I wasn't all that excited about this event-planning gig, and even though not long ago I'd decided to get my bachelor's degree in procurement and become a corporate buyer, I'd been in my breakup fog at the time, so I wasn't sure that counted.

I realized then that the murder of Lacy Hobbs was rambling around in my head. It took up more room in my mind than Sheridan's party—which just shows how I was feeling about working at L.A. Affairs.

When I'd talked to Paige earlier she'd told me that Belinda had come up with the money to buy Lacy Cakes—which was immediately after the ransom was delivered. Darren had left town at the same time, supposedly.

I was pretty sure one of them had murdered Lacy. I didn't like to think that anyone deserved to be murdered, but really, Lacy had been pretty awful to both of them for years—right up until the end, it seemed.

They both had motive—money. Lacy's life insurance was surely substantial, plus the bakery was worth a fortune whether Darren sold it or Belinda kept it operating.

They both could have had the opportunity also, since there was no way, at this point, to be sure where either of them had been at the time of Lacy's murder.

As for the murder weapon, coming up with a handgun wasn't hard to do these days.

For a moment I considered calling Detective Madison with my suspicion, but I doubted he'd take me seriously. Shuman would have, but I hadn't heard from him in a while. I thought about calling Jack, but I wasn't exactly loving all his good advice lately.

I needed more evidence, I decided, as I stepped out of the way of a guy pushing a dolly stacked high with cases of wine. But I had no idea where to find Darren or Belinda at the moment. I didn't see how I could come up with anything—not today, anyway, with this whole Beatles event going on.

The only option was to talk to Paige. She was here somewhere putting the finishing touches on the Yellow Submarine cake. I put in a call to her; it went straight to voicemail.

I wondered if, since they were buying Lacy Cakes together, Belinda might be on hand helping with the cake. I didn't really expect her to be here since she was handling the business end of the bakery, and it would be unseemly to solicit orders at an event of this caliber. Jack had told me to stay away from her, but I called her cell phone, anyway. She didn't answer.

At this point there was nothing I could do but perform some actual work for L.A. Affairs.

I hate it when that happens.

Luckily, everyone involved with the party preparations had done this before and knew what they were doing.

I caught up with Lyle, the guy who owned the construction company. He assured me that everything was under control and on schedule; ditto the sound and lighting guys, the landscapers and the caterers.

Just so I'd appear concerned and involved, I telephoned the guy who ran the security firm I'd hired for the event and asked for an update. He reported the number of uniformed personnel on duty, the number of plainclothes who would arrive later—then everything turned into blah, blah, blah, so I thanked him and hung up.

There really wasn't all that much for me to do—unless I was missing something huge—so I basically just strolled around and chatted with people, texted friends, took a picture of myself in front of the huge aquarium and sent it to Marcie, and updated my Facebook page.

As I made my way past one of the bars, my cell phone rang. It was Bella.

"You're not going to believe this!" she screamed. "You're not going to *believe* it!"

Before I could answer, she went on.

"My hairstyles are on YouTube!" she said. "I videoed the show and posted it! I edited out the clothes because they were so damn ugly and just showed my hairstyles! I've gone viral! A half million hits—already!"

"Oh my God!"

"I got to go!" Bella said. "I got to call my nana!"

How totally cool, I thought as I put my phone back in my pocket. Thank goodness something worthwhile had come out of that horrible fashion show.

Then I noticed that most everyone around me—people who were doing actual work—were giving me stink-eye. I decided it was a good time to find Paige.

I made a sweep of the grounds and didn't spot her, so I went into the service wing. I walked by the kitchen— something really smelled great in there—and continued past the staircase. I figured there had to be a temperature-controlled room in the building that was cool, a place where the desserts and cold foods could be prepped.

On my left was a lounge intended for the hired help— not that they got much of a chance to use it—complete with tables and chairs, a TV, a refrigerator, a microwave, and vending machines. Jackets and totes hung from a row of hooks, but nobody was in the room.

A little farther down the hallway a door opened and a woman in a white chef's jacket came out followed by a gust of cold air. I went inside and spotted Paige and the guy who did the baking at Lacy Cakes working on the Yellow Submarine cake. Around them a couple dozen people were assembling scrumptious-looking desserts.

"Hey, girl," Paige called as I walked over. She gestured to the cake. "What do you think?"

The blue sugar work ocean that surrounded the submarine was populated by colorful fish, seahorses, dolphins and coral, and an Aztec pyramid, as well as characters from the movie—the Blue Meanies, Lord Mayor, and Old Fred—and, of course, the mates themselves, John, Paul, George, and Ringo.

"It looks fabulous," I said.

"I'm pumped," Paige said.

Jack's words of caution flashed in my head, but I pushed them away.

"Where's Belinda?" I asked. "I thought she'd be here helping today."

I didn't, of course, but what else could I say to get info out of her?

"Oh no," Paige said, eyeing the cake. "She had to work today, or something. I don't know. I wasn't really paying attention."

Since Paige didn't know—or seem to care—where Belinda was, I figured that squashed my one last chance to discover any more evidence today and I'd have to put my murder investigation on hold until tomorrow.

I circled the estate grounds again. The workmen were gone. The sun had dipped low on the horizon, so all the lights were lit. The bands were on their stages, tuning up. The caterers had set up their food and drink stations. Guests would start arriving soon.

I headed toward the service wing to dress for the party and found Tiberia putting the finishing touches on the display of gift bags. She looked great in a red linen pantsuit and sandals.

"Haley, so good to see you," she said.

We hugged and exchanged air kisses.

"I have something special for you," Tiberia said.

From one of the boxes, she took a gift bag and presented it to me.

"Courtesy of Sheridan Adams," Tiberia said.

This was totally cool. When I'd been in Tiberia's office

and seen the gifts she'd assembled, I'd wanted absolutely all of them. I didn't expect I'd get one of the bags, though.

She gave me a knowing grin. "Sheridan asked me to select something special for your gift bag. I hope you'll like it."

"Thanks so much," I said, cradling the bulging bag in my arms.

"I have to run," Tiberia said. "Another delivery across town."

I waved good-bye and hurried up to my room in the service wing.

My first thought, of course, was to open the gift bag and check out everything inside, but something this fabulous must be savored—plus, I had to be on hand when the guests started to arrive.

I took a shower, did my hair and makeup, and put on the fabulous cocktail dress I'd bought for the party. Since I didn't think I'd need anything in the portfolio, I put some essentials into my Judith Leiber clutch and opened my door.

A black garment bag hung in the doorway.

Okay, that was weird.

I stepped around it and saw that someone had hung it on the door frame.

What the heck was going on?

I looked up and down the hallway but spotted no one, so I went downstairs. Through the double doors I saw the valets hustling to park a long line of cars. Strains of "Please Please Me" drifted in.

Muriel stood at the entrance to the floral room—at least I thought it was Muriel. She was dressed kind of odd in a gray uniform—pleated skirt, a jacket with brass buttons, kneesocks, a crossbody leather bag, and one of those big dome hats the policemen in England wear.

"Who are you?" she asked.

Jeez, did she really not recognize me in my hot cocktail dress? Or had working for Sheridan Adams sent her over the edge?

"I'm Haley," I said.

She looked me up and down. "You can't be Haley."

I started to get a weird feeling.

She pulled at her skirt and said, "I'm Rita. As in 'Lovely Rita.' The meter maid in the song."

My weird feeling got weirder.

"Where's your costume?" Muriel asked.

Oh my God—this was a costume party?

"Everybody *has* to wear a costume," Muriel said.

How could it be a costume party?

"Mrs. Adams will lose her mind if somebody shows up without a costume," Muriel said, bordering on all-out panic.

How come nobody told me I needed a costume?

And then I knew—Vanessa.

She'd taken the costume requirement info out of the file—just like she'd done with the other things. She hoped nobody would tell me and I'd show up without a costume, and look like a complete idiot—which is exactly what I looked like.

Total panic set in.

Where the heck was I going to find a Beatles costume *now?* The party had started; people were already arriving. What was I going to do?

And what would happen when L.A. Affairs found out I'd attended this high-profile event without a costume? Would they fire me?

But would it matter—after Sheridan blabbed to all of her important, influential friends about how the planner from L.A. Affairs had snubbed her costume requirement and put the company out of business?

"Oh, wait," Muriel said, and heaved a sigh of relief.

"That must have been your costume that was delivered for you."

Okay, now I was totally lost.

"The garment bag," Muriel said, pointing up the stairs. "I hung it outside your door."

I nearly collapsed with relief.

"That other girl dropped it off," Muriel said.

My anxiety amped up again.

"What other girl?" I asked.

"The one Jewel worked for," Muriel said. "Vanessa."

Vanessa had brought me a costume?

"She had on the most beautiful dress," Muriel said. "A deep garnet red made of lace. She's Julia Lennon, John's mother—the woman who inspired it all."

What was Vanessa doing here? This was my party. She'd dumped it off on me the very first day I met her.

And why was she wearing the most totally awesome costume imaginable?

Oh my God—this could *not* be happening.

I dashed up the stairs, grabbed the garment bag, and hurried into my room.

Vanessa had deliberately tried to sabotage me—again—by taking the costume info out of the file—then she'd brought me a costume?

I dropped the garment bag on the bed.

Why would Vanessa have done that?

I unzipped the bag.

Had she suddenly had an attack of conscience?

I pulled my costume out of the bag—white elephant leg pants, a white bell-sleeved jacket, a black blouse, and small, round eyeglasses with yellow lenses.

My mind sorted through all the characters I'd seen in every Beatles movie. I didn't remember anyone dressed like this.

Then I pulled from the bag a huge, white floppy-brimmed hat and a wig of long, thick, frizzy, unkempt black hair.

I couldn't recall ever seeing anyone on a Beatles album cover wearing this outfit.

But no time for that now. Vanessa was at the party, parading around in a fabulous costume, no doubt taking credit for all my hard work—well, mostly it was Jewel's hard work, but still. I wasn't going to let her get away with it.

I threw on the costume, took a quick glance in the mirror, and—froze.

My mouth fell open. My eyes bulged.

Oh my God. *Oh my God.*

Vanessa had stuck me in a Yoko Ono costume.

Crap.

CHAPTER 26

I wove my way through the crowd looking for Vanessa. I intended to blast her for all the crappy things she'd done—even if Yoko Ono putting the smackdown on Julia Lennon at a premiere Hollywood event made it on YouTube before midnight.

Judging by the looks I was getting from the guests, I didn't think I could count on anybody for backup.

These partygoers—or maybe their personal assistants—really knew how to put together a costume. I spotted Sgt. Pepper, an old guy who was probably supposed to be Paul's grandpa in *A Hard Day's Night*, and Father McKenzie from "Eleanor Rigby."

Another guy wore white face paint and a pale gauzy robe—I'm pretty sure it was his take on the whole Paul-is-dead thing—and next to him was a woman with long blond hair parted in the center whom I thought was supposed to be Cynthia Lennon.

A creepy man was carrying a hammer—no way did this guy look anything like Thor—whom I think was the serial killer mentioned in "Maxwell's Silver Hammer." The old couple Paul had sung about in "When I'm Sixty-Four" was there, along with Ed Sullivan, a clean-cut fellow in a suit who was probably Brian Epstein, and George Martin represented by a man with swept-back white hair, a loose tie, and rolled-up sleeves.

A group of partygoers had all dressed as blackbirds, somebody else had on a walrus costume, and several other people had on Nehru jackets and love beads inspired by the *Magical Mystery Tour* album.

Even the waitstaff was in costume. The waiters had on black turtleneck sweaters and Beatles wigs from the cover of the *With the Beatles* album. Bartenders wore bright pastel military jackets with braids and brass buttons from the *Sgt. Pepper's Lonely Hearts Club Band* album.

Everyone looked fabulous.

Everybody but me.

"Can't Buy Me Love" played as I passed the Strawberry Fields dessert buffet. Paige's Yellow Submarine cake was the centerpiece, surrounded by hundreds of rich, sumptuous desserts—all of which I desperately needed at the moment.

Apparently Vanessa didn't need a chocolate boost to get her through the rest of the evening, because I didn't see her there.

I pushed on, and calliope music drew me to the Mr. Kite event area. The whimsical circus theme of "Being for the Benefit of Mr. Kite" featured dancing horses, fire eaters, jugglers, stilt walkers, trampoline, and acrobats. The Hendersons were dancing and singing, but no Vanessa.

A group of partygoers wearing blue ponchos and black hats from the *Help* album passed me as I made my way to Penny Lane. Here, Lyle and his construction company had built the façade of a town and populated it with cutouts of a barber, banker, fireman, and a pretty nurse selling poppies from a tray.

Still no Vanessa.

There were over two hundred guests here, plus half that many in the support staff, so realistically I could roam the grounds for hours and not find her. My anger was winding down—plus everybody was glaring at me—so I decided to take a break.

I passed the stage where the two Cirque du Soleil performers were dancing to "Lady Madonna." The woman's cutaway top exposed her huge pregnant belly, and both she and her male partner had on bright yellow rain boots. I didn't get it, but the audience seated around the stage loved it.

I caught sight of Sheridan. It looked as if Muriel had put together a Lucy in the Sky with Diamonds costume for her. The full-length dress was sky blue and covered with crystals. Her hair was colored white and whipped into a massive updo to represent, I suppose, a cloud.

Beside her stood her husband, Talbot. He looked as if he were John Lennon and had just stepped off the cover of the *Abbey Road* album, wearing a white suit and sporting shoulder-length hair and a full beard.

No way did I want either of them to see me in my hideous costume.

I knew Eleanor and Rigby were here somewhere. I hoped they wouldn't spot me—they'd probably eighty-six me if they saw what I was wearing.

I endured more glares, stinky looks, and a few outright sneers as I made my way back to the service wing. I desperately needed a chocolate fix—it was the only way to salvage this evening.

I ducked into the room where the desserts had been prepared. A number of people were still working. I grabbed two slices of Black Forest cake, went to the employees' lounge, and collapsed at a table.

Luckily, I had the place to myself. I devoured the cake, as anyone in my position would have, and was contemplating going back for more when I caught sight of a tote bag hanging from one of the hooks on the other side of the room, partially covered by a sweater.

Huh. Something about it looked familiar.

I sat there for a minute waiting for the chocolate cake to turbo boost my brain cells.

Nothing turbo boosted.

Another minute passed, and I decided that if I was going to figure out why that tote had caught my eye I was going to have to get another piece of cake. I got out of my chair and headed for the door.

Then it hit me.

I spun around and looked at the bag again.

Oh my God. That tote was a Coach bag from several seasons ago when, for unknown reasons, the designers had thought women would actually want to carry a bag covered with huge fuchsia flower blossoms.

Then something else hit me.

I'd seen that bag at the Hollywood & Highland Center when I'd gone there for the ransom exchange. Belinda had been carrying it.

So that could only mean that—oh my God, Belinda was here.

The Black Forest cake kicked in big-time.

Somehow, she'd gotten past security onto the grounds and into the service wing. From here, she had access to the entire estate—the party, the main house, everything.

Since Paige had told me earlier that Belinda hadn't accompanied her to the party to help with the cake, I could think of only one reason for her to sneak into the event.

I yanked my phone out of my pants pocket and called the guy who headed up security.

"Where are the Beatle collectibles?" I asked when he answered.

"On display near the serenity garden," he said.

"Double security on them," I said. "I think someone may be trying to steal the bobbleheads."

It was the only reason I could figure that Belinda would be here. Apparently, she intended to take the bobbleheads again.

"Her name is Belinda Giles," I said.

"Hold on," he said. A few seconds later he came back on the line. "Belinda Giles is an employee with the Ever Clean Janitorial Service."

"What?"

"She was cleared through the security checkpoint this morning with the rest of the cleaning crew," he said.

Okay, now I was really confused. What the heck was going on?

"Do you have reason to believe she's planning a theft of the memorabilia?" he asked.

Yeah, okay, my head was buzzing with all sorts of questions about Belinda, but I managed to tell this guy the most important thing.

"Yes, I do. You have to stop her. She's old, sixty maybe, kind of thin. Dirty blond hair." I hesitated a couple of seconds, then said, "And I think she might be involved in the murder of Lacy Hobbs. Stop her, if you can find her."

I needed to locate her myself, though I didn't have a clue how that would be possible in this crowd.

I closed my cell phone and spun around—and there she stood.

She had on a pale green smock that matched the color of the janitorial service van I'd seen parked outside Lacy Cakes, here at Sheridan's estate during a previous visit, and on the freeway coming back from the ransom money delivery.

The real outstanding feature about Belinda at the moment was the pistol she was pointing at me.

"I guess you figured it all out," she said, giving me a tired smile.

Actually, I hadn't—but this didn't seem like a good time to say so. Things were falling into place, though.

"Let's get some air," Belinda said.

I hesitated. I figured I could take her easily. I was younger, stronger, and faster—plus I was jacked up on two slices of

Black Forest cake—but no way did I want to try anything while she held the gun on me.

She backed out of the door, checked the hallway, and motioned for me to walk ahead of her.

At the end of the corridor was a set of double doors. I opened one of them and found myself outside on a covered porch; a single light gave off a feeble glow.

I realized this was the rear of the estate. A thick row of trees and shrubs separated it from the neighboring lot.

To my right only a few yards away was the first floor of the parking garage. On my left was a row of Dumpsters. I figured this must be another entrance to the service wing.

Belinda walked out behind me. The door slammed shut.

"I guess you know this place pretty well," I said.

"Every inch of it," she told me. "I've been cleaning it for years."

I glanced at the garage. The place was packed with vehicles. Not one person was in sight.

"You must have been surprised to see me here tonight," I said.

"I knew you'd be here. You'd have to be, working for that party planning company. I've been looking for you." Belinda shook her head in dismay. "Why on earth did you pick that costume?"

Okay, this whole Yoko Ono thing was getting on my nerves big-time. I was going to let Vanessa have it when I saw her—provided I got to see her again, of course.

"I recognized you at the ransom drop," I said.

"I thought you'd figure it out sooner or later, which is why I'm here." She glanced around. "I don't see Batman lurking in the shadows to help you this time."

I sure as heck could use a partner right now.

Why hadn't I called Jack?

That made me think of something else.

"What about you?" I asked. "Where's your partner?"

"Partner?" Belinda uttered an ugly little laugh. "What partner?"

"Your cousin Darren," I said.

Her ugly little laugh morphed into an ugly growl.

"Darren? My partner?" she demanded. "I've got nothing to do with that self-righteous, tightfisted miser."

I glanced at the nearest car parked in the garage, then at the Dumpsters, and calculated how quickly I could get to them. I was pretty fast—especially with this combo of adrenaline and Black Forest cake pumping through me—but I'd never get to them quicker than a bullet fired from Belinda's gun.

"So it's just Paige you're partnered with?" I asked.

Paige had told me Belinda worked as a housekeeper. I didn't know if she was just shining me on or if she really didn't know the truth about where Belinda worked and what she'd done.

"She's desperate to buy the bakery and so am I," Belinda said, and shook her head. "Paige knows nothing else."

"Not even about how you broke into the bakery and stole Lacy's things?" I asked.

"Those things were due me," Belinda said, her anger rising. "I deserved something after everything Lacy put me through."

Something clicked into place in my head.

Belinda had just admitted she'd staged the robbery at the bakery. To do that, she needed the key to get inside. And, probably, she'd gotten that key from Lacy after she shot her.

A yucky feeling pooled in my belly. This wasn't just a thief holding a gun on me. This was a murderer. And she'd come here tonight, using her job with the janitorial service for cover, to kill me.

Jeez, I really wish I'd called Jack.

"Darren didn't want you to have anything of Lacy's," I said. "That was pretty crappy of him."

Honestly, I didn't care one way or the other, but I definitely wanted to keep Belinda talking.

"Everything Darren did was crappy," Belinda said. "He could have helped me, defended me years ago, but he didn't. He just stood by and let Lacy turn the whole family against me."

There's nothing like family when it came to screwing someone over.

"I heard about how you won those concert tickets," I said.

Belinda's face contorted with anger. "Those concert tickets—those damn concert tickets. Yeah, Lacy and I were both crazy about the Beatles. Yeah, we both wanted to go. But I had a boyfriend and I wanted to go with him, so I took him instead of Lacy."

"She was pretty mad about it, huh?" I said.

"She turned on me like a dog," Belinda said. "She made up stories about me. She even told people I'd gotten pregnant and had an abortion. Lies, lies, nothing but lies from her. She'd say anything to get her way, or make herself look good."

That was really bad, all right, and from what I'd heard about Lacy she'd never changed her ways.

Still, I didn't see how Beatles concert tickets had led to stolen bobbleheads and, of course, Lacy's murder.

"So you were working here at Sheridan's estate, cleaning," I said, "and you spotted the bobbleheads—"

"They are *my* bobbleheads," Belinda said, her anger spinning up again. "I bought them years ago—along with every other Beatles item I could find. I recognized them the minute I laid eyes on them from the dent in the box lid."

Okay, now I was confused.

"Hang on a second," I said. "The bobbleheads that

were donated to Sheridan's charity auction had a connection to British royalty. How could—"

"Royalty? They've got nothing to do with royalty." Belinda's face flushed bright red. "Lacy stole those bobbleheads from me years ago because I didn't take her to the Beatles concert with me. Then she donated them—*my* bobbleheads—to the auction so she'd look like a big shot in front of Sheridan Adams."

I threw a quick look at the ceiling of the parking garage and spotted a security camera. I couldn't tell whether Belinda and I were in its line of sight.

"Those bobbleheads are mine. I bought and paid for them with babysitting money I'd earned." Belinda's anger rose. "Lacy lied about taking them, she lied about me, she lied about everything."

It was all starting to fall into place now.

"So when you saw the bobbleheads," I said, "you—"

"*My* bobbleheads," Belinda said.

"Okay, *your* bobbleheads," I said.

Jeez, now I see why it was called *Beatlemania* back in the day. These Beatles fans were maniacs, all right.

"I was here inside this big, fancy house—doing that back-breaking job I've been doing for years—and I saw my bobbleheads with the other auction collectibles. I couldn't believe it," Belinda said. "There they were just sitting on the shelf—*my* bobbleheads."

"And you realized they were the set you'd bought, the set that disappeared," I said.

"The set that Lacy stole," Belinda said. "I knew she took them—I always knew she was the one who took them."

"How did you find out it was Lacy who'd donated them to Sheridan's charity auction?" I asked.

"You'd be surprised how much the servants know about what goes on. I found out Lacy had donated the bobbleheads," Belinda said. "But I hadn't heard that ridiculous story about British royalty. I should have known, with Lacy involved."

"You must have been furious once you knew for certain that Lacy had stolen them, that she'd kept them all these years," I said. "So you, what, confronted her at the bakery?"

"I told her I wanted them back," Belinda said. "I have health problems. I didn't have a smooth, easy life like she had baking cakes for thousands of dollars. I had to work—work hard—for nearly nothing."

Jeez, I really hope those security guards can see us on their video screens.

"But she wouldn't give them back," I said.

I knew that Lacy's reputation meant everything to her. No way would she ask Sheridan to return the bobbleheads after she'd donated them—especially after she'd made up that story about them being connected to British royalty.

"She laughed in my face!" Belinda's anger bordered on out of control now—not that I blamed her, of course. "I went to see her over and over and tried to reason with her, but she wouldn't give them back."

"So the next time you went to see Lacy, you took that gun with you," I said.

"It belonged to my dad. I took it with me when I left home after high school—when I was forced to leave because of all the things Lacy had said about me. I moved here to L.A. to get away from everything, and here came Lacy with her fancy cakes—just to throw it in my face that she was better than me," Belinda said.

I didn't know what to say to that.

"So, yes, I went to see Lacy and I took this gun with me." Belinda trembled with rage, then drew in a couple of big breaths and said, "I just wasn't going to get screwed over by Lacy again."

"You shot her," I said.

She nodded. "And I enjoyed it."

We were both quiet for a minute while Belinda's words sunk in. The color drained from her face. I decided I should try to keep her talking.

"It must have really hurt you to learn that Lacy hadn't left you anything in her will and that Darren wouldn't let you run the bakery," I said. "That's when you decided to steal the bobbleheads and hold them for ransom, wasn't it? That way, you'd have a big chunk of money to retire on, or invest in Lacy Cakes with Paige."

Belinda's anxiety level revved up, as if the magnitude of what she'd done had suddenly occurred to her. Her eyes darted back and forth. The gun seemed slippery in her hand.

"You should leave," I said, gesturing to the parking garage.

That got her attention.

"Just get in the janitorial van and go," I said, in my what-could-be-simpler voice.

Belinda looked at the parking garage, then back at me.

I figured if I could get her to go to the van—which would benefit me, of course—I could alert security and the cops in time to catch her before she got too far.

It was the only plan I could come up with on short notice, and Belinda looked as if she liked it.

"Good idea," she said, then waved the pistol at me. "You're coming with me."

Oh, crap.

What could I do but roll with it?

I headed for the parking garage, then swung around and slapped Belinda's arm. The gun flew from her hand, skidded off the porch, and disappeared. She pushed me hard. I fell backward and landed on my butt. Belinda took off running.

I scrambled to my feet and followed her into the parking garage. Wow, for an old gal she could really move. I wove between the cars, vans, and trucks, then spotted two security guards running toward Belinda. Another one came from the opposite direction. They grabbed her just as she got to the Ever Clean van. When I reached them, she was screaming and crying, and the guards had her up against the van cuffing her hands behind her.

Tires squealed and a black-and-white LAPD patrol car pulled up. Behind it was a white Crown Victoria. The doors opened. Detective Madison got out along with—oh my God—Detective Shuman.

I called Muriel and let her break the news to Sheridan and Talbot, gave my statement to Detective Madison, and went to the employee breakroom—after I stopped off for a half-dozen scrumptious desserts, of course. I got stink-eye from the pastry chefs, but nobody was willing to cross Yoko Ono, it seemed.

I had the lounge to myself, which was good, so I immediately ditched the wig and hat—better to look poorly dressed than like the person who'd caused the breakup of the Beatles—and started in on the gooiest treat I'd pilfered. Halfway through, the door opened and Detective Shuman walked in.

I'd been surprised to see him roll up with Detective Madison. I hadn't heard from him and didn't know he was back on the job.

He looked as much like his old self as possible, under the circumstances. He'd cut his hair, shaved his beard, and wore his traditional mismatched shirt, tie, and sport coat.

But his eyes seemed empty. He looked thin, withered, as if the weight he carried over Amanda's murder had caused him to shrink.

"Good job," he said, nodding toward the door.

I was glad to have a chance to talk to him alone. He'd been busy with everything in the parking garage and we'd only nodded at each other.

I licked the chocolate off my fingertips and walked over to meet him. I wanted to give him a hug, but I sensed he wouldn't want me to.

"How did you and Madison know to show up?" I asked.

"The security guard notified LAPD that a possible murder suspect was on the grounds," Shuman said.

I'd forgotten that I'd mentioned Lacy Hobbs's name when I'd called about the bobbleheads possibly being stolen again.

Jeez, was I wrong about that or what? Belinda was really here to kill me.

I guess my private detective skills still needed some work. But at least I'd been right about the security guards spotting Belinda and me on the surveillance camera.

"Are you all right?" Shuman asked. "She didn't hurt you, did she?"

I'd answered that question a couple of times already, but I guess Shuman wanted to be sure.

"I'm good," I said. "When did you start back to work?"

"This morning," he said.

A few minutes passed with us just staring at each other. I wanted to ask him a zillion questions about where he'd been, what he'd done, why I hadn't heard from him, if he was okay. But Shuman had put some sort of wall up around him, and I couldn't bring myself to try to get through it.

The door to the lounge opened and Detective Madison walked in. He looked as if he'd aged since the last time I'd talked to him.

Amanda's murder and Shuman's disappearance had taken a toll on everyone.

"You're free to leave," Madison said.

I guess he was content with the confession I'd heard Belinda screaming as I left the parking garage and no longer considered me a suspect in Lacy's murder, but I wanted to make sure.

"You're closing the case?" I asked.

The case that wasn't closed seemed to spring up between the three of us as if someone had said Amanda's name aloud.

Detective Madison's expression turned grim. He looked at me, then at Shuman and said, "We'll find the man who murdered Amanda. We'll find him."

Madison walked away.

I turned to Shuman and asked softly, "Are they going to find him?"

He shook his head. "No. They're never going to find him."

CHAPTER 27

My apartment was only a semi-mess now, thanks to Cody, but several things still needed to be done. I figured I could get Lyle and his construction crew to handle them.

I sat on my couch wearing sweats, my hair in a ponytail, a package of Oreo cookies on my left and a one-pound bag of M&M's on my right, watching the History Channel. I'd grown to appreciate their programming—who didn't love *Ancient Aliens*—during my extended stay in breakup zombieland, but today I was just tired and wanted to veg out.

Yesterday had been one heck of a day. So much had happened I couldn't even process it all. After leaving Sheridan's estate last night I'd come home and fallen into bed. I'd have to face reality sometime today—maybe after I'd gotten through the Oreos.

Just as the narrator on TV started in on how aliens had come to Earth to mine for gold, my cell phone rang. I hoped it was Marcie—I could really stand a good, long talk with my BFF—but Jeanette's name appeared on my caller ID screen. What the heck could she want?

Since I'm not big on suspense, I answered.

"Good news, Haley," Jeanette said. "We won!"

I had no idea what she was talking about.

She must have realized that because she said, "The con-test. Our store sold the most fashions from the runway show—the most in the entire chain. We won!"

Jeez, so much had happened I'd forgotten all about the contest.

"And you know what that means," she said, in a third-grade somebody-likes-you chant.

Oh my God. We'd won the contest. That meant I'd have to go to the corporate office and work—with Ty.

My heart started to race. A thousand thoughts flew through my head.

I really needed to talk to Marcie now.

"You know, the most exciting thing about the fashion show was all those young girls who were there," Jeanette said.

I remembered seeing dozens of stylishly dressed girls in the audience.

I got a weird feeling.

"Who would have suspected it?" she went on. "We've never had a concentration of that demographic before. I don't know where they all came from."

One of my conversations with Amber flashed in my head. She'd told me Ty had her hire a group of actresses.

My weird feeling got weirder.

I needed a distraction.

I spotted the gift bag from Sheridan's party that Tiberia had given me. I grabbed it off my kitchen counter.

"Those girls bought armloads of fashions," Jeanette said. "They could hardly carry them all to the checkout lines."

I dumped the gift bag out. Something sparkly caught my eye.

"Of course, it would have been better if they'd used a Holt's credit account to pay for everything," Jeanette said.

My doorbell rang.

"The interest the store would have earned from those purchases would have been a real boost," she said.

I dug down through the gift items and found—oh my God, the Enchantress evening bag.

Tiberia had told me Sheridan wanted me to have something special. She must have remembered how much I wanted an Enchantress and gotten it for me.

My doorbell rang again.

This was so awesome. I couldn't wait to tell Marcie.

"But I'm delighted all those girls bought our fashions," Jeanette said. "Even if they all used gift cards."

Gift cards?

A knock sounded on my door.

Hadn't Amber mentioned something about gift cards?

I opened my front door. Shuman waited outside.

"Hi," I mumbled, and stepped back.

He walked inside.

Then it hit me—Amber had told me that Ty had her buy zillions of Holt's gift cards for him.

"I'll personally handle your schedule so you can report to the Holt's corporate office immediately," Jeanette said. "You can work with you-know-who right away."

Several things clicked into place—but could they really be true?

"Haley, I need to talk to you," Shuman said.

Had Ty engineered this entire fashion show contest to get me to the corporate office? He'd changed the grand prize at the last minute so the fashion show coordinator would work there. Jeanette had given me that position, but was it at Ty's suggestion?

Shuman pushed the door shut.

"You're on the schedule for tonight," Jeanette said, "but don't come in. You deserve some time off."

Had Ty hired all those actresses and bought them gift cards with instructions to buy everything in our fashion show—so I'd win?

"I'll get back with you on your transfer to the corporate office," Jeanette said, and hung up.

I stood there holding my cell phone, my thoughts in chaos.

Had Ty really done that?

And, if he had, what did it mean?

"Haley, I—I really need to talk to you," Shuman said.

Did it mean Ty wanted us to get back together? Was this his way of having me near him?

Shuman moved closer.

Did it mean that Ty missed me? Or did he want me there so I could see that he was perfectly all right without me?

"Haley?" Shuman said.

Then something else hit me—had Ty been spying on me in my parking lot? Was it him who'd warned Cody to step off?

"Oh, Haley." Shuman sighed.

Hang on a minute.

"I've—I've done something . . . something terrible," he said.

Oh my God, what was going on?

Shuman pressed his palm against my cheek and leaned in.

"I don't think anybody could ever . . . ever love me again," he said softly.

I froze.

Shuman leaned down until his lips hovered over mine.

"What about you, Haley? Could—could you love me?" he whispered.

Oh, crap.